THE
MISSING
POEM

JOHN W. PARSONS

Wasteland Press

www.wastelandpress.net
Shelbyville, KY USA

The Missing Poem
by John W. Parsons

First Printing – April 2013
ISBN: 978-1-60047-850-5
Library of Congress Control Number: 2013935784

Printed in the U.S.A.

0   1   2   3   4   5   6

Other books by the author

A JOURNEY THROUGH LIFE – 2008

UNSELFISH – 2010

STONE AND MORTAR – 2011

ETB – 2012

CHAPTER ONE

Introductions

I couldn't wait for Spring break, as it had been a long and trying year. My students, gifted as they all are, have been very demanding. I need to get away from it all, even for a brief time. My name is Doctor Kaitlin Graham and I am a professor of Studies of the Universe here at one of the most prestigious halls of higher learning in America. We are fortunate to have some of the greatest minds ever to walk this Earth, teaching and sharing their knowledge and life experiences with a very select student body.

I am 37 years old, never married or had a serious relationship. My loving father always said it was because my one true love was for the Universe and that no man could even come close to competing with that. Many have wanted to become romantically involved, but none of those matured into a lasting love affair. I have often wondered if the road I have chosen, one of commitment and devotion to my work, was the correct one, but most likely I will never be able to answer that question.

One of my greatest heroes and most likely the most brilliant mind to ever grace this planet, Albert Einstein, once said, *"ONLY TWO THINGS ARE INFINITE, THE UNIVERSE AND MAN'S STUPIDITY AND I STILL AM NOT SURE ABOUT THE FORMER."* As I follow this world's conflicts and tragedies I often think of his words of wisdom. Maybe someplace we will be fortunate enough to locate, out in that vast wilderness we call the Universe, a world of creatures that have learned to live in peace with one another. I often dream what a blessing it would be to be able to visit such a utopia someday, before or possible even after, I go to my reward.

So much for daydreaming. Not only is what I dream impossible, but even our government, which has up until now led the exploration of space, is so bankrupt that space exploration is all but forgotten. If only the vast treasure that this species called man has spent over the centuries in annihilating one another with more and more sophisticated weapons of war could have been spent on exploring the Universe for a more peaceful world. I have long dreamt that there is life out beyond our capacity to envision, and that it is also a serene life. When God created the Universe, He must have, with a twinkle in His eye, decided to seed it with many different forms of life. In the case of this Earth He most likely got a chuckle out of the fact that He chose the bottom of the barrel to inhabit this planet we call Earth and see if they could rise above their idiocy. Unfortunately, they have not met His challenge.

I must remind myself every now and then that I cannot change mankind and to stop trying to. Maybe when I pass from this Earth, into God's loving arms, he will allow me to live on a more peaceful planet somewhere in space. Many a lively debate in my classes at the university have centered around this thought and provoked many theories from my talented and gifted students. Without such interchange, from such an intense and exceptional group, my life would certainly be even duller than it is. I am not complaining however as this is the life I have chosen, and my dreams of the magnificence of the Universe and God's hand in it carry me comfortably from day to day.

Due to my standings here at this institute of higher learning, and my reputation on the world stage of my subject matter, I have a full time assistant, Mark. We all sometimes forget that this Earth is but a speck in this vast Universe and that we as individuals are smaller than a grain of sand so having an assistant hopefully will not go to my head. I wonder how I could function without his devoted support in looking after my daily schedules but, hopefully, I will never have to find out. He also reminds me often not too take myself to seriously as in the vast galaxy and even greater Universe I am as we all are, but a fleeting moment in time. He has been tidying up my schedule so I could get away without leaving too many loose ends for my spring break.

"Mark, would you mind checking the mail for me and seeing if anything is so important that I should deal with it before I leave."

"Doctor, there is one letter here marked personal which I did not open and it has no return address. In fact, the other strange thing about it is that there is no postmark as to where it originated, however, it was delivered along with the rest of the mail. Everything else is routine and I will take care of anything that needs attention while you are at Cape Cod enjoying many an evening gazing into space. Take my advice and spend some of those evenings staring into some handsome fellow's eyes as you and he enjoy a drink together. Remember, there is much more to life than what you cannot see or imagine beyond human eyesight."

"Mark, what would I do without you, always looking after my well being? You know me all too well I am afraid and the only excitement I will be having is watching our Milky Way with Sally and Debbie, my two dear friends and colleagues, who also have as the loves of their lives the Universe.

"To each his own, but just remember doctor life is too short and so far you have not been able to connect with that lover from Planet X so enjoy what time you do have here on this Planet Earth."

"Mark, enough of the lecture, when I am ready for a relationship I will look no further than my personal assistant. Go ahead and open the letter and read it to me while I tidy up a few last minute items, as I have no secrets from you." We both enjoyed a snicker over the thought of the two of us as anything but co-workers, so to speak, as Mark was in his early twenties and frankly not interested at all in the opposite sex. I am sure romance between us was the furthest thought from both our minds. Whatever his personal desires, that is his business, I could not ask for a more generous, devoted and wonderful assistant than he is. Mark proceeded to read the letter.

"My dear Doctor Kaitlin Graham.

In my extensive research into the area of space exploration, both physically and mentally, your name repeatedly comes to the forefront. You do not know me and I wish to remain anonymous at present. I noted in my research concerning your qualifications that you are a world renowned expert in the field of the study of the Universe or at least as much of an expert as anyone living on this planet can be. You have given many lectures on your research and insight, and I was privileged to attend one and was most impressed. I have long held a deep desire to learn all there is to know about our galaxy and the Universe beyond with all it's secrets and mysteries, as I am sure you have.

I herein enclosed some pictures, which I recently took from beyond our galaxy, and I was hoping you would take a moment of your time to study them. You will note in the first picture the Earth is plainly visible from outer space as a speck with all the other planets shown as well. I can assure you that the pictures were not taken from any satellite but from much further out in space. Even with your extensive research you have no idea what lies beyond your ability to see and understand. The mystery of the Universe has unfolded before my eyes and continues to do so. I wish to share that which I have seen with someone, and I have chosen you.

We all have our needs, and having no family left, or any close trusting friends, I was praying that you might see fit to, at the least, receive communications from me on occasion concerning my exploration of that wonderful Universe that we both love so dearly. I need to share with someone, and I have selected you, the fact that I have conquered space travel. Very simply I have mastered movement throughout the Universe and have traveled extensively about our galaxy, and well beyond. I well realize that when you read this letter you are first going to think it is from another crackpot, of which there are many I am sure. You will probably think here is another one that belongs in an institution. Please believe me that I am far removed from what your initial reaction is. I have enclosed these pictures that I recently took from far out in our beloved Universe to help convince you of my truthfulness and sincerity.

If you were to meet me on the street, or after one of your lectures, I would certainly not be very impressive. I am an average guy, hold a mediocre position in a high tech company, and lead a quiet, unassuming, very lonely life. I cannot be reached and prefer to remain anonymous as I stated. I will, however, at some point in time make contact with you again to see what questions you might have concerning what I have revealed to you and what the pictures have meant to you. I sincerely hope that you take the time to review them. Please keep them confidential, as I am sure that almost one-hundred percent of the governments in this world would relish this technology, sadly for the advantage it would give them in future conflicts with one another. I plan on taking my secret to the grave with me but wanted at least one other person, an expert such as yourself, to realize what I have accomplished and what is possible with such a gift God has chosen to entrust to me.

Sincerely:
Yours in the unlimited brilliance and beyond human comprehension, the Universe."

"Dr. Graham, I know you have received many weird communications but this one takes the cake, so to speak. This person doesn't sound stupid, but to make such announcements with such conviction is interesting. Do you want me to toss it out with the rest of the trash?"

"Mark, do you even need to ask. On second thought, however, since myself, Sally and Debbie are going to have such an exciting time sitting on the beach with my drinking diet cokes and watching the heavens, maybe I will take the pictures with me to entertain them with. One of these vacations I might actually take you up on your advice and spend my time, and convince my dear friends to do the same, in some friendly bar with three handsome men. But, alas, I believe that time is yet to come."

"Kait, please don't wait to long. You are an extremely attractive, desirable woman, but even someone as pleasant to look at as you are and of course your two dear friends, need to make such a move before waiting forever. Time has certainly been kind to you, however if you truly want to love and be loved do not wait an eternity."

"Enough already Mark, throw those pictures in the bottom of my briefcase and hopefully I won't forget they are there with all the excitement I expect the ladies and I will be facing in the next couple of weeks." With that we wrapped it up. Mark went about his business of caring for my obligations while I am away and I finished packing and gave Mark a little peck on the cheek and headed out for my Mercedes. I was elated to be on my way and couldn't wait to meet up with the ladies at the Cape for what should be a memorable time. Maybe if we are fortunate we will even discover a new star in the heavens using our latest telescopic technology. I had a fleeting moment thinking what a dull life I truly lead, and then the thought faded rapidly and I was back on my never ending monotonous track.

I was the first to arrive at the tip of the Cape and checked into the hotel. The hotel personnel remembered me from my semi-annual trips up here and, as usual, were most hospitable and furnished me with our usual suite with the magnificent view out over the ocean and into my beloved heavens. I headed for the dining room and ordered my diet and also some delicious Cape Cod lobster tails while I awaited Debbie and Sally's arrival. As I sat there I glanced around and one handsome gentleman seemed to be staring my way. For a fleeting moment I wondered if it was my mysterious letter writer who claimed to be a space traveler, but that thought passed quickly as he was soon joined by a well tanned, very attractive lady. So much for moments of excitement in my otherwise humdrum existence.

The ladies showed up as I was drinking my after dinner coffee and savoring my great meal. We embraced, as only dear friends can, and they joined me at the table. Sally ordered a scotch and water, easy on the ice, and Debbie ordered her usual diet. She and I had long kidded ourselves about which one of us would be the first to finally break down and try a glass of wine or a mixed drink but so far neither one had been brave enough to. Sally was the first to speak.

"Kait, pray tell what have you been doing lately? Are you and Mark a thing yet or are you still going steady with the love of your life, Mr. Universe?"

"I didn't want to mention it but Mark and I have definitely become a twosome and are planning a trip shortly to Las Vegas to get married in the Viva Las Vegas Wedding Chapel. After that we plan on having a very wild time doing the town and many a night of hot and heavy sex." Those comments really broke the ice early on and we all enjoyed a tremendous chuckle over them. I thought maybe it was time to get serious, however, so I went on to say.

"I figure we have about two hours to kill before we adjourn to our favorite spot on the beach to soak up the beauty and majesty of the Universe this night. I also have some breathtaking pictures that I received from someone who claims he has conquered space travel to share with you two. I thought it might give us about as much hilarity as three college professors interested in outer space could handle for the time we are here. I received them in a blank envelope from an anonymous source just before I left to come up here." Debbie was the first to respond.

"Kait, are you still getting those crank letters and pictures of outer space that you have been getting for years? Ever since you went on the international lecture tour you have attracted every nut job in the world it seems. So far Sally and I have managed to keep ourselves off the world stage so fortunately those odd persons out there concentrate on sending this material to you. I can't wait to see your latest collection. I think that we ought to wait until Sally is on her fourth or fifth scotch and water before showing them to her. Maybe when I see them I might even have to partake to absorb the authenticity of them.

Seriously Kait, I also have something to share with the two of you. My mother found a poem that my beloved dad wrote when he served in the Korean War and I want to read it to you folks. She had been searching for it for years, as she remembered he had written these two very moving poems and she never could find them. She was rummaging around in the attic the other day and came across the one but the other one is still missing and she continues to search for it. She said they remind her so much of the love that she shared with my dad and his wisdom in looking at this world out of the eyes of someone who had seen the dark side of it. She almost thought she could remember that when dad was laid to rest she put one of them in his pocket but the years have taken their toll and she is no longer sure.

What say you Sally, do you have any spurious pictures to share with us or maybe a poem that your most recent lover wrote you?" The only thing I have to share with the two of you is this scotch and water and many more where this one came from. I still can't believe that the two of you can get through every day college life, especially without Mr. Right, and not partake of at least a small glass of wine. I need to go freshen up a bit before we meet

Mr. Universe on the beach in a short time. Why don't we figure we will meet at nine as that will give me enough time to get ready and also to spend another hour at the bar checking out the guys. If I didn't love you two so much you would have a hard time dragging me away from the bar and some of the handsome fellows there. See you at nine." With that Sally left us, Debbie and I drank our diets and passed the moment with much small talk for the remainder of our waiting time. At nine we headed out for our favorite spot and as we arrived Sally showed up arm and arm with a much younger handsome fellow.

"Ladies, this is Keith, I brought him along as I realized this was show and tell and Keith agreed to show it all if we were so inclined. Keith and I have shared several drinks along with his special friend, Larry. They are two of the sweetest guys you would ever want to meet." I thought it was time I intervened before things got completely out of hand.

"Sally, Keith seems like the salt of the Earth, however, we are not here to share the human anatomy but the vastness of space. I think you may have had one too many and it is time to cut you off. Thank you for the offer Keith, but I think we can manage just fine without any display that you might see fit to share with us." At that he gave Sally a smooch on the cheek and headed back to the hotel. Sally seemed downhearted but she did manage to help Debbie and I set up my newest telescope so we could take turns exploring the heavens. I thought for a moment what an exciting way to spend a vacation on beautiful Cape Cod, but then again that is who I am.

We were about an hour into our star gazing when we needed a levity break so I decided to share the pictures that Mr. Anonymous had sent me that he claimed he had taken from outer space. I laid them out in our makeshift cabana and told Sally, who was finally sobering up, and Debbie that they were taken by my secret admirer when he was on a recent trip into the depths of the Universe. Sally asked if I had been with him and enjoyed the trip and Debbie just looked at them for a long time and then finally spoke up.

"You know ladies, these are fascinating photographs. Whoever Mr. Anonymous is he certainly went to a great deal of effort to make sure the alignment between the various planets was perfect. I have seen many mockups of the planets in our galaxy but these are the most accurate that I have ever observed. You may be dealing with a major league crackpot here Kate but he is certainly not an ignorant weirdo. You may want to be cautious about becoming involved with this one as he might outshine you with his knowledge of the vastness and mysteries of space."

"Ladies, I need to share with you also the letter he sent me along with the pictures. Debbie, you have now peaked my interest and all of a sudden I am thinking I can't wait to hear from this man of mystery again." Sally interjected some levity into the conversation as only Sally could do.

"Kait, when he does contact you again, and offers to take you for a ride in his chariot into the vastness of the Universe, just remember who your friends are and make sure we are invited along also."

"I doubt very much I will be hearing from him again as the travels he is talking about, into the far reaches of space, might just take him a few million years. I doubt if we have to concern ourselves with my secret admirer, at least in our lifetime." Debbie spoke up and asked if she could share with us one of the poems that she and her mother loved so well that her father had written while serving during the Korean War. We needed to become serious again after the absurdity concerning the pictures and letter I had shared so we were eager to hear it.

"THE BOYS IN THE DAY ROOM WERE TALKING
OF THE HELL HOLES THEY'VE BEEN IN AND SEEN
AND THE TALES THEY TOLD WERE HEARTBREAKING
THEN UP SPOKE A GUY NAMED BILL GREEN

I SERVED OUT SOME TIME IN THE ARMY
FROM HAWAII THEY SENT ME TO NOME
BUT THERE'S NOTHING I'VE HEARD IN YOUR STORIES
LIKE THE HALL WAY THEY CALLED THE ZONE

DOWN WHERE THERE'S NO TEN COMMANDMENT'S
AND A MAN RAISES HIMSELF A THIRST
LIE THE OUTCASTS OF CIVILIZATION
THE VICTIMS OF LIFE AT IT'S WORST

NOBODY KNOWS THEY'RE LIVING
AND NOBODY GIVES A DAMN
BACK HOME THEY'RE SOON FORGOTTEN
THESE BOYS OF OUR UNCLE SAM

LIVING ALONE WITH THE NATIVES
DOWN IN THE TORRID ZONE
DOWN BY THE MAN MADE RIVER
MORE THAN THREE THOUSAND MILES FROM HOME

DOWN IN THE RUM SOAKED ISSMUS
ARE THE MEN WHOM GOD FORGOT
BATTLING THE SNAKES AND LIZARDS
THE ITCH AND THE CHINESE ROT

DRENCHED WITH SWEAT IN THE EVENING
THEY SIT ON THEIR BUNKS WHILE THEY DREAM
THEY'RE KILLING THEMSELVES WITH LIQUOR
TO DAMN UP THE MEMORY STREAM

WAKE ALL NIGHT ON THEIR PILLOWS
THEY'RE ILL'S NO DOCTOR CAN CURE
HELL NO, THEY'RE NOT CONVICTS
JUST SOLDIERS ON A FOREIGN TOUR

"That was beautiful Debbie. Since I feel so strongly about the futility of war after war, I think your father nailed it with that poem. It reinforces, as far as I am concerned, Albert Einstein's famous saying about man's stupidity. I sometimes wonder if God is looking down from the heavens and saying to Himself, 'Those humans that I populated the planet Earth with certainly never rise above their foolhardiness.' Thanks so much Debbie for sharing it with us." Sally, who was about eighty percent sober at this point, spoke up and offered her input.

"That was so thought provoking. You mentioned there were two poems but that your mother had been unable to locate the other one. Was she positive she had put it in your father's pocket when he was laid to rest?"

"She often said that both poems were so moving and they had brought tears to her eyes many a time when she had read them. They certainly reinforce the fact that, as that famous quote of years ago by an anonymous author goes, *'MAN TOO EASILY SETTLES CONFLICTS WITH WARS INSTEAD OF WORDS*.' God help us all. Is your mother still trying to find the other one? If she does please share it with us as I, and I am sure Kait, have been so moved by it."

We spent another couple of hours sharing glimpses into space through my telescope and then we finally succumb to heavy eyelashes and decided to call it a night. One brief moment during my time with the telescope I thought I glimpsed a moving object far out in space, but dismissed it as a meteorite or a satellite. I didn't need any more mysteries in my life at the present time so I didn't even file it away in my mind to dwell on while trying to fall asleep. Frankly, I seldom have any problem falling asleep since my imagination takes me to the far reaches of the Universe and that always delivers me into dreamland almost immediately.

The remainder of our time here passed by rapidly. Sally enjoyed the fellows at the bar and on several occasions tried to get Debbie and I to choose a couple of the more attractive young men, but to no avail. All of our evenings were spent at our favorite observation point, with myself and Debbie sipping our diet cokes and Sally indulging in her scotch and waters. She also brought along, on several evenings, a young man from the bar to entertain us. One of the more talkative young fellows mentioned that we were the talk of the bar crowd as the weirdest trio most of them had ever seen. In fact he went on to say that for three very attractive middle age ladies to be spending their evenings gazing into space was almost sacrilegious. We all got a kick out of this but I must admit that it made me wonder why our lives were so mundane. On more than one occasion I thought there must be a more fun filled time out there someplace compared to what we were doing. Several times, when we were indulging in our staring into space, I thought again I glimpsed an object sailing across the heavens in my lens, but again dismissed it as a meteor or a satellite.

I arrived back at the university. Mark had everything well organized for me as usual. Classes were to begin tomorrow and I wasn't quite sure I was up to the challenge quite yet. In my position, however, I had little choice so I set the agenda for my very talented students for an open discussion. Some of these young minds that were as eager as I was concerning the Universe could, on days assigned to open discussion, come up with some interesting topics to raise, and I was sure tomorrow would be no different.

CHAPTER TWO

Heaven and Hell

After we all became reacquainted again from our spring break I opened the floor to whatever they wanted to discuss. One of my more brilliant students, Robert, who hailed from Northern Norway, said he had been home during the break and been privileged to observe the Aurora Borealis several nights. He remembered the tales that had been handed down from generation to generation about those who had passed from this life to the next riding chariots along these beautiful Northern Lights to their reward in Heaven. He asked if we could discuss the relationship of those tales to the thought previously raised in the class of the Universe and it's relationship to Heaven and Hell.

Gail, never at a loss of words, asked him if he believed in those old wives tales and if Robert actually thought Heaven and Hell resided in the vastness of space. "Robert, do you honestly believe we all end up out there someplace, after we pass from this life, depending on the record that the Lord accumulates on each and every one of us during our lifetime." Robert, never at a loss for words answered Gail back.

"Tell me Gail, you are a student of many disciplines, just where does the Bible suggest that Heaven and Hell are? The last I checked the Bible makes no reference to Heaven being at a certain longitude and latitude any more than Hell is. Why then can we not open our imaginations to the possibility that some of the infinite number of planets in the Universe actually are God's destinations for each and every one of us when we pass. I would suggest that we are at some point loaded into a chariot and launched into space with preset destinations arranged by the record of our lives that the Lord has kept. Those of us that are caring and considerate members of the human race, such as Doctor Graham, would be taken to the number one Heaven planet, where all outstanding, caring humans will be and will share peace and harmony for eternity." I felt obliged to interject at this point.

"Robert, I am enjoying your supposition up to this point but please do not evaluate my lifetime record for the class as to my chances of making it someday to the planet of the most worthy." Just because I spend my vacations, as you all are well aware, gazing into space with my fellow college professors, is no reason to think that I am as pure as you suggest". This brought some laughter to those in the class and I was sure they were thinking some very strange thoughts about their college professor. Robert went on to expound on his theory.

"For arguments sake let us assume there are twenty-six planets in outer space that the Lord has designated, from Heaven to Hell. The first planet, let us call it Heaven A, is reserved for those from this life with unblemished records and without sins. Mother Teresa would be an example of an occupant of this most cherished planet. There, those most deserving spend eternity in peace and harmony as the Lord was hoping mankind would spend their time on this Earth. Sadly, it has been anything but that. The last planet in the cycle of Heaven and Hell planets, called Hell Z, is reserved for those amongst mankind that have been most evil, Adolph Hitler, Joseph Stalin, Genghis Khan, just to name a few. That list could go on forever. On that planet those most evil among man live out eternity trying to destroy one another as only those most unworthy could do. It is man against man at its ugliest. In between Heaven A and Hell Z are 24 planets where all those masses of mankind that fall between most worthy and most evil reside. The Lord assigns each of us to one of the planets according to our sins or lack thereof while residing on Mother Earth."

"Robert, as the leader of this group of marvelous students of the Universe let me say that your imagination is second to none. Does anyone else have any thoughts on Robert's theory?" Gail spoke up again as she loved to tweet Robert's theories.

"Professor Graham, I think as an assignment you should order each of us to make a complete list of all one hundred and twenty two students in this class and we will assign each to a planet. These assignments, to one of the twenty-six planets in Robert's Heaven and Hell, would be based on our perception of the scale of worthiness or unworthiness of each of our classmates. I would want to assure Robert that he would not, in my opinion, end up in Hell Z, but I would most likely keep him on the Hell side of the twenty-six planets, possibly Hell P." This brought a bit of laughter from the class and many a side comment.

"Gail, since you are the main challenger in my theory that the Universe is in actuality the location of Heaven and Hell, I would not have a difficult time with your assignment. In fact I suspect we might both end up on the same planet." It was time to inject a little professorship into the conversation so I thought it best to end it.

"I will say that this has been an interesting discussion and I am not sure we will be able to top it in future open discussion sessions. One bit of homework before you are sent off to evaluate Robert's theory. I want each of you to take with you a copy of the pictures that I recently received from an anonymous source and study them and be prepared to discuss them during our next session. The author claims to have taken them from far out in space and also claims to have conquered space travel." Robert had to inject his thoughts here.

"Professor, possibly you could ask your source of these pictures to check out my theory and visit a few of the Heaven to Hell planets and get back to us on his or her observations."

"Robert, I will say you are persistent, and as a favor to you for your out of this world imagination I will be happy to ask my mysterious space traveler to check that out for us." With that we all broke to a great deal of amusement and each of us went on our way. I still had a number of items to deal with back at the office that Mark had organized for me so I headed back there.

When I arrived back at the office Mark was waiting for me. He couldn't wait to find out how the trip went and if Debbie, Sally and I loosened up some. "I heard reports Doctor, that three extremely desirable women were the wild ones up on Cape Cod this past week. Word has it that the police had to be summoned to the hotel several times in response to calls to bring order out of chaos. I couldn't believe it when they reported that the policemen were lined up to answer the calls to the hotel as these three handsome ladies put the moves on the officers whenever they showed up. Please tell me that it isn't true professor."

"Mark, your information source must have been drinking a little in excess as our week was anything but what you describe. The most excitement we had was when Sally had one too many scotch and waters and invited various young men to perform for us on the beach, which of course Debbie and I rejected immediately. We did manage to get in many an exciting hour however star gazing in the evenings, if that is what you mean by a wild time. I even observed, on more than one occasion, a streak of something going through the heavens when I was manning the telescope. I could hardly contain the excitement of that observation but that was about all this old soul could take. I believe the record speaks for itself and that this trip was no different than past trips for the three of us, quiet and unassuming."

"Well, I can at least hope and pray that my favorite professor someday will loosen up a little and start to see life from a perspective other than staring into outer space. Staring into the eyes of some handsome fellow might open your eyes that there is a whole other world out there."

"Enough Mark, you should know by now that this lady will never change, no matter how handsome the fellow might be. Since you are already taken that closes the door on any other possible relationships. No one could top my handsome, debonair assistant."

"If I ever did decide to change my sexual orientation, Kait, it would certainly be for you. By the way, you have considerable mail backed up and there is even one there marked personal and it has, again, no return address or postmark or anything else to identify its origin. I truly believe you have a secret admirer and you have been keeping him from me."

"I see Mr. Efficiency has already opened all the mail and sorted it to its importance so open that one also and let us see what my man of mystery, assuming it is the same fellow, has to say now." Mark proceeded to open it and read it and the look on his face peaked my interest. He asked if he could read it to me.

"Dear Doctor Kaitlin Graham:

I enclose yet again some pictures I recently took while traveling in outer space. You would have to look very close but if you had superhuman eyesight you might see yourself and your two lady friends sitting on the beach in Cape Cod staring out into space. I trust you might have caught a glimpse of me traveling around the outer heavens those evenings when you were occupied with the Universe rather than with some good looking, interesting fellow. I realize in my last communications with you I mentioned that I was boring, but I have been told I am fairly good looking and I am in hopes someday of taking a beautiful lady such as yourself on their first trip into the far reaches of this magnificent Universe. I would love to introduce you to some of the mysteries of what I have seen out beyond one's deepest thoughts. To even peak your interest more I would also love to introduce you to some of the most wonderful creatures that are even beyond your imagination that call the Universe their home. You would be amazed to visit some of the planets and I would truly love to share the experience with you at some point in time.

I trust you have had a chance to study the pictures I sent you in our previous correspondence. I am sure you thought that I had built a mockup of the planets and then faked the photographs from that. That is the furthest from the truth and I dare say, knowing your expertise, that you were surprised by the accuracy of the layout if in fact I had built such a mockup.

Someday I hope to be able to prove to you, by providing evidence that you request, of the truth of what I say. I well realize the enormity of what I am relaying to you but believe me when I say it is all true. I have been to the far corners of the Universe and yet have only begun to explore such an infinite area, which is beyond the average persons ability to comprehend. The human mind, however powerful, cannot begin to imagine what lies beyond what can be seen with even the most powerful, advanced telescopes built today. I have visited planets occupied by what you might consider very strange creatures, and also planets occupied by many beautiful creatures.

As I mentioned in my previous correspondence please do not share the pictures or letters I have sent you with anyone. I have become increasingly conscious of my surroundings, as the gift that the good Lord has bestowed upon me would be invaluable as a weapon of war if any nation were to uncover my secret. I will send you some more pictures that I will take on my next trip into the far reaches of the Universe shortly. Many mysteries await myself and all mysteries await you.

God be with you. I pray we will someday be able to share the beauty of my other world together.

Bless you
Joseph"

"Kait, you either have connected with the world's greatest imagination or the most brilliant mind to walk this Earth since Albert Einstein. Whichever it is I would certainly call him, assuming it is a he, a man of mystery. When I read this second communication I was wondering about your sharing with anyone else, such as Sally and Debbie, his pictures and correspondence. I am not saying I believe him, but if what he is saying were even remotely possible his life would not be worth anything if any world government even had a hint of what he has conquered. Mankind's insatiable thirst for power would be unquenchable if they ever had a suspicion of what he has mastered."

"Mark, are you beginning to actually believe this weirdo. I not only think we are dealing with a major league wacko here, but hopefully he is not also dangerous. I shared the pictures and his letter with Sally and Debbie and also shared the photographs he sent with my entire class, so if what he says is true his cover is blown."

"Just be careful Kait, as stranger things have happened, I think, over the history of mankind. There is much speculation, as you well know that aliens from somewhere in outer space in history visited this Earth many times. You and your class have discussed this before, and drawings from prehistoric times that you have studied are evidence of such visits. Maybe years ago they conquered space travel from other worlds out there and now your mysterious stranger has done the same. Who is to say what is possible and if possible what lays well beyond our imagination."

"Mark, if I didn't know better I would suspect that you were sending these mysterious letters and photographs yourself. If you are the perpetrator I would suggest you stifle it as I have about had it."

"Doctor, you certainly know me better than that, if I wanted to send you any intriguing photos they would be pictures of some very handsome, middle aged men that would love to date a fine looking woman like you."

"Enough Mark, it is time to move on as I must prepare my lecture for the next class. I can't wait for next Friday when we have another open forum day to see what some of my students who have such vivid imaginations come up with. One of my more verbal students even has raised the issue of the Universe containing planets, which the Lord has set aside as Heaven and Hell planets. He has suggested that we are all assigned a planet where we will end up on for eternity after we pass from this life, based on our sins or lack thereof while being on planet Earth. One of the class assignments for the next open forum is to assign every class member a planet and explain why."

"Kait, I don't think I even want to comment on that, talk about going around the bend. All I will say is that you should get top billing for being without sin as your life is generally so dull that the good Lord would have to set aside a special planet for you for the most untainted. You want to give that idea some serious thought doctor, as life does not go on forever and sometimes a little sin is what makes life interesting. If we are going to be assigned a planet to spend forever on, then possibly if you loosen up some we might both end up on the same one? Mine certainly will not be Heaven A so I would just hope to end up in the top ten."

"I cannot imagine that you and I would end up in the same place. That is not to say you are not as deserving as me but we just travel different roads in life. I frankly think that theory makes as much sense as my mysterious space traveler. Someone would certainly have to prove it to me if in fact that is where Heaven and Hell reside. Enough of this talk, I have too much work to do so I will touch base with you later Mark. Just in case I go to my reward before we see each other again, I will reserve a place for you on say, Heaven K."

With that we reluctantly broke off our conversation and I settled down to my office work. I was checking my email and I had a note from Debbie. She mentioned that her mother had come across some papers she had accumulated when she laid her husband to rest. In those papers it was noted to the undertaker to add one of the poems to his suit coat pocket. That mystery being solved Debbie went on to say how much she had enjoyed our time together. I wrote her back and said that I looked forward to our next encounter and even went on to suggest we might wish to loosen up a little.

It was just after I responded to Debbie's email concerning the missing poem when Mark interrupted me. He told me there were two gentlemen waiting to see me. I asked him what they were here for and he said they would not tell him and only flashed a couple of badges of some sort when he questioned them. He mentioned they were not, at first glance, the type of guys he would want to spend an evening with at the local watering hole. He said they were sort of sinister looking. I told Mark to send them in, not knowing what to expect.

After the less than believable introductions they said they represented the Federal Aviation Administration. I asked them what was on their minds. The taller of the two introduced himself only as Tim. "Doctor Graham, we understand you have received some photographs which allegedly were taken from beyond our galaxy and along with the photos a letter or two. We would like to have copies of the photos and the letters. Since we have become aware of these photos and letters the Federal Aviation Administration has been concerned about commercial air traffic and the possibility of some kind of an encounter with this mysterious space vehicle." I immediately became suspicious that these two certainly were not from the FAA, anymore than I was a barfly.

"Tim, or whatever your name is, you are wasting your time. Even if I had received such photos and letters I don't believe they would be anyone's business except mine and I certainly would not share them with strangers. I fail to understand your concerns about commercial air traffic since the last I was aware they do not fly beyond our galaxy. Whom did you say told you that some photos and letters had been sent to me concerning out of this world travel so to speak?"

"I would suggest, doctor, that you not take this visit lightly and that you cooperate in sharing whatever you have with us. This is a serious matter and your failure to cooperate could put you in jeopardy with several government agencies."

"Gentleman, and I use that term loosely, I have to believe that wherever you found out about the alleged materials you also obtained a copy of them. If your purpose in coming here is to try and intimidate me into buying into this story be advised I do not take to threats or intimidation easily. Frankly, if such photos exist they are one hundred percent bogus, in my opinion, as is the fact that you two claim to represent the Federal Aviation Administration. Now if you will excuse me I have a great deal of work to do, or I would be happy to call security." With that the two abruptly turned and left my office. Mark came, almost running, in to find out what they wanted as they were arguing when they walked through his office as to how I should have been handled.

"Kait, who, pray tell were those fellows? They sure were a sinister looking pair. I am certainly happy they aren't hanging out at the gay bars that I do."

"Mark, they claimed to be from the FAA but that was, I am sure, fake. They wanted a copy of the photos and letters our mysterious stranger had sent. I'm sure they already have a copy or they wouldn't have been here. I did share them with Debbie and Sally but I am positive they were careful not to share them with anyone else. I also shared them with my class on open discussion day and my guess would be that one of my students had a friend or relative whose interest was aroused by them. I still think the photos are doctored from mockups but I will say the mystery seems to be deepening."

"Doctor, you do recall that Mr. Space Traveler did ask you to keep all of this confidential as he was concerned that any world government that was even slightly made aware of his mastering travel within the Universe would be after him. I certainly agreed with your assumption at the time that all you were sent was a hoax, but now I am beginning to wonder. I would recommend that you cool it a little from this point on and do not share, if in fact you receive anything else, information from your mystery man and secret lover."

"You and your imagination, are you honestly taking these communications seriously and think he has any interest in me outside of my knowledge of the Universe? It would take a lot more than a few doctored pictures and some well-chosen words to convince me that our Mr. X is who he says he is. Enough of this for now, these two visitors are enough excitement for me for one day, especially as sinister as they acted and appeared. I must email Debbie and Sally and mention this to them."

"Kait, I would be cautious about emailing anyone about this entire affair. I don't want to be Mr. Suspicious but if this goes as deep as it might from what we have encountered so far our email and even your phone calls might be monitored. I would suggest you call the ladies and just tell them you miss them and want to get together this coming weekend if they are free."

"Talk about a suspicious mind, Mark, do you really believe what you are saying or are you pulling my leg? Whatever, I will take your advice. We have often talked, you and I and the ladies and I about the military superiority of any government that could learn how to conquer space travel. With mankind's less than stellar past in using every technological advance to built more efficient weapons of war to annihilate each other with I would hold out little hope that such a discovery would be used for peaceful purposes. If what we are in the midst of were even slightly legitimate there would be the race to end all races for every government in the world to discover what our mysterious stranger has mastered. For the sake of him and for all of mankind let us hope this is all a well-designed fraud. In all my years of loving the Universe and it's mysteries I never in my wildest dreams expected anything even remotely close to what this could all suggest."

I excused Mark and decided to call the ladies and see if they were free to meet this weekend.

When I picked up the telephone I did so with apprehension, as I could not get out of my mind the fact it might just be bugged. Here I am a professor of Studies of the Universe and my life was becoming complicated more than I ever dreamed. Sally said she was free and we would meet at her watering hole up on the Cape. She couldn't wait to renew acquaintances with some of the fine looking young men that frequented the bar. Debbie said she had plans but would change them to get together. Debbie also asked if I had received any further communications from Mr. Space Traveler and I was somewhat abrupt and cut her off on that subject. In fact, to get her immediate attention away from that, I suggested we tip a few glasses of wine in the bar with Sally. She said, which surprised me, that she thought it was about time. I hung up feeling a little better but still nervous about everything that was going on. I decided to move up the class on open discussion for this Friday and see if I could ferret out who might have spread the word on the pictures and letters. I was not upset about anyone that might have shared them as I did not ask the class to keep it confidential but thought maybe I might get some clue as to who the two mysterious visitors were.

Friday rolled around soon enough. I had not received any more correspondence from the so-called space pioneer or any more visits from strange men to complicate my life. I welcomed the class back into session and I could sense the anticipation from the group. Not surprisingly Robert opened the discussion. "Professor, I wondered if you had any additional feedback from anyone on those photos you shared with us? I ran them through an analytical calculator at my uncles business and was surprised at the accuracy of the planet placement. Whoever did the mockup had to be brilliant as the location of each planet was so perfect that even my uncle was amazed. He, frankly, is the type that is always skeptical and that is why the Pentagon uses his expertise in so many cases, since he is so precise and never fooled no matter what the challenge is."

"You say your uncle does work for the government Robert. How long has he been involved with them?"

"He is on call twenty four hours a day, fifty-two weeks a year, as so many mysteries seem to need expert analysis and he is one of the few they turn to. Why are you so interested in my uncle and his expertise?"

"No particular reason, just always interested in brilliant, analytical minds and where they fit into our society. Did anyone else deem anything interesting from these obvious hoaxes that I received?" Several students spoke up and supported Robert's observations about the planet placement and then, fortunately Gail changed the subject.

"Professor, I did a lot of thinking since our last open discussion class about the theory of God setting aside a number of planets in outer space for those that have gone to their reward or punishment to occupy. I even talked at length to our pastor to see what his opinion of the theory was. Our pastor is a brilliant man and has always kept an open mind on most every issue. He often preached that man is so closed mind about so many subjects that it works against progress. He agreed that the bible does not identify the location of Heaven and Hell or what lies therein. He even went on to say that the theory that the worst of the sorts of mankind sharing the same planet would in itself be enough of a Hell to compensate for sins perpetrated while on this Earth. To share the same space with like scum of society would be payback enough for what happened while on this planet we call Earth. He mentioned that we think of Hell as a place where the devil dictates the pain and suffering but what better way than to have the most evil amongst us create it for each other who share those planets designated for the worst of mankind. From the opposite ends of this theory the best of mankind share the Heaven planets and live out eternity in peace and harmony with each other. He said the entire theory was extremely interesting to say the least."

"Remember, we agreed to give everyone in the class an opportunity to rate each of us on which planet in this realm we would eventually end up on. We agreed that the most coveted planet on the Heaven side would be named Heaven A and the most feared planet on the Hell side would be named Hell Z. The remainder going unnamed unless any of you wish to add a handle for your choices for the others of us. The further down the alphabet one goes from Heaven A to Hell Z the less desirable the destination. Planet M would be the tipping point between good and evil, so conduct yourselves accordingly so you would end up in one of the top thirteen anyway."

Everyone got a big laugh out of my identification of these destinations and several students offered their thoughts about the final destination for many of us. Gail again reiterated that Robert would be lucky to make it to M with his reputation as a ladies man and bar fly. It was all in good nature and everyone had a chance to participate. Many an interchange took place as students were placed into their final destination with many interesting names given to the various planets. One was named 'Just Made It' and another one someone called 'Oops' and everyone enjoyed the interchange. The class finally broke up on this note and I suggested we find another issue to discuss concerning the Universe the next time we have an open discussion get together.

I returned to my office, packed up a few things and headed for my Mercedes and the trip to the Cape with great anticipation. When I arrived I glanced into the bar area and Sally and Debbie were already there. As I approached I was shocked that Debbie had a glass of wine sitting in front of her. I gave each of the gals an embrace and then threw caution to the wind. "Would you believe I received a mysterious visit from two sinister looking people concerning the photos and letters I had received from my mysterious, so called space traveler. They claimed they were from the FAA but if they were I would be very surprised. They wanted copies of the items, which I am positive they already had, and they wanted to question me about them. During discussion in one of my classes, which incidentally I had shared the photos and letters with, one of my more brilliant students said his uncle had taken an interest in them. He further said that his uncle was associated with the government and I would guess these two visitors were also somehow associated with them. Our discussion was anything but pleasant and they left prior to my calling security. I did tell them that I thought the photos were bogus and were taken from mockups and that the person or persons that had sent them was certainly certifiable.

I am beginning to vaguely believe what the author of the letters claimed when he says he has achieved, unlimited space travel, would be the ultimate ambition for world conquest to any nation that achieved it. Just imagine the possibilities for peace on Earth if man could travel freely throughout the Universe rather than use that knowledge to create more sophisticated weapons to annihilate one's fellow man with. Here I am on my soap box again about mans failings." Sally beat Debbie to the punch with a response.

"I thought you were somewhat evasive on the telephone when you called about meeting here this weekend. Are you actually beginning to believe that there is someone out there that has mastered unlimited travel throughout the Universe? I think it is time that you joined us in a glass of my favorite wine, or possibly several glasses. Even if someone had mastered space travel why would they choose to share this feat of all times with you? I think this entire episode is getting way out of hand and it is time we put an end to it once and for all. The last thing you need is to be caught up in is some intrigue involving questionable characters and government powers. We are all just plain college professors and we are not involved in issues involving suppositions and mysteries beyond our control." Debbie also added her two cents after she ordered me my first glass of wine, but as things were going certainly not my last.

"I think there is a simple answer to this mystery. Kait has a secret admirer and he is desperate to make contact with her no matter what it takes. I also agree with Sally that it is time to end it and move on. Whoever it is that is communicating with you, in my opinion, could be dangerous to your well-being. You are being drawn into a situation which, if true, could involve multiple world governments and much more intrigue than even you could handle. I have a suggestion, the next time the Master of the Universe communicates with you tell him you want absolute proof of what he says. You mentioned your open forum class discussed planets that the Lord had set aside for each of us when we go to our reward or punishment. Since we are talking far out in space, literally, let us assume that is a fact. Each of us ends up with others of the same rewards or punishments, depending on how we conduct ourselves on this Earth, on one of these planets. My father was a very good man, thoughtful of others, charitable and kind so he should have been assigned one of the higher lettered planets and be easy to locate. When your mystery man next contacts you, if in fact he ever does, ask him to travel out in space and find my father and ask him for The Missing Poem that my mother loved so much. He can then send you the poem to prove that he has mastered space travel. That way you will know he is for real."

"Ladies, since I am the central character in this unfolding drama I vote we move on to other subjects, like a second glass of wine. This entire drama is just too bazaar to comprehend. I am beginning to think that that handsome fellow over at the other end of the bar might be more interesting to discuss." Only Sally could top these remarks.

"I am amazed that my oldest and dearest friend, the stalwart of propriety, is even suggesting spending some time studying the opposite sex. It is even more remarkable that she is doing it with her second glass of wine in her hand. I do agree that we should combine these two bazaar theories and ask your secret admirer to visit several of the Heaven planets, find Debbie's dear departed father, and ask him for the poem. He could then send you the words, which of course you would share with us and prove that both he and the theory of the location of Heaven and Hell are correct. Just think, over night Kait you would become the most famous person in the world, with headlines in the paper reading, *'PROFESSOR OF STUDIES OF THE UNIVERSE MASTERS UNFETTERED TRAVEL IN SPACE AND ALSO FINDS HEAVEN AND HELL*.' That should certainly bring you fame and fortune like nothing you ever dreamed of."

"Ladies, I have had enough of this talk. I pray I never have another communication from Mr. Mysterious, and never hear anyone again speak of planets far out in space being the locations of Heaven and Hell. I am going to order my third glass of wine and go and see if that gentleman who has been eyeing us wants to start a conversation."

"Debbie, I think you and I need to cut Kait off before she gets in way over her head. Has she ever approached a stranger of the opposite sex anywhere, let alone a bar, to strike up a conversation?" I didn't even hear Sally's remarks to Debbie, as I was half way to the other end of the bar and the good-looking fellow when she made them. In fact he was looking more intriguing as I got closer. I glanced back and the gals were looking at me with admonishing eyes and laughing their heads off. I saddled up in the bar stool beside handsome and asked him if I could buy him a drink. Needless to say I was shocked when he said to me, Doctor Graham, I would love to have you buy me a drink.

I almost completely lost it right there and then and almost fell off the stool. The ladies saw that I was coming unglued and rushed over and at that very moment the gentleman abruptly got up and exited the bar. Debbie grabbed me by the arm and asked what was wrong.

I struggled for breath and to gain my composure and told them that he had called me by my name and then, as we all saw, left immediately as if his cover was blown. "Who was that Kait, you say he called you by your name? Do you think it was one of those henchmen that visited you at your office?"

"I have no idea who he was and I am still shaking. It wasn't either of the questionable characters that visited me at the office. I have no idea how he knew my name; I just want this over with. Let's get out of here, my first glasses of wine and an encounter with some mystery man are enough for one night." As we turned to leave the bartender called over to us.

"Ladies, that gentleman that you were just talking to asked me earlier to give this envelope to you after he left. I'm not sure why he asked me to give it to you, since he was talking with you, but here it is." He handed us a manila envelope and the three of us just stared at it for a minute. Finally Sally spoke and said she was going to go to the lobby and the parking lot and see if he was anywhere around. My hands were still shaking as I tried to hold on to the envelope. Debbie calmed me down and told me to open it immediately. I tore it open and out fell a picture and a letter. I picked up the picture and could not believe it as it appeared to be a picture of Saturn taken from far out in space. I shared it with Debbie, as Sally was still trying to find our mysterious stranger, and she too was astonished. I opened the note with trembling hands and read it aloud.

"Dear Kait:

I trust you do not mind my referring to you as Kait, as I heard your two very beautiful, petite lady friends refer to you. I realize this is a strange way to meet but thought it best that we had an opportunity to see each other in person. For obvious reasons I did not want to linger at the bar with you, even though I find you extremely attractive. I would love to just sit and discuss my intimate view of the Universe with someone as knowledgeable and striking as you. I truly believe we would have a great deal in common to share. I would like to again ask you to be discreet in discussing my achievements with anyone, with the possible exception of your two lady friends.

I have become increasingly concerned about my welfare and unscrupulous persons, representing governments, zeroing in on my achievements. I have taken an oath with God to go to my grave before divulging any of my secrets that the Lord has seen fit to endow me with. The fewer persons that are aware of what I have mastered the better. I also realize that two questionable characters visited you trying to find out whatever they could about the strange photos and letters. I appreciate your being evasive with them. The source of their suspicion came from one of your students that shared the photos with a top-secret government consultant.

I forgive you for what has transpired and assure you that under the circumstances I would most likely have done the same. As I mentioned, however, please be as discreet as possible in the future in order for this secret of the Universe to remain undisclosed. If you ever wish to contact me, put an ad in your local newspaper under the heading of *'SPACED OUT TRAVELER LOOKING FOR DESTINATION'* and I will contact you. If you wish to add your telephone number reverse the last two numbers for your protection please.

I sincerely hope and pray we will meet again and someday I will be able to share with you the millions of secrets of our vast Universe.

Yours in space,
Joseph, which by the way is my real name."

Debbie was the first to speak up. "Kait, I am beginning to be a believer that Joseph is much more complicated than we originally thought. He certainly is not certifiable and actually may have conquered travel in space, how far into space remains unanswered, however, never the less into space. There are far too many coincidences here to ignore this completely." Sally had returned from her search of the lobby and parking area without any success in spotting him and we shared the memo with her.

"My God, Kait, this mystery is getting deeper by the day. I want to believe Joseph, if in fact that is his real name, as it would be the greatest discovery of this century, or any century. As we spoke before, in the past, with so many ancient cave drawings and carvings of what appear to be visitors from space in ancient times conquering travel throughout the Universe may not be so allusive after all. We need to put our collective heads together and find a way for Joseph to prove to us what he is saying? We also need to raise our guard and keep this entire undertaking confidential between the three of us."

"Do you two realize what you are suggesting? I do agree, as we have discussed many times in the past, that space travel may well have been achieved in earlier Earth times, but nothing even close to what Joseph is suggesting has even been dreamed possible in what we call modern times. It goes without saying that I will, and I expect you both will, button our lips about all this from now on. If what Joseph says is even partially true the ramifications for mankind would be earth shattering. I don't blame Joseph for fearing for his life, if in fact he has achieved what he says he has. Supremacy in space would be the ultimate aphrodisiac for many government leaders on this Earth intent on ultimate control of all the nations on Earth.

Sally, I agree proof is what we require, however I would not have a clue as to what we would ask our space traveler to bring us as evidence. Wouldn't it be wonderful if my gifted student Robert's theory was correct and there were planets set aside where we all go to our reward or punishment after we pass from this Earth? It would be easy then to ask him to bring us back proof from someone we have previously laid to rest. Without such an avenue I fear this mystery will never be resolved. Frankly ladies, I for one want to drop the subject and return to the lounge and have another glass of wine. I have had more than enough excitement for one day."

We returned to the lounge and ordered another round. There were several new faces in there and immediately I looked around to see if I saw our mystery man. I also was conscious of the fact that maybe one or two of the fellows were from the clandestine government agency and were there to keep an eye on me. Sally noticed my anxiety and told me in no uncertain terms to cool it. As we sat there enjoying our wine, and my suspicions of who all these gentlemen were passed, Debbie raised an interesting point.

"Kait, maybe it is not such a far fetched idea to ask Joseph, if in fact that is his name, to bring us back proof from beyond our imagination that in fact he can travel in space. We discussed your gifted student's theory, I believe you said his name was Robert, that when we pass from this life we are transported to a planet in outer space to spend eternity on, with others of the same record of rewards or punishments. That theory might not be so far fetched after all. I remember some time ago lying in bed at night asleep and a vision came to me of all my ancestors standing alongside what appeared to be a garden path. It was so vivid I awoke with a start, expecting to see them standing beside my bed. Tie this vision in with Robert's theory and we have a challenge for Joseph. Find one of our ancestors that have gone to their reward, and bring us back proof of their existence and the fact that he has mastered travel throughout space."

"Debbie, you are being absolutely ridiculous now and I believe it is the wine talking. Number one, you don't seriously believe that Joseph has discovered the secrets to unlimited travel throughout the Universe, and you are not buying into Robert's Heaven and Hell theory also are you? I cannot believe what is happening to me and now to you two also. Just a short time ago I was just a run of the mill college professor leading a semi boring life and now, along with the two of you, we are caught up in mystery and intrigue and possible intervention by government agencies."

The morning newspaper left at our rooms as a complimentary copy contained the headline, *'UFO SPOTTED OVER CAPE LAST EVENING.'* It went on to explain that a number of folks who had been strolling the beaches of the area had witnessed what appeared to be an unidentified flying object in space. The newspaper even had a picture of it. They went on to explain that it was being investigated by the Homeland Security Department of the government. I thought to myself, that is just great to have another government agency involved in all this mystery. Can't we just set all this aside and move on with my humdrum life?

I met the ladies for breakfast and it was the talk of the town in the restaurant with everyone abuzz about it. Debbie was the first to speak. "So much for putting this issue to rest. I think our mysterious space conqueror has chosen to expose himself and has created quite a stir. Even on one of the late night airline flights onto the Cape the pilots mentioned seeing the object very plainly and trying to identify it. I am becoming a true believer and insist,

Kait, that you put that ad in the paper and present Mr. Space Traveler with an ultimatum. Prove it or leave us alone, put up or shut up. I think it is time to either get on board or end it all. Frankly I am about fifty percent convinced our mystery man is what he says he is."

"Enough is enough, if I agree to put the ad in the paper and ask him for proof when I return will you then drop this forever?" Debbie agreed and thankfully we all dropped the subject for the remainder of our time here at the Cape. It was sad leaving my dear friends, but duty called and I reluctantly climbed into my Mercedes and headed back. On the way I could not get out of my mind that I had promised to put the ad in the paper and thought how foolish this all sounded. I said a silent prayer that no one, even Mark, would find out about it. If anyone did I think I would be the certifiable one and would be an unemployed college professor.

I didn't even ask Mark to take the ad to the newspaper. I composed it, as directed, and sent it to them via email. I said a silent prayer that it would never be answered and I could get on with my life, even as boring as it has been.

Several weeks went by. Sally and Debbie both called me and emailed me multiple times and discretely asked the question on all our minds, has he responded? After a full month went by I had all but forgotten the episode and one day when Mark brought in the mail there was a manila envelope without any postmark or return address. Mark commented on it, but I asked him just to leave it unopened for me. I certainly didn't want him to become involved in this. After he left I opened the envelope and I noticed my hands were shaking as I cut it open.

"Dear Kait:

Please forgive me for not responding sooner to your ad. I have literally been on the run as my foolish display in the heavens, when you and your fiends were at the Cape, aroused much suspicion in the wrong government circles. You would think that someone who has been granted a gift that no other person has would be more discreet. As I am sure you are well aware, when one possesses such knowledge the deepest desire to share it with others is overwhelming. I have no one to blame but myself as to the present danger I am in. For some unknown reason the government, or I should say governments that are suspicious, have sent many drones, which are of course unmanned airships, over the area where I live.

Maybe I am being paranoid by the drones as I also understand they are evident in many other areas of the country. I read the other day that our government is making even more widespread use of drones to literally spy on its own people. This is in my opinion, and of course many others share this feeling, which frankly is a frightening scenario. I must be extremely careful, if and when I next take my space explorer out into space, to try and not raise further suspicion.

Enough of my problems, since you contacted me I assume you have something you wish to discuss. If whatever you desire is within my power to grant I am prepared to do so. Needless to say if it is proof you desire, in whatever form, I am ready and willing to go to the ends of the Universe to provide it. Taking all the necessary precautions please keep your request as brief as possible and tuck it under the wing of the statue of the eagle which as you know stands outside the local space museum. If you do this at seven in the evening three days from today, I will retrieve it shortly thereafter. Please do not remain in the area, as I will be extremely conscious of anyone around the vicinity. I do not anticipate your being followed, or under surveillance, but we cannot be too careful. I look forward to hearing from you Kait; you are an extraordinary woman who I pray will someday share the greatest mystery of all with me, the unbounded Universe.

Joseph"

I debated for some time what to ask him to bring me as proof. I decided to leave it general, as I am a firm believer that we, on this tiny planet called Earth, are not the only living creatures in this immeasurable Universe, so I asked Joseph to bring me any kind of proof from a distant galaxy. I would not be specific and left the proof up to him. As I composed the note I thought, this should end this once and for all. If I were looking for a suitor I would hope they would be more straightforward in their desires to get to know me more intimately than to go through such a charade as Joseph has perpetrated.

"Joseph, you mentioned providing me with proof of what you say you have mastered. Since I am a firm believer that we are not the only creatures in this vast Universe, I would ask that you bring me back some proof of life in another galaxy. What type of proof I leave up to you. In a previous letter to me you mentioned that such wonderful and magnificent life forms occupy the vastness of space. Those who think that man is the only seed that the good Lord planted in the Universe must have insurmountable egos. I look forward to hearing from you; I think?

Dr. Graham"

I dropped the note off as instructed and was beginning to find this clandestine life sort of exciting. This, of course, is the furthest from the truth of what I should really be thinking. I was even so paranoid that I kept looking around to see if I was being followed or watched. As far as I could tell those folks in the area all seemed like tourists or locals visiting the space museum. I didn't spot Joseph either and, as instructed, I left the area immediately. There was a slight pocket where the wing connected to the body so it was the perfect place to leave the note. I returned to my office reluctantly wondering if I would ever hear from him again, and if I did what type of proof he would produce.

When I convened the class for open discussion the next day the students were all abuzz about the UFO, which had recently been spotted off the Cape. Robert asked me if I had been there and if I had seen it. Most of the students were aware that I met my two college professor friends there on a regular basic so Robert's question was not surprising. I decided to be evasive as I did not want any of the class, especially Robert with his relative being inquisitive about the letter and picture to be any further involved. "I must admit, just between us that I was indulging in several glasses of fine wine when said UFO was supposedly observed. I have found it releases the tension built up in my rather routine life so I am beginning to indulge somewhat." Gail was the first to speak up and it was all in good fun.

"I cannot believe our gifted professor who has only one love in life was indulging in wine. You have told us in the past that you spent most of the time on the Cape on the beach gazing into the heavens. I believe there may be hope for you yet." The class had a few chuckles over Gail's comments, all in good fun. I suggested we leave the subject of the supposedly UFO and open the discussion up to whatever anyone wished to contribute. Several of the student urged Robert to expound on his Heaven and Hell theory of planet assignments but I quickly put a stop to that as I felt we had covered that subject thoroughly. One of the other brilliant students raised the issue of life in space and so we spent the entire hour with an open discussion of that concept. After some time I did a survey of the class as to whether they believed in some form of life on other worlds in space. I was somewhat surprised that every one of these gifted students was absolutely convinced that other forms of life existed in the Universe. One of the students confirmed what I had always said, that God did not create the Universe and then populate it with only those called humans on this planet Earth. A lively discussion followed and we finally broke it off as the class time had come to an end. Robert did ask at the conclusion of the class if I was convinced in our lifetimes that any of us would be fortunate enough to confirm other life forms in other galaxies. All I could say was I thought someday it would happen, in the far future, but unfortunately not in our lifetime. I enjoyed the open discussion as I always did and found it ended to soon. I returned to my office and Mark was waiting there for me.

"Professor, your mail again contains a non-postmarked, no return address envelope and I must assume it is from your mysterious stranger who claims to have opened the door to the knowledge of free travel throughout space." I hesitated but noticing how anxious Mark was to see what was inside I told him to open it. He glanced at it and then almost shouted as he read it.

"Doctor Kaitlin Graham:
Please forgive the blank envelope, without any return address or postmark, but I must also remain anonymous. I am well aware of the letters and pictures you have received from a mysterious stranger who is claiming the mastery of travel throughout the Universe. I am associated with the highest levels of our government involved in clandestine and covert operations. Your name has recently been mentioned in regards to the claims of this mystery man and I wished to relate to you that several powerful

persons at the highest level of our government and military have taken an intense interest in this issue. As I am sure you are well aware, any government trying to come into possession of such knowledge of unlimited space travel would be willing to go to any measures in order to acquire it. We are certainly not at that point yet, but I have seen these things unfold before and if it does not die a natural death for lack of proof it could become extremely ugly in the future. I realize you were randomly selected by this mystery man to share his knowledge, but I wanted to warn you that for your safety I would strongly suggest you distance yourself from this stranger and the issue. I know why he chose you, as an expert in the study of the vastness of space and your reputation as one of, if not the most knowledgeable scholars on this subject. You are for all intensive purposes an innocent bystander, and as such please heed my advice and detach yourself from any further contact with him. My interest in telling you all this is strictly humanitarian, as in my many years in the government I have seen too many innocent persons fall victim to clandestine operations of questionable intrusion by a government supposedly of a free people.

Please destroy this letter and do not share it with anyone.

A friend for a more peaceful world."

Mark just stared at me for a moment and then back at the letter. "Doctor Graham I always thought you led a pretty lackluster life but the way things are going it is anything but boring. If I may be so bold as to suggest that you back off some and bid a fond fare well to your mysterious suitor, for want of a better term. I think you are treading on dangerous grounds and getting in way over your head in this situation. If you worked for some clandestine government agency, such as the CIA, then this type of intrigue might be acceptable, but you are a run of the mill college professor. Well maybe not run of the mill, but never the less this is way out of your league. The longer this goes on the deeper you are getting into it. I beg you for your own good to distance yourself from this entire sordid affair."

"I am afraid I am already much too deep in this to back out now. Can you imagine, if what this man Joseph claims is even partially true, the earth shattering ramifications of it. To be able to freely travel throughout the Universe is beyond the comprehension of most humans. Even though many believe that in ancient times, in Earth measurements of time, space travel by aliens from other worlds was achieved, it is unheard of as a possibility today. Blasting off into space via rocket-propelled ships is one thing, but to actually travel freely from galaxy to galaxy is unheard of and only thought of in one's wildest dreams. I'm, frankly, captivated Mark, for whatever the future holds. Not in my wildest dreams did I ever see myself in this position, but it would be the ultimate achievement, especially in my field of study, to conquer travel into space. I cannot and will not back down at this point, or any point, no matter what the risks."

"Kait, I am always here for you and understand the aphrodisiac this is to someone in your field of endeavor, or for that matter anyone. I will always be here for you and I will do my best to watch your back. Do you want me to destroy this latest letter?"

"Put it in my briefcase Mark as I plan on sharing it with Debbie and Sally the next time we get together. I know whoever wrote it said to destroy it, but at this point in time I am not going to fall in line for anyone or any group be they friendly or hostile. I am in this to the finish, whatever that may be. If Joseph and his claims prove to be true it will be the greatest story since mankind first walked this Earth and, frankly, I want to be a central part of it whatever the consequences. I have spent my entire life being intrigued by the mysteries of the Universe so I am not going to turn my back on this until it is proven to be for real or a possible hoax." With those words we broke off our conversation and both returned to our duties.

Weeks went by and I heard nothing from Joseph as to what proof he was going to furnish and I heard nothing from either the two gentlemen that claimed they were from the FAA. I also received no further communications from whoever was warning me to keep my distance from these affairs. My classes went on as usual and neither Robert nor Gail brought up anything about the pictures or letters and Robert didn't even raise the issue of the location of Heaven and Hell. After all the excitement of the past months I was beginning to wonder if I had dreamt all of this and would awaken suddenly to the world of reality again. My world of dull and unexciting routines.

CHAPTER THREE

The Rock

It was about two months after I had left the letter for Joseph at the Space Museum when Mark came in one day with the mail. The look on his face immediately peaked my interest. "Doctor, this small box again has no postmark or return address and I believe it is from your mystery man.

"Mark, I can see you are chafing at the bit to see what is inside of it. Just remember, if it comes from the outer most areas of the Universe who knows what it might contain. Let us hope that our mysterious space traveler is well aware of the safety of what he brought back as proof." As Mark opened the box he reached in and, with a strange look on his face, brought out what looked like a plain and ordinary rock. We both looked at the rock and then each other with a look of confusion and amusement on our faces. Mark found his voice before I did.

"I think the mystery man who claims to have conquered space travel has just revealed his true self. He traveled into deep space and brings back a rock?" As Mark was speaking I picked up the rock, which was no more than five inches long, and as I was staring at it I noticed that it had a glow to it. I looked closer and could not believe my eyes. The rock was glowing on the inside as if it was on fire yet the outside was cold to the touch. I handed it to Mark and told him to look closely at it. The expression on his face said it all as he noticed the fire burning deep inside the rock.

"Kait, I cannot believe what I am seeing, this rock is cold to the touch, yet it is on fire deep within itself. What is fuelling the fire, and why is the outside cool to the touch if in fact it is burning within itself?"

"Mark, I think we may have to take back our doubts concerning Joseph and his claims. This is truly amazing; I have never seen anything like it. I'm not sure if it qualifies as proof of life in outer space but it certainly comes close. I would love to try and split the rock open, but something in my better judgment tells me that might be extremely dangerous."

"Doctor, there is also a note in the box that we overlooked. If you will allow me I will read it for us?"

"Dear Kaitlin,

This specimen from the third galaxy beyond the Milky Way, that we call home, may not be proof of life in outer space but I am sure it has peeked your interest. Please do not try in any way to open the rock, as that could prove extremely dangerous. This sample contains enough energy, if properly tapped, to fuel an entire city the size of San Francisco for many years. The life forms, I will not refer to them as humans, which inhabit this particulate planet, use these natural forms of unlimited energy to provide all their needs. I would further suggest that you not use it as a paperweight, as prying eyes might arouse even more suspicion as to my accomplishments. A safe deposit box would be appropriate and I can assure you those persons that work in the bank would be perfectly safe. Thank you again.

PS: Feel free to share it with your two lady professor friends but, again, try to be as discreet as possible. I do not feel as threatened as I was feeling, as the drones are no longer circling over this area of the country.

With all my affection,
Joseph"

"Kait, I think your mysterious space traveler is also rapidly becoming your very affectionate significant other. I know you mentioned meeting him briefly at your getaway on the Cape and I hope you found him attractive."

"Mark, that is none of your business, however, all I will say is that if I ever become interested in someone of the opposite sex it could very well be this handsome mysterious man."

"One other observation, doctor, just think you could be the only human to have intimate sex in the far reaches of the Universe with your noteworthy other."

"Mark, I truly believe that if Joseph were to take me on a trip into the far reaches of space, the last thing on my mind would be sex. Enough of this discussion, I want to call Debbie and Sally and see if there is any chance of our getting together again, either this weekend or next, at our usual rendezvous. It seems like we should move there permanently as we are spending so much time at the Cape."

After Mark left, and I swore him to secrecy, I placed the first call to Debbie. I had to leave her a message and was purposely evasive, as I was still worried over the warning letter I had gotten and if those mysterious gentlemen that visited me might still be nosing around. In fact I was so paranoid that I even thought I heard a clicking noise on the phone connection. After that I placed a call to Sally and she did answer the phone. Again I was evasive as I spoke with her.

"Sally, I had such an exciting time at the Cape last time that I was wondering if we could do it again this coming weekend or next?"

"Oh my God Kait, you received proof from your mysterious lover of his travels in outer space." I almost lost it right there and told Sally in no uncertain terms to stifle it. I went on to explain to her that it wasn't anything of the sort and it was just a get together for a weekend to pick up where we left off. She immediately became aware of my concern and changed the subject completely. We agreed to meet and I told her if Debbie could not make it I would let her know and we could pick another weekend. As it turned out Debbie did call back, was very discreet, and said she would be there. I was so anxious to share with them not only the special rock but also the other letter of warning that I had received from another anonymous source. When one is in possession of such great mystery it is so human to want to share it with others rather than keep it all to yourself. That is not necessarily the wisest move, but certainly the one where most folks would find themselves.

I was extremely nervous when I threw a few items in my overnight bag and tucked the rock in my briefcase for the trip to the Cape. All I could think of was if I became involved in an accident how would I ever explain what the strange object in my briefcase was. I did arrive without incident however and met the ladies in the lounge as they were already there. Sally was so excited she could hardly control herself but Debbie was much more discreet. I took the warning letter out of my briefcase and shared that with the girls. They couldn't wait to read it. Debbie was the first to speak. "Kait, I said it before and this further reinforces my feelings wondering what you have gotten yourself into. Again, I am concerned if you want to continue to go down this dangerous road or distance yourself from this entire affair. I can't wait to see what your space traveler sent you to prove that there are other life forms in the Universe.

As it turned out Sally was so caught up in this entire sordid affair that she urged us to adjourn to our mini suite so they could see what I had, supposedly from deep in space. I also shared Joseph's note with them and they could not believe the ramifications of what he was saying. When we arrived at our room I checked carefully to make sure everything looked normal, as I was still paranoid that we were being watched. Things seemed to be ok so I took the rock out of my case and eagerly handed it to them. They almost fought over which one of them was going to get the first close look at it. After they had examined it Sally was the first to speak.

"All doubts have been erased from my mind at this point. This is truly amazing and I am one hundred percent convinced that your secret admirer has in fact mastered unbounded space travel."

Debbie agreed and we spent about an hour discussing what we should do next. We finally agreed if I was going to stay connected to this entire issue that I should just wait and let Joseph make the next move. We had an enjoyable supper in the lounge and, as usual, I kept looking around at the other patrons wondering if we were being watched. There were two gentlemen together at a far table that raised my suspicion but Debbie said not to let it bother me as she thought they looked like a couple and the last thing they were interested in would be three ladies. I wasn't convinced, but finally let it pass.

We sadly parted company in the morning and headed back to our home bases reluctantly. As I drove along the expressway I noticed a large black SUV behind me and being as paranoid as I am I wondered if I was being followed. I purposely exited the expressway, about half way home, to see if the SUV would exit behind me. When they kept going I was relieved and turned around to return to the thruway. I soon needed a break so I pulled into a rest area to get a cup of coffee. I re-entered the superhighway, and within a short time I again happened to glance in my rear view mirror and there again was a big black SUV behind me. I wasn't sure if it was the same one and thought that I was certainly getting apprehensive by all that was going on. I swore under my breath to relieve the tension and decided right there and then to take the stone to the bank and put it in the safe deposit box before returning to my office. As I left the expressway at my exit, the SUV again continued on straight ahead so I breathed a little easier. I arrived at the bank, checked my surroundings carefully and took the rock in and left it in the safe deposit box. I said a silent prayer that I would never have to see it again and breathed a little easier as I left. Of course I knew I was much too deep into this entire business to back out now.

I arrived back at the office and Mark was curious as to how the ladies had reacted when they saw the specimen from space. I filled him in and then went into my office to check the accumulated mail and the emails. I was not surprised when I checked the emails that I had one from both Sally and Debbie as they had a shorter time to travel home than I did. Both emails mentioned that they each felt they had been followed at least part of the way home. We were certainly all getting mistrustful. I wrote them both back and mentioned my concerns about possibly being followed also. I mentioned again to be discreet in all future emails and phone calls and told them I couldn't wait until our next get together.

Weeks went by without any contact from Joseph, or the mysterious letter writer that had warned me to abandon my contact with anything to do with this mystifying space traveler. I fell into a comfortable routine with my classes and with Mark taking care of all my organizational needs. Neither Mark nor I talked about the issues that had been haunting me for so long now. Sally and Debbie kept in touch and seldom, even discreetly, mentioned anything about it also. I was beginning to again be comfortable as just plain Dr. Kaitlin Graham, professor of studies of the Universe, when I received a strange call on my cell phone one afternoon.

"Kait, I cannot talk long, please go to the bank and immediately remove the item that I entrusted to you and find a secure hiding place for it. Our clandestine friends have spent a considerable time interrogating your close friend Sally and she has mentioned the rock. They stopped short of actual physical interrogation, but they made her life so uncomfortable that to end the torment she mentioned the rock and that she thought you were going to secure it in your safe deposit box. I will get back to you again, soon I hope. Love you, Joseph."

With that the phone went dead and I just sat there speechless, wondering again what we had gotten ourselves into. I immediately picked up the phone and placed a call to Sally. I got her answering machine and left a message for her to call me immediately. I also called Debbie and told her what had happened and she was shocked. When she recovered her voice she said we should immediately go to the authorities and ask for help and protection. I asked her what authorities she was thinking of as so many of the government agencies would be anxious to get the inside information on what Joseph had mastered. I told her I would get back to her and headed out for the bank.

When I arrived at the bank and asked the attendant in the safe deposit box area for access to my box she said that two men had just been here and were extremely insistent that they wanted to see my safe deposit box. They had flashed some badges and demanded to talk with the manager when she refused their demands. She said the manager had told them they would need a court order. They became belligerent and he called security and when they showed up the two characters reluctantly left and shouted that they would soon be back. I immediately opened the box in the private room, removed the rock and placed it in my briefcase and left the bank half running. I looked around outside. Everyone appeared to be going about their business, so I thought it must be that they didn't expect Joseph would have found out about their interrogation of Sally so quickly.

As I drove off, constantly looking in my rear view mirror, my mind was racing as to where I should hide this secret. I decided not to go back to the office as they might be waiting for me there, and rather to go to the space museum. As I drove there I thought what better place to hide it than with the display of other space rocks that have fallen to Earth and are on display there in an open case. I acted as a normal tourist and had the rock in my pocket as I entered. I wandered around for a while, as I knew the entire area was under surveillance cameras and certainly didn't want to arouse suspicion. I edged my way toward the space rock display and noted the camera positions. When the closest camera swung to the other side of the room I leaned into the display and deposited the rock near the far back. I then just stood there and dusted myself off so the camera would only see the tail end of my clandestine deposit and hopefully not arouse suspicion. The sign at the front of the display said not to touch the rocks as the case was alarmed. Thankfully adding one did not activate the alarm as removing one most likely would have since it is a weight sensitive alarm system. I left immediately and returned to the office intending to put an ad in the paper without delay requesting contact from Joseph. I had every intention of telling him where the specimen was, and also that I wanted nothing more to do with this entire sordid affair.

When I arrived back at my office I had a telephone call that I had missed from Sally. I immediately called her and she answered the phone in tears. "Kait, I am so sorry for telling those monsters about the stone. You cannot imagine what they subjected me to. They didn't do any physical harm to me but the mental strain was unbearable. I am so sorry Kait, but I have to tell you that I must distance myself completely from this entire incident. Until you have divorced yourself completely from this mysterious stranger, who says his name is Joseph, I am afraid I will no longer be able to meet at the Cape or for that matter anywhere else with you and Debbie.

These people, who claim to be from some government agency, are intent on finding your puzzling mystery man and his secrets of supposedly unlimited space travel. You know how much I love you but I cannot subject myself to any such treatment in the future, so please let things drop and distance yourself from him entirely. It is not worth it. These so-called government agents that are allegedly on to his accomplishments will stop at nothing to find the answers they are seeking. I love you, Kait, as I do Debbie. You are like sisters to me, but until this is completely behind us I cannot be part of your life. Forgive me for being so weak, but please do not contact me until such time as you are no longer associated with this man who claims he has conquered space travel. You are in grave danger Kait, please heed my warning. I love you." With that the line went dead and I sat there stunned.

I called Debbie and threw caution to the wind. "Debbie, you will not believe what has happened to Sally. I feel it is entirely my fault and I am devastated about it." I went on to tell Debbie all about what had happened to Sally and told her to watch her back also. She said she had already hired a private security firm to keep her safe since she was sure she had been followed home from the Cape, and she was very comfortable that the security firm could do the job. I did tell her this was the end of my contact with Joseph and that I was going to put an ad in the paper and leave him a note at the space museum that I never wanted to hear from him again. We agreed we would not communicate with each other for the time being until this was all behind us. Debbie said she was going to call Sally next to see if she needed any help and assure her that she was there for her at all times. We ended the conversation, both in tears, and I immediately sent an email to the local paper with Joseph's pre-arranged contact code. I couldn't wait to hear from him and tell him exactly what had happened, and also tell him in no uncertain terms to get lost, in space or on this Earth, but nevertheless to get lost.

The ad appeared in the local paper the following day and I anxiously awaited a response from Joseph. I didn't have to wait long as I received another envelope from him with the usual lack of postmark or return address.

"Dear Kait:

I am appalled that our so called government, that talks peace so often, would stoop to the level of evil as to subject Sally to such treatment. They are desperate to discover my identity before some other world power ends up with it. Several times I have thought to myself, maybe it would be easier to just fly off into space to some more peaceful planet, never to return. I realize Debbie has hired a private security firm to watch her back, and I would urge you to do the same. I regret involving you in all this, but I so wanted to share my accomplishments with someone of your advanced knowledge of the mysteries of the Universe. It is such a sad reflection on mankind to think that the evil amongst us is so intent on world domination, including many in the United States, that we must be terrified as to their potential use of such understanding that I embrace.

I realize I should never have involved you as much as I did but you are so intelligent and desirable that I needed your connection. I pledge to you this day that our contact will cease forever. I have subjected you and your two dear friends to danger that I never thought was possible, especially from our government. If you need in the future to ask the assistance of law enforcement I would urge you to call local authorities, as they would be much less corrupt. Someday possibly, we will meet on a planet assigned by our Lord for the two of us, based on our record of our time on this Earth. Your prized student, Robert, was not far off in his theory of the location of planets called Heaven to Hell, or whatever one wishes to name them. The Universe is amazing Kait, even beyond what a brilliant imagination you have.

I will always hold you in the highest regard. Forgive me and please do not think ill of me. Love always.

Joseph."

So that was that, it was ended, as it should be. For a brief moment I had this strange feeling that I would possibly miss out on the greatest adventure of the centuries, but only for a brief moment. Even as exciting as it might be to travel to the far ends of this vast Universe, it has turned out not to be worth the sacrifice. If it had been only myself that was involved and confronted by those evil investigators it would have been one thing, but since it involved my oldest and dearest friend it was not worth it.

In retrospect I was surprised that Joseph had not asked me where I had hidden the rock that he brought back from the outer reaches of the Universe. I did wonder, however, if he already knew since he seemed to have such a grasp of everything that was going on.

Months have gone by and all has been quiet with myself, Sally and Debbie, thank God. On two occasions I did wander into the space museum and observed the rocks from the outer space display. Without fail the rock was still there and undisturbed, so my hiding it in the open was at least something I had done right. It crossed my mind that Joseph, if in fact he knew where it was, might have retrieved it by now. Maybe someday years from now, when they decide it is time to clean the rock display, someone will notice the glow from within this one and such excitement will gather around the scientists that are called in to study it.

I have missed our getting together at the Cape, but the three of us agreed that we wanted at least six months to go by before we decided to again get together. All of us, within a few weeks of deciding to distance ourselves from Joseph, have given up the private security personnel. We each did take a few routine precautions with our security, but fortunately none of it was necessary.

On at least three occasions the newspapers did carry articles in this six-month period stating that citizens of Argentina, India and Ireland had seen UFO's in the skies above those countries. The spokespersons in each case for those governments tried to explain it away as a natural occurring phenomenon, as I am sure they did not want to panic their citizens. It crossed my mind that possibly Joseph was involved but I didn't dwell on it. This gal had had enough excitement for one lifetime.

The three of us, after such a long period apart, did make a date to visit the Cape and get together for a holiday weekend this coming week. I could not wait to see Sally and Debbie and excitedly jumped in my Mercedes and headed out when the time came. I constantly checked my rear view mirror to see if I was being followed as I had been doing for months, as obsessed as I was. Everything seemed to be normal however, and I arrived and headed for the lounge. As I entered, there sat Sally and Debbie at the bar having a drink and seemingly relaxing. Sally turned around first and she almost flew off the stool as she saw me. The embrace was overwhelming and my embrace of her was equally loving. Debbie and I then embraced and we all settled in at the bar for a drink of our favorite wine. The first thing Sally said to me was that her experience with those monsters months ago was not a topic she ever wanted to discuss, and we all agreed. The other matter was we agreed not to discuss Joseph, and/or his rock, under any circumstances.

We spent an enjoyable three hours just sharing small talk about our jobs, classes and such exciting topics as the planets that we would all be assigned to as our reward or punishment when we leave this life. Robert made sure, when I last had a class of open discussion, that we didn't forget his theory and the class enjoyed the thoughts as I did. The ladies and I all had a good laugh talking about his vivid and wild imagination and finally after several drinks and much small talk we retired to our suite. We also agreed gazing into the heavens would not be part of our trip this time around, so the beach was off limits. It didn't take any time to fall asleep, but I did hear Sally tossing and turning often during the night and wondered if her memories of such an unpleasant experience were still disturbing her.

When Monday afternoon rolled around we enjoyed a late lunch and sadly said our goodbyes with many an embrace. It was so great to spend time with my dear friends again, but so upsetting to part. We all agreed to try and get together for a weekend again about a month from now.

My trip back to the college was uneventful. Mark had everything organized well for me so it was not long before I fell back into my routine. About a week later I had been out for a forlorn supper by myself and decided to visit the space museum and check out our rock. I thought to myself I just can't seem to put that entire sordid affair behind me. I was shocked when I approached the display case that the rock I had hidden there was missing. My mind raced as to what might have happened and I had the strange thought, wondering if my fingerprints could have still been on it. It worried me and I left in a hurry, still confused by what had happened to it.

It was about two weeks later and Mark brought in the mail and there again was an envelope without a postmark or return address. My hand was shaking as I opened it. Mark asked me if I wanted him to open it but I said I didn't want anyone else involved after the experience Sally had. He left and I reluctantly read the note.

"My dearest Kait:

You may already have noticed that the souvenir I brought you back from the depths of the Universe is no longer where you hid it. That was an ingenious place where you placed it and I doubt anyone would have uncovered it for many years, if in fact they ever did. I know that I promised to never involve you in my achievements again but, frankly, I cannot get you out of my mind. If you choose not to acknowledge this note with our prearranged method of communicating I will certainly understand. You may have seen in the news the UFO sightings over several countries across the seas. Just for your information, that was I. I certainly didn't want to arouse any more suspicion in this country so I took my adventure abroad. Not that other governments wouldn't love to get their hands on this understanding, but so far none seem to be as caught up in my activities as our government. I did see in the paper the other day that some official came forth in the States and said that he had been involved in the Roswell, New Mexico UFO incident and in fact it happened and the government covered it up, not surprisingly.

Kait, if you ever desire more proof of my accomplishment and knowledge of the Universe don't hesitate to contact me. I can even bring you back proof that mankind does in fact spend eternity in space on various planets assigned from our accountable behavior or lack thereof while on this Earth. Your brilliant student Robert's insight is astounding. I pray you will decide to contact me.

My love, Joseph"

It wasn't too much later that Mark came in and by the look on his face he just couldn't wait to find out what was in the envelope. He pressed me and I told him in no uncertain terms that I was not going to involve him or anyone else. "You know Mark what those so called government agents subjected Sally to and that is not going to happen again to anyone that I know. Just let it be, Mark, as I have no intention of taking up again with Joseph."

"Kait, at least share the note with me. If those fellows that say they represent the government want to get a little rough with me I might even enjoy it. I certainly would make it interesting for them."

"Mark, enough of this talk, if you insist on reading the note help yourself but don't blame me if you also get caught up in this intrigue." Mark proceeded to read the note and couldn't contain himself.

"Kait, you must realize you are involved in the discovery of all times. You cannot let it rest here. If someone contacted you and said they wanted to give you the world on a silver platter you would jump at the chance. Here someone is offering to give you the entire Universe on a silver platter, don't throw away the chance of a lifetime or for that matter the chance of many lifetimes. If you don't want to become involved with Joseph please ask him if he has ever entertained any sexual preferences besides the opposite sex and if he has I would love to travel through space with him as my lover. Go for it Kait, you have been chosen from billions of people on this Earth to share this excitement which is beyond human comprehension."

"Enough Mark, I will think about it but believe me when I say I do not intend to ask Joseph about his sexual orientation. I believe from his letters he has made it abundantly clear where he stands in that regard. The only flight into space you will have with one of your lovers, I believe, would only be produced in a strong drink or something else which I will not discuss. Thank you Mark, please close the door quietly when you leave." With that Mark reluctantly left and I sat there wondering what my next move would be. I started to work on some lectures for my next two classes and about fifteen minutes went by and I could not stand it any longer. I picked up the phone and dialed Debbie. I was pleased when she was there and took the call.

"Debbie, do you think it is safe to talk on the phone? I assume you well know what I am implying?"

"Kait, when I had temporarily hired that private security firm to watch my back I spent considerable time with the chief of the firm and he was fascinated by what little I told him. He did suggest at the time, and I took his suggestion, that I place a safety net arrangement on my phone so it would be impossible to tap into a conversation. You can pick one up at your local Radio Shack and according to him they so far are impregnable. All you have to do is unplug the cord from the wall jack and insert this in the jack and then connect your phone to it. I would suggest you get one when possible and then call me back after you have it. I will be here for the next few days, when I am not in class, so if I don't answer leave me a message and I will call you back post haste.

By the way Kait, if you ever need any private security assistance or advice on a safeguard matter I strongly recommend this company and the man in charge. He shared with me that their greatest area of work now comes from individuals or corporations interested in counter intelligence and protection from invasion of privacy from an ever more intrusive government in this country." I thanked Debbie, and since my next class did not start for a couple of hours I jumped in my car and headed out to Radio Shack.

I found what she had suggested and bought two of them, one for my office phone and one for my townhouse phone. I didn't have any idea if they made anything to protect privacy when using a cell phone so I just make a conscious decision that in cases involving Joseph and his claims I would not ever use the cell phone unless forced to. The next morning before I left for class I called Debbie back.

"I sure hope your security gentleman knows what he is talking about as I have something important to talk to you about. I received another communication from Joseph and he is almost pleading for me to become involved again. Would you believe he actually knew where I had hidden the space rock he brought me back and he has recently retrieved it. Even more amazing is the fact that he confirmed that there are planets in the vast Universe where we do all end up when we go to our reward or punishment for the time spent on this Earth. He thought it was certainly insightful of my prized student, Robert, to come up with such a theory without any actual knowledge of it. Frankly Debbie, I can't decide if I want to become involved again or not. Mark said I am missing out on the discovery of all times if I distance myself from him, but I just don't know what to do. After the incident that Sally had, and by the way I have honored her request and have no intention of calling her at this point, I am at a loss as to pursue this or not. I need help Debbie in making a decision."

"Kait, I'll make it for you here and now. Throw caution to the wind and contact Joseph and tell him you want final and absolute proof from him, and if he can provide it you will travel to the far ends of the Universe with him. If you are annoyed again by persons claiming to be government agents, or whatever, I will have Rick, the head of the security firm, get in touch with you immediately. Once you spend a little time with him you will feel much more comfortable no matter what the circumstances are. I even have a foolproof request you can make of Joseph that if he can produce will forever put to rest any hesitations we might have.

You remember I read you a poem that my father had written when the three of us were at the Cape sometime ago. I also mentioned that my mother had remembered he had written two poems when he served during the Korean War. Mother has searched high and low for the second one and she vaguely remembers she had placed it in his pocket when she laid him to rest a number of years ago, as it was so moving. Joseph is claiming that Robert's theory of the fact that we all end up in space on a planet, depending on our conduct while on this Earth, gives me this idea.

Kait, make contact with your mysterious stranger and tell him you want him to travel into space to the planet where my dad ended up and ask him for the other poem and bring it back to you. If he could do this then prepare to be transported to the many mysteries of the Universe and Sally and I will be there to see you two off and wish you God's speed. All Joseph would have to know was that my father was a good man, honest and hard working. If anyone deserved to be on one of the planets for the best amongst us it would have been him. Maybe not Mother Teresa's planet, but certainly in the top few. With that information, if Joseph is telling the truth, he should be able to find my father and deliver the note."

Debbie, you have always had a vivid imagination. I just cannot decide if I want to continue to be involved in this escapade. On the one hand I still find it hard to believe all of this is true and on the other hand, if it is, I want desperately to be part of it. I will give your suggestion some serious thought and get back to you. How Joseph would actually find the planet your father was assigned to, and then how he would find him, is beyond me, but then again the entire theory is beyond my comprehension."

"That is the entire point Kait, the Universe, as you know better than most, is the greatest mystery of all, so the answers to its riddles may not be within our grasp but may well be within

Joseph's. I'll wait anxiously to hear from you, go for it gal." With that we bid our goodbyes and I was left with this uneasy feeling, trying to decide my next move. This was like a colossal chess game being played out in space.

It was a week later, of restless nights that I finally decided to put the ad in the local paper to contact Joseph. If he can fulfill this almost impossible request that Debbie suggested, then I am totally hooked. I thought to myself that there was no way he could pull this off, or if he did he and Debbie were old friends pulling the biggest practical joke on this unsuspecting person ever perpetrated on anyone. I sent the ad into the paper on Friday afternoon so it should appear in the Sunday edition. Once I had sent it in I breathed a sigh of relief that I had at least made a decision to move ahead with contacting him.

My ad appeared on schedule and I waited anxiously to hear back. Several weeks went by and nothing. I was beginning to wonder if that was the last I would ever hear from Joseph since all that had transpired, then late one afternoon Mark came rushing in and told me some gentleman was on the telephone asking for me and would not identify himself. I calmed Mark down and told him I would take the call and instructed him not to listen in. I told him it was most likely nothing, but from the look on his face I just knew who it was. Mark reluctantly left and closed the door behind him. I heard Mark hang up his end before I spoke. "This is Doctor Graham, to whom am I speaking?"

"Kait, I believe you know who this is. I understand your phone is now secure and appreciate Debbie making you aware of the security firm that Rick heads up. I have done a bit of investigating concerning them and they are top notch and can be trusted absolutely. Keep them in mind for you and your friends if you ever need assistance. I saw your ad in the local paper but I have been busy taking additional security measures myself. I have an acquaintance in the highest level of government and they have alerted me again that certain unscrupulous individuals are again expressing an interest in my activities. I believe you even received a communication from said individual warning you to distance yourself from me also.

I was so excited when I saw your ad in the paper alerting me to contact you. Kait, even though we have only met briefly in the past at the Cape I can not get you out of my mind. I think we were meant for each other both emotionally and spiritually. Especially as it comes to traveling the Universe together. Traveling the Universe is beyond anyone's imagination, but traveling with you would even be more breathtaking. I'm sorry Kait, I am too long winded, as I am so excited talking with you."

"Joseph, just so I know this is you, tell me what I was wearing when we had a brief encounter in the bar at the Cape?"

"Our meeting was so brief I can only remember you were wearing a red blouse and a pair of white slacks. You had red shoes on and a beautiful ring on your left hand. As you can tell, I was very observant, especially when it comes to remembering you. I can even remember your voice and your walk as you approached me."

"I remember you well also Joseph and it is good to talk to you. I appreciate your getting in touch with me after I put the ad in the paper. I did in fact get an anonymous note a while back warning me not to become involved with you. I assume this is the same person who is advising you as alerted me.

"It is in fact the same gentleman and renews my faith in human nature to know there are still decent folks out there that care about their fellow man. The only thing that could make this day more meaningful for me is if we were sitting together enjoying a glass of our favorite wine and looking deeply into each other's eyes. Kait, I so want to share with you the mysteries of what I have experienced in my travels throughout this vast and beautiful Universe. There are sights in the Universe beyond human intellectual capacity and I can think of no one I would rather share them with than you."

"Joseph, I have become almost ninety percent convinced that what you claim is true, however I am still not one hundred percent convinced. I recently spoke to Debbie, whom I am sure you remember from the Cape, and she suggested that I ask you for absolute proof to what you claim you have conquered. We all agreed, Sally, Debbie and I that we would then be on board with you in the adventure of the millennium. We three are all professors of the vastness and indescribable mysteries of the Universe. We all agreed that it is not beyond the realm of possibility that in the past, especially due to cave drawings and other evidence, some creatures of this vast cosmos have conquered inter-galactic space travel. You mentioned that Robert's theory of the location of Heaven and Hell is in fact to some extent accurate. As wild as that theory seems, Debbie and I have come up with a fool proof request that would absolutely convince us that you have in fact mastered unshackled space travel."

"Kait, Robert's theory is in fact almost on the mark. He mentioned, as you relayed to me, that he thought there were twenty-six planets where every human that ever walked this Earth are assigned upon their passing. There are not twenty-six of them as he suggested but Heaven and Hell do in fact exist in space and all mankind spends eternity there according to their record of good or evil accrued while on Earth. I, in fact, have actually visited a few of these planets, those with kind souls on them, and seen it first hand. Families are together as often as possible, if in fact our Maker gave them all the same grade when they passed from this life. It is amazing to see and experience the thrill of visiting ancestors, who one would think would never be possible, but this of course is but one of many mysteries of the vastness of space. I have in fact visited my parents and deceased sibling on several occasions. What is it you want me to do to prove what I say?

"Debbie shared with Sally and I a poem that her father had written when he served during the Korean War. She told us that her mother had said that he had written two poems, but after searching for weeks they could only find one. She then remembered that she put one in her husband's pocket when they laid him to rest. Debbie has suggested I ask you to visit him on the planet that her father was assigned to and bring back 'THE MISSING POEM.' Is this within your powers to do?"

"I believe it is. What I would need to know is what kind of life Debbie's father led while on this Earth. That would give me information as to which planet he may be resting on for eternity. I will need to know all the details of his life, family, job, church affiliation, belief in our Savior. I especially will need to know if he was kind to his fellow man, strangers and friends alike. Was he ever accused of a crime? Did he love his wife and family? Everything you can tell me about him. I'll make a pact with you Kait; if I agree to this assignment, and I am successful, you will agree to accompany me in my spacecraft into the far reaches of the Universe within a reasonable time after I provide the proof?

"Joseph, I will ask Debbie to compile a complete history of her father's life for you and I will leave it under the wing of the eagle at the space museum two weeks from today at seven PM. If you can provide this proof you will not have to ask me twice about accompanying you into space. By the way, even if what Robert says is true, and you confirmed it, how is it possible to find one individual in all the deceased persons occupying a particular planet? You mentioned these planets are the locations of Heaven and Hell and that all Earthlings end up on one of them. How then is it possible to locate any one person on any one of them? Even if you were fortunate enough to pick the correct planet what guides you to an ancestor, or in this case Debbie's father?"

CHAPTER FOUR

Book of Life-Book of Death

"Kait, I am sure you have read in the bible about the Book of Life and how each of us are listed therein. We have all thought that we were listed in that book, but there is also a Book of Death where our Savior notes those who have committed multiple sins on this Earth. These books, of course, are not available, but each of the planets we have referred to that house all of us once we go to our reward or punishment, does contain a record of those that reside there for eternity. I have been privileged to see such journals in my search for family that have gone to their reward before and, as I mentioned, located them. If I receive enough detailed information as to Debbie's father, and can pin things down to just several planets on the Heaven side, I will be able to locate him. It will be a demanding task so bear with me as far as time is concerned. I have voluntarily terminated my employment so time will not be a factor. I really do not need to work anyway as my family left me well off, bless them."

"This all sounds so fascinating I can hardly wait to leave the information that Debbie gives me for you. She is working on it as we speak and I will leave it for you at the appointed time at the drop spot. I so wish we could meet face to face again and this time for more than an instant."

"I will see that it happens, Kait, when I retrieve the information about Debbie's father. I want to remind you to please remain cautious and don't share anything about our conversations with anyone except your two close professor friends. Also keep in mind that if you are ever in need of protection or security don't hesitate to call on Rick and his firm. As I mentioned, he is one hundred percent trustworthy and more than capable. He has a fabulous staff, of both men and women, who are the most talented and motivated when it comes to any and all needs in the area of security. I will await the information from you at the appointed time. Let me be so bold as to sign off with love Kait, as you have touched and warmed my heart."

"It was good to have a conversation with you Joseph. I cannot yet however, end our conversation with love but given time let us see what materializes. Goodbye and God be with you Joseph"

"And God be with you also Kait, goodbye."

With that the line was silent and within a few moments Mark knocked on the door as I expected him to. He was so curious he could hardly contain himself and immediately wanted to know what we had talked about. Much to his disappointment I remained closed lipped concerning the conversation. All I did tell him was that it definitely was Joseph and that we had an enlightening conversation. He was so excited and asked me repeatedly if we were going to meet soon as lovers. Mark was much more interested in my love life than I was!

"Doctor Graham, just remember that you are not getting any younger and I can tell you from great experiences you are wasting precious time. You said you found him very attractive when you briefly met him at the Cape, so squander away no more time."

"Mark, I think I know my needs much better than you and, bluntly, I would rather not hear anymore about it. When the time is right I will take up with the right gentleman and maybe have a tryst with him in the far reaches of the Universe."

After Mark left I immediately dialed Debbie and left a message for her to call me back. My head was spinning from the events of the past hour and it was hard to concentrate on the mundane work of being a college professor. When Debbie did get back to me I again alerted Mark to not listen in on my conversation. He assured me that never happens, but knowing Mark as well as I do and knowing how he likes to mother me, I could never be certain.

"Debbie, just a short time ago I got off the telephone with you know who. He told me what we talked about is possible for him to do. My mind is having a difficult time getting itself wrapped around the enormity of what we are talking about. He told me that he will need a complete history of your father's life including marriage, church affiliation, family, career, anything you can think of. It might be well to receive your mother's input also. She of course knew him intimately and there might be something that she could add that would give our mutual mystery man an important clue to finding the poem we have talked about. I am leaving the material for him shortly at a previous drop spot we had arranged, so the sooner you can get it together and fax or email the better."

"Kait, do you realize what is upon us. There is absolutely no way he could know the contents of the poem. If he in fact produces it we will become a part of the greatest story in the history of this world. I will see mother tonight and begin to put together the dozier and get it to you in the next couple of days. The biggest hurdle I see as I look down the road is, if in fact this proves true, that it can never be made public. The desire of our government, and so many other governments, wanting this knowledge for whatever world domination purpose they might use it for is a reality. As we have talked, wouldn't it be marvelous if at some time in the future he and the three of us could actually come forth and announce his accomplishment of conquering unfettered space travel. I could only pray that after said announcement mankind would find only peaceful uses for such information, but we both know that is wishful thinking. I will call you in the next two days and let you know when I am sending the material to you. I love you Kait, try to stay calm."

"Love you also Debbie and when you talk with Sally send her my love."

I left for the day and tried desperately to sleep. After a couple of glasses of wine, and reading the remainder of the book **STONE AND MORTAR** that I had started some time ago, I finally fell asleep. When one talks about breaking new ground like Joseph is doing, that book also dramatized the importance of crusades and many mountains to conquer for mankind. Tomorrow my first class is the open discussion forum, and I am hoping I can restrain myself from telling Robert that his theory of the location of Heaven and

Hell is almost one hundred percent accurate. At least at this point it seems to be, while I await confirmation from Joseph and his retrieval of the second poem.

The class went well and the only reference to Robert's theory was when Gail responded to a question Robert raised about sex in space. She reminded him that he best be careful, as the record that is being accumulated for his final resting place assignment just dropped down one planet or two. I was happy the issue did not come up again as with what I know I would have to be extremely careful of my input. Much of the class time was spent on speculation of previous space travel to the Earth in ancient times and the references left in the distant past from early man. Many in the class raised the issue of the world's current technology advancements and how long it might be before man conquers the total freedom of space travel. I could only bite my tongue as to this issue and thought to myself, 'if only you knew.'

Debbie, as usual, was true to her word and called to tell me she was faxing the materials that afternoon. As Joseph and I had agreed on a date and time for the drop this would work out well. When I received the dozier on Debbie's father I thought she had written a short book, as it was about fifteen pages of materials. I thought to myself Joseph shouldn't have any problems finding him with all this information, but then again I had no idea what Joseph would be up against in his quest.

On the day we agreed upon I headed out for the space museum at the appointed time. The packet of material I was carrying was quite bulky, since Debbie had supplied so much history, and I was hoping there would be room to leave it hidden under the eagle's wings. When I reached the spot I looked around to make sure there were no prying eyes and was just about ready to discreetly place it where we had agreed when a voice behind me said to stop. My heart went up in my throat and I turned abruptly and to my surprise Joseph stood there.

"I know we agreed for you to drop it here for me but I needed so desperately to see you especially after our recent talk. I was hoping, actually I was praying, you would spend a little time with me before I leave on this mission you have given me. Depending on the difficulty of the search I could be gone for some time. It looks like Debbie gave you a great deal of detail about her father so that should make my task easier. Would you join me for a drink at the restaurant across the street and make the end of this day one I will always remember?"

"Joseph, you startled me so. I didn't expect to actually see you here. Aren't you still concerned about rouge agents that were after us earlier trying to track you down?"

"Things have quieted down considerably since I have not been giving human eyes, especially in this country, any glimpses of UFO's. As you know my activities have been limited to other countries lately, therefore I am not raising suspicion in the United States at present. Will you please join me and fill my empty day with your beauty and intelligence?"

"Joseph, how can I resist such an offer? I have so many questions I am dying to ask you? You have brought intrigue and mystery into my otherwise very mundane life."

With those words we headed for the restaurant and ordered our drinks. I noticed Joseph picked out a corner booth where he could see the other patrons, as well as watch the door, and wondered if he felt as secure as he had mentioned to me. Whatever the case I became enthralled in the moment, as he was one of the most handsome men I had ever seen and I had to catch myself several times from becoming too attached to this man of many mysteries. It was private enough where we were sitting that we felt free to discuss his journeys into space and he told me a great deal about his experiences visiting several of the planets on the Heaven side of Heaven and Hell. I was awe struck just listening to him. Finally he suggested we forget his escapades and talk about my life.

"Joseph, I am sure you know as much about me as I know of myself. My life has been pretty unexciting, born in a small town in Nevada of parents of the Mormon faith, I was raised in that wonderful church and it's devoted followers. I sadly never continued with a close relationship with that group or as a matter of fact any other religion. My religion has always been the mysteries of the Universe and God's hand in creating it. I went to Yale and there took up my studies of space and received my doctorate in The Study of the Universe. Here I sit with someone who claims to have conquered unfettered space travel and most likely puts to shame what little I actually know about the far reaches of space."

"Kait, your knowledge is in the love of the Universe and it's many mysteries. The splendor of infinite space only surpasses your beauty, as I frankly cannot get you out of my mind. I cannot wait to share the secrets of the Universe with you someday. I will hold you to your promise to travel with me into its vastness once I return with the poem that Debbie's father wrote. You have filled my life with meaning and excitement, even more so than my travels in space. God bless you Kait. I must be off shortly as I have an obligation that now means more to me than any other in my life. You will never know how much you mean to me and I cannot wait for the day when we meet again and I read you **THE MISSING POEM**."

We spent an enjoyable half hour talking about our beloved Universe, and I was amazed as far as some of the things that Joseph related to me that he had experienced. We enjoyed our wine and I had to actually remind myself that I didn't really know this man that well. I was still waiting for absolute proof of what he said he had mastered. When it finally was time to leave and go our separate ways he leaned over and gave me a kiss on the cheek. I almost wanted to throw my arms around him but at the last second I pulled back into reality. We shook hands and he was off with these parting words. "Much love to you Kait, and my memory of our time together, and the vision I hold of you in my mind, will make my upcoming journey complete."

With that he was gone and as I stood to leave I happened to glance over at the end of the bar and there was Mark and another fellow with him. He came rushing over and could not restrain himself. "Doctor, was that handsome fellow your mysterious space traveler and it now appears your lover? I cannot believe you actually solicited a kiss from such a distinguished looking man. Frankly it is long overdue. Life goes by too quickly to not partake of all it's pleasures and that fellow certainly looked like he could give you many fantastic moments of pleasure"

"Mark, I have said it before and I will say it again, we have only briefly met twice and we certainly are not in the midst of any love affair. He and I share the same dreams but I am far from being his lover in any sense of the word. I will admit I find him handsome and mysterious, but there is a long road ahead of us and it is strewn with many obstacles before anything significant might happen between us."

"Kait, please tell your handsome stranger that if he has any tendencies towards the same sex to give me a call. Spending a night with such a handsome specimen would be a night of enchantment for me."

"Enough already Mark, I think your friend is looking lonely over at the bar. Please forget what you saw here today and, again, I want to remind you that this gentleman you refer to is off limits to any conversation with anyone else. What you have observed and what we have talked about remains between the two of us only. Please do not even share it with your friend at the bar."

"Kait, my lips are sealed, as you and I previously agreed. Just let me leave you with this thought, life is much to short to not embrace all those emotions that the good Lord bestowed upon each and every one of us. I guarantee that, from the look on your face when he kissed you, someday you will look back upon this moment and think, why did I wait so long?"

With that Mark also gave me a peck on the cheek and with an enormous smile on his face he headed back to his friend and, I assume, lover. I don't know what I would do without Mark, he brings me back to this world often and with such a boring life that I lead I certainly need someone like him to remind me of all that I am missing. I have recently taken to enjoying a fine glass of wine and, who knows, maybe I will soon partake of another of life's pleasures and mysteries.

I returned to my abode with many mixed emotions. I didn't know if I was falling in love or just enjoying an infatuation with someone who claims to hold the key to unlocking the greatest mystery of all times. I put my head down on my pillow and for a brief instant I envisioned Joseph lying next to me. I shook those thoughts immediately out of my head and wondered for a moment what had become of just plain Professor Doctor Kaitlin Graham and her mundane life. I vowed to call Debbie and Sally and see if we could spend a weekend together, hopefully someplace except the Cape. I wondered if Sally was ready to become one of the three of us again after her unpleasant experience.

As it turned out Sally was very anxious to get together and suggested we meet in the Hampton's. She also said she had experienced no further threats or suspicions and felt much more comfortable knowing she could call on Rick and his team of experts if she needed them. She mentioned again those rouge agents that claimed they were representing our government. She hoped the bastards would rot in the worst of the worst Hell planets someday. I could not help but think maybe they would end up on one of the planets that Joseph claims are locations of Heaven and Hell. They might be assigned to the same one as Hitler, Stalin and the rest of the most horrible of mankind. I could only hope. She mentioned Rick, whom she had hired for awhile, had asked her why these low life's were harassing her and she didn't tell him anymore than she had to. She did say she completely trusted him however, and even felt if she had told him the entire story he could be trusted with the knowledge.

I could not wait to get together with my friends and called Debbie after talking with Sally. We arranged a date and time to meet at a hotel we had previously spent some time at in the Hampton's and time could not go by fast enough for me to meet there. I had so much to share with my dear friends. I had to remind myself to continue to be cautious, as what we were dealing with was certainly a volatile and potentially perilous issue.

The day finally came and I headed out for the Hampton's. I couldn't wait to see Sally and Debbie and share with them my time with Joseph and his assignment. When I arrived at our agreed upon meeting place neither one of them was there yet. I went in and registered and then headed to the bar to loosen up with a drink or two. Now that I had found pleasure and relaxation in a fine glass of wine my waiting time was much more pleasurable. I did notice a couple of men sitting at the corner table that I immediate became suspicious of. After I observed them for a while, however, they seemed to be more occupied with each other than anything else, so I forgot them as I waited?

Debbie showed up first and found me in the bar. She was so anxious to hear what had happened when I actually spent some time with Joseph. I told her I didn't want to repeat myself so we should wait for Sally and pass the time with some small talk. It was only a short time later and Sally showed up. We all ordered a round and I proceeded to tell them about my tryst, if one were to call it that, with Joseph. They were both so excited and had a million questions to ask me. I had to calm Sally down as she was bubbling over with enthusiasm for the task we had sent Joseph on and couldn't wait to see if he could produce the second poem.

During the conversation I did ask Sally about the security firm she had temporarily hired to watch her back. She said they were top notch and Rick, the CEO of the company, was fantastic. "I felt one hundred percent comfortable when they were taking care of me. I have to tell you also that Rick and I have been seeing each other on several occasions and, frankly, I am excited when I am with him. He is smart and runs a tight ship. His personnel are hand picked and totally trust worthy, and very capable of handling any situation. I even found several of the ladies that were assigned to me to be persons no one would want to trifle with. I almost wished on a couple of occasions that the bastards that intimidated me would try it again while Rick's folks were watching over me. They would have found more than their match in any of his staff, including the ladies. One thing that impresses me about Rick is his utter distrust of the government and his commitment to challenge them in any issues where he is hired for security purposes. He is convinced this country is headed for a dictatorship eventually and the citizens must stand up for our rights or all go down with this ship we call America. Beyond all that, girls, he is truly handsome and very appealing. I dare say I might be falling in love. I find it exciting and wonder why I waited so long.

We enjoyed the evening immensely and had a few too many glasses of wine. It felt good to unwind, kick our heels up, and have some fun for a change. This life of just being a plain old mind-numbing college professor is all right, but as far as a steady diet I am finding there may well be other, more gratifying things in life. Seems strange it took so long to come out of our shells. We wrapped it up around midnight and hit the hay and I don't think it took more than five minutes before we were all asleep.

Morning came around too soon, as it always does, and we had a great breakfast conversation. While we were eating we noticed some of the folks with newspapers were talking excitedly about something in their papers. Sally went to the newsstand and picked up the paper. When we looked at the headline on the front page we could hardly believe it. ***'NEAR COLLISION OF DRONE AND UFO OVER KANSAS***.' So there it was for all the world to read, Joseph must have taken off on our mission late in the night last evening and in so doing almost collided with one of these new unmanned aircraft. He had shared with me that his craft was hidden in Kansas in a barn whose roof opened hydraulically at the touch of a button. The article went on to say that the military was looking into the incident and had yet to positively identify the object as a UFO. They said they had ruled out a commercial aircraft since the altitude was so low, but except for the cameras on board the drone there were no eyewitnesses. No one on the ground reported seeing anything strange in the ski that night. There was even some speculation that the cameras on the drone had malfunctioned and caused the blip, which had raised the question of what it was.

"Ladies, I think we can assume this was Joseph headed for one of the Heaven planets to retrieve Debbie's father's second poem. I think we should lay low until the entire episode has blown over. Joseph did say, with all the drone activity it was becoming more perilous to try and leave the Earth unseen." Sally spoke up and reminded us of her contact with the security agency in case we needed them.

"I remember when I talked with Rick about the government becoming more intrusive in everyone's life, he was saying how extensively the use of these unmanned aircraft, to literally spy on people, was becoming a major problem. He mentioned that he thought this country was moving closer and closer to a totalitarianism state and that the consequences of a massive central government would only eventually lead to a revolt in America. As Thomas Jefferson once said, 'every generation needs a new revolution,' and maybe it is overdue. I think I should call Rick, I want to hear his voice anyway, and we should bring him into our circle of knowledge and solicit his advice at this point. What say you ladies?"

Debbie had no qualms about Sally contacting her newest close friend and even said she would feel more comfortable under the present circumstances to have an expert guiding us. My only concern was whether he could be completely trusted if we opened our hearts to him totally about Joseph and his accomplishments. I wasn't sure, however, at this point if we had a choice. I somewhat reluctantly agreed and Sally placed the call. She told us Rick's organization covered almost all of the fifty states and was made up of largely ex-military personnel. She said they were in demand now almost constantly for security, as well as their investigative skills. After Sally hung up her mostly very personal call, placed outside our earshot, she said he happened to be in New York City at a conference and would meet us tomorrow morning here in the Hampton's. I kidded Sally about what seemed to be an intimate call. She just shrugged it off and said Rick had never been married and needed her to mother him. I was sure that motherly love was not what either of them had in mind. The remainder of the day went by with our going on a shopping spree and having a great supper at the hotel. The only thing to concern us was two suspicious looking gentlemen in the restaurant that seemed more than once to glance our way and showed some interest in us. Maybe it was purely attraction by the opposite sex but it still concerned us some after all that was going on.

We enjoyed a continental breakfast and the only distraction was the same two guys that seemed interested in us during supper were also at the restaurant for breakfast and again seemed to show some interest in the three of us. Fortunately none of us recognized either of them from our past unpleasant encounters, which led us to believe they were innocent, opposite sex interested guys, only.

Rick walked in at the appointed time and Sally jumped up and gave him an extended kiss and they embraced for a minute or so. Rick immediately impressed me as totally self-confident, without concerns for anyone else's opinion of his actions. He was self-assured and that confidence automatically was passed on to those around him. One thing that did disturb me slightly was when Rick walked in the two suspicious gentlemen immediately became engrossed in a heavy conversation and within a minute or two they left. I wasn't sure if that was just coincidence or if in fact they were spying on the three of us. I mentioned it to Rick and he said not to let it bother us, that it was most likely just a coincidence.

"Dr. Graham, I am always one-hundred percent observant of my surroundings when I enter any public place and those two fellows did not raise any alarm on my internal radar. Believe me when I say that I would recognize about ninety-five percent of any unscrupulous agents our government employs to literally spy on its citizens. Sally filled me in slightly on what is going on but I was wondering if you wanted to bring me completely into the loop. I think Sally would agree that I can be completely trusted and I hold no loyalty to our current government. I fought in two wars for the United States and have nothing but the deepest love for this country, however the current leadership is becoming much too intrusive in everyone's lives and much to domineering. We are almost to the point of a dictatorship. It is, of course, your decision if you want me to be fully informed, but remember we can do a much better job of providing security and advice if I fully know what we are dealing with."

"Rick, please call me Kait. Of course you have met Debbie and I take it you and Sally have become close friends. I, for one, feel that I would like us to share everything we know to this point with you if Debbie and Sally agree." Both ladies spoke up and were one hundred percent behind opening our minds completely to him so I proceeded to fill him in.

"Rick, a number of months ago I received an envelope which came in the mail, even though it was unstamped and had no postmark. That in itself I thought was strange, but upon opening it I found pictures of the planets supposedly taken from far out in space. There was a note attached and it stated that he, the author of the note, had taken the pictures from well beyond any human being's capacity to travel into the depths of the Universe. He claimed he has conquered boundless space travel and wished to share his knowledge with me. He said he had chosen me, since I was a professor of the studies of the Universe, and he had also attended at least one speech I had given on the subject. He said he desperately needed to share his achievement with another person and had selected myself, due to my expertise in the field. He further stated he was extremely concerned that our government, or some foreign government, would do almost anything to obtain this knowledge as they would use it to achieve world domination."

"Let me stop you right there for a moment Kait. If what he says has even a grain of truth to it I wholeheartedly agree with his concerns that our government and many others would kill for such knowledge. Have you had any further contact with him?"

"I am sure Sally has shared with you the unpleasant experience she had with so called government FAA agents in trying to coerce her to reveal what she knew. In one of my classes of, if I may be so bold, brilliant students, I shared with them the pictures that he sent me of the planets. Many of the class, along with Debbie, Sally and I, thought the pictures were taken from an elaborate mock up of the various planets and sent to me by someone who could be committable. It would not be the first time I have received such questionable items, since I gained some fame from my numerous speeches I have given on the mysteries of the Universe. The one fact that seems to many of us to set these pictures aside from other mock-ups was the absolute precision of the spacing of the planets. One of my more outspoken and especially brilliant students, Robert, did mention that he had shared the pictures with his uncle who worked for the Pentagon as an on call expert in deciphering the hidden agendas in any documents they deemed suspicious. I believe that is the reason the government got wind of this and subsequently sent allegedly FAA agents to question each of us. If they were from the FAA then I am the Queen of England. Since this initial contact I have received more pictures and communications, and even spent some time with this man of mystery personally." Debbie interrupted me at this point.

"Kait, don't forget to mention to Rick that you did ask Joseph for some type of proof and he sent you what looked like a plain and simple rock that turned out to contain a constant power source within its core. The fact that you hid it in plain sight at the space museum and Joseph, he claims his name is Joseph, retrieved it later on is important. Whether it is proof of his conquering space travel is not one hundred percent, but it did raise our level of conviction considerably. Also, the fact that we have asked him for absolute proof in the form of retrieving the poem my father wrote during the Korean War and the issue of the planets designated as Heaven and Hell."

"Rick, I think Debbie has pretty much covered the rest of the story. I am sure you are wondering what we are talking about when we mention planets that are the final resting places for those souls that leave this Earth. The brilliant student I mentioned earlier raised the issue in one of my open discussion classes some time ago. He suggested there were planets in the Universe where each of us ends up for eternity, depending on the record of good or evil we accumulate while on this Earth. At the time Robert raised this theory we laughed it off as so wild it wasn't worth spending time thinking about. It did arouse my interest however, as talks with several religious leaders and others confirmed the fact that the exact locations of Heaven and Hell are not mentioned in the Bible or any other religious record. I became intrigued when thinking about this over several months and then one day my mysterious stranger, that claimed he has conquered space travel, confirmed the existence of said planets. He further said he had actually visited several of them on the Heaven side and even saw his parents. I know this sounds strange, Rick, but this entire undertaking is to say the least far out. Far out possibly is not the term to use since we are talking the entire Universe as one's backyard, but I'm sure you get the picture."

"Kait, I hope that is the 'end of the story' so to speak, as I am not sure I can even begin to absorb what you have laid out in front of me up to this point. As wild as this all appears, again let me say that even if a small part of what you say is true the ramifications for mankind are enormous. I would also repeat, in the strongest terms, that if this were even close to the truth governments would kill for the knowledge. I want to do whatever is necessary to protect you, Debbie and Sally. You have already had visitations from so-called government agents, so they are at the least slightly suspicious that something major is unfolding so we need to be ever vigilant. At the least I want each of you to carry with you at all times the latest technology for personal protection. This small device can be worn as a ring or a necklace and when pushed would immediately contact my crack staff and they would pinpoint your exact location, alert the local police, and also my people would be by your side in a matter of minutes. It is foolproof and should provide the protection each of you need from inquiring persons. Since they are already suspicious and have no idea, I assume, at this point who Joseph is, you three are the links they are going to pursue, especially as more and more UFO sightings occur. My paramount mission at this point is the safety and security of all three of you, and indirectly protecting the intellectual property of Joseph. As I have mentioned, I have little loyalty towards our current government so my priorities are clear to me, as I trust they are to you. All of those that I employ, who are mostly ex-military or ex-police, are of the same mindset. Your safety and security are my main concern and you can rest assured that of my staff."

With that we finally called it a night and went our separate ways, and in the morning bid a sad farewell as we each headed back to our separate colleges. I felt much more secure knowing that Rick was there for us and several times I found myself rubbing the necklace as if it were a security blanket, which of course it is. The return to my monotonous life was not what I was looking forward to, but since it was who I am I was not too downhearted.

At this point it was a time to reflect and see if Joseph could produce what he said he could. I didn't expect any results soon as he had said it might well take weeks or even months for him to locate Debbie's father and retrieve the poem. Several times I had to pinch myself to make sure I was awake and not dreaming this entire scenario. I also found myself thinking about this mysterious, handsome stranger on more than one occasion, and wondering where our relationship might travel if in fact I hear from him again in the future. I must admit, on more than one circumstance I felt some envy of Sally and her relationship with Rick and again wondered if I was missing out on many of life's pleasures from a loving relationship.

It was back to my routine and my open discussion class to start off the new week. When the class began I asked if anyone had a topic they would like to discuss and Robert raised his hand. "Dr. Graham, I was wondering if you had received any more pictures from your so called space traveler. My uncle, who I mentioned is a consultant to several branches of government, asked me recently if we had discussed this any further."

My alarm antenna immediately went up. I wondered if this was the connection to the matter that had been raised in the past, and generated the visits by those unscrupulous characters.

"Robert, nothing further has ever been raised as far as the initial contact I had with the pictures and the note. I would dare say that whoever sent those items to me has been committed or moved on to other fields, such as predicting the end of the world as we know it. I saw on the news the other day some sordid looking fellow standing on a corner in Boston holding up a sign saying,

'The end of the world is upon us.' I would venture a guess that might have been the same person who communicated with me." I hoped with this explanation to diffuse the situation significantly so Robert's uncle would dismiss it entirely.

"Dr. Graham, he and I were again examining the photographs the other day and we came to the same conclusion that the spacing was so precise it would be almost impossible to be a mock up. My uncle said he had shown the photos to a number of experts and they all agreed on how accurate they were. He said whoever did them was most likely either a genius or just plain lucky in his setup. He asked me to ask you if you heard from this person again to let him know immediately as he was concerned about what might transpire. I told him I would pass his request along to you."

This last comment by Robert really raised my antennas, as now I wondered if maybe his uncle might have been the one who had sent me the warning letter. "Robert, just how involved is your uncle with the clandestine underbelly of these government agencies?"

"He is deeply involved to the point of it taking a toll on his health. He has confided in me on a number of occasions just how demanding some of the various government agencies are and also how ruthless some of the persons involved can be. He said the other day just how far this country, in his opinion, has moved towards being totalitarianism and away from the democracy it was for so many years. He said that some of those in power have an unquenchable craving for absolute domination at any cost. He did admit the many outside threats to the United Sates exist, and the need to be vigilant, but he said many in Washington have gone beyond that point and want unfettered control over everyone and every nation. He told me that was why there were so many eyebrows raised about the possibility of someone having mastered limitless space travel, because that knowledge would be the ultimate world control mechanism."

"Thank you for the update Robert, it is reassuring to know that there are some in government, or at least associated with our government, that have a sense of decency and the rights of the individual. Fortunately, I have had no further contact with anyone claiming to have mastered free travel throughout the Universe. If I do I will ask the person if I can ride along, as I would dearly love to see first hand all of those marvelous and beautiful displays of God's making that we have so often talked about. I also would definitely want to visit the planets that are designated as Heaven to Hell locations." This brought some laughter from the students and hopefully defused the situation from getting too serious. In no way did I want Robert, or for that matter anyone else in the class, to think that in any way I had any further contact or knowledge of anyone having mastered travel throughout the Universe.

We spent the remainder of the class discussing what the National Space Administration had recently reported of seeing what looked like UFO's flying around Mars. It was an interesting discussion and I believe we all left with many questions on our minds as to whether there actually was life of some kind on other planets, and if in fact the other forms of life had conquered space travel. Someone brought up the point of why, if the Universe actually teemed with UFO's filled with life forms of one kind or another, they did not visit planet Earth more often. Gail ventured an answer to the question and said that with the record of mankind's endless wars and other evils, who would care to visit here. I wasn't sure that was relevant but it did leave us with some fairly deep thoughts.

CHAPTER FIVE

The Poem

At least two months have gone by, and nothing. My life is again so predictable and routine that I find myself almost praying for some excitement to come back and be my companion. Rick several times has contacted me about the situation and to make sure everything is secure. Debbie, Sally and I each check in with his organization weekly, as far as our alert system is concerned, to make sure all the devises are working properly. They certainly have so far lived up to their reputation as highly reliable. Fortunately, none of us have had to activate our protective device but I am sure if we did it would only be a matter of minutes before his personnel and the local police responded. He told us he has had one hundred percent cooperation with all local police authorities over the years, as many of his staff are past police officers as he had mentioned.

I had totally given up and decided this an elaborate scheme, or maybe I was dreaming all of this. I called Debbie and Sally and asked them to come up and spend the weekend with me as I was depressed and needed their company. Being the wonderful friends that they are they both agreed and showed up on Saturday evening. We headed out for our favorite local restaurant shortly after they arrived and they immediately lifted my spirits. While we were eating we overheard some folks at the next table talking about an article in the human-interest section of the paper. When they mentioned a poem my antenna went up immediately. Debbie was the first to speak.

"Did I hear what I think I heard? They were, I thought, talking about a poem that was published in today's paper that had been written by a soldier who served during the Korean War. Ladies, if this is what I think it is then our mystery is deepening. I am going to ask those folks if I can see their paper. Hang on a minute and I will get it."

When Debbie got up Sally and I just stared at each other. I finally found my voice. "Sally, what is going on? I can't believe this. Do you think there is any chance that this is the missing poem from Debbie's father? Why on Earth would Joseph have it published in the paper rather than send it directly to me?"

Debbie came rushing back with the section of the newspaper that contained human-interest articles. She was speechless as she handed it to Sally. In a stuttering voice Sally read from the paper the poem that was printed there.

"HERE IN THE CAMEL SUN LAND
RAMEY IS THE SPOT
BATTERING IN THE TERRIFIC HEAT WAVE
IN THE LAND THAT GOD FORGOT

DOWN WITH THE SNAKE AND LIZARD
DOWN WHERE THERE IS NO DEW
DOWN IN THE BOTTOM OF NOWHERE
THREE THOUSAND MILES FROM YOU

OUT IN THE DIRT WITH A SHOVEL
DOWN IN THE DITCH WITH A PICK
DOING THE WORK OF A BULLDOZER
AND THERE IS NO USE TO KICK

SLAVING OUT IN THE RAIN AND MUD
WORKING FOR OUR HARD EARNED PAY
WHILE GUARDING FOLKS THAT HAVE MILLIONS
FOR A DOLLAR AMD A DIME A DAY

*SOON AS WE LEAVE OUR HOME WE ARE SOON
FORGOTTEN
AND NOBODY GIVES A DAMN
WE'RE NOT MERELY CONVICTS
WE ARE DEFENDERS OF THE LAND*

*ONLY THREE YEARS CAN WE STAND IT
ONLY THREE YEARS OF OUR LIVES ARE MISSED
BOYS, DON'T LET THE DRAFT BOARD GET YOU
AND FOR GOD'S SAKE DON'T ENLIST*

*LIVING WITH ONLY MEMORIES
AND ONLY TO SEE OUR GAL'S
AND HOPE THAT WHEN WE RETURN
THEY HAVEN'T MARRIED OUR PALS*

*WHEN WE GET TO THAT PLACE
THAT PLACE KNOWN SO WELL
ST. PETER WILL PROUDLY SAY
THESE MEN ARE FROM THE CANAL ZONE
THEY SERVED THEIR TIME IN HELL"*

ANONYMOUS
The eagle at four on the fourth

The poem was signed anonymous and under that were these few words that almost seemed like they were a message of some kind. After we all caught our breath Debbie had this look on her face, which said it all. "Kait, Sally, I cannot believe it, this is the poem that my mother loved so well and that she placed in my father's pocket when we laid him to rest. Do you know what this means? Joseph has conquered unlimited space travel. Why he had the poem published in the paper rather than sending it directly to you is certainly a mystery. What does the last line he submitted to the paper mean, the eagle at four on the fourth? Kait, what does that look on your face imply?"

"I was just trying to wrap my mind around the promise I made Joseph that I would accompany him into space if in fact he produced this poem. Ladies, do you realize I am going to journey into the far corners of the Universe and see first hand what only Joseph has seen before. This is utterly amazing news. The last line in the article under anonymous is a message for me to meet him at four on the fourth of next month at the eagle by the space museum. I truly believe he has accomplished what he claims he has, the complete mastery of unlimited travel throughout the Universe. This is earth shattering news ladies, I am so excited I can hardly contain myself." Sally brought us back down to Earth.

"I am also a true believer in what he claims and I agree it is miraculous. I think we need to calm down a bit, take a deep breath, and think this through. My first thought is that we should immediately alert Rick and bring him up to date on what we know. I think that Joseph most likely communicated indirectly with you in this fashion to try and distance you from any inquiring eyes. This way it is just a very deep and moving poem that someone had written while serving during the Korean War. The editors of the human-interest section of the paper thought it worthy to publish. There is no trail leading directly to you this way Kait. If you agree I will bring Rick one hundred percent up to date, and frankly I will feel much more secure once he is totally on board with this latest information. I am sure he will be as astounded as the three of us."

Debbie and I both agreed to Sally's suggestion and we finished our meal and drinks, having a great deal of difficulty calming down. Since it was almost the end of the month I wouldn't have long to wait to again meet my mystery man and, perhaps, future lover. Finally this humdrum life may be getting some excitement in it, and I will experience many of life's pleasures and mysteries with this man of many faces. Am I falling in love, as if I should know, as I have never experienced any feelings like this before.

Sally called a couple of days later and said that Rick desperately wanted to meet with the three of us prior to the fourth when I am to meet Joseph at the Space Museum. She said he felt we needed to talk over where we were at this point as far as security is concerned, especially with this latest development. I agreed, as did Debbie, and we tentatively set the day after tomorrow to meet at the space museum coffee shop. Rick thought the more public the meeting place the safer it would be.

The day before we were to meet I held another open discussion class with my prized students. I stood there before them and almost shouted out, *'MANKIND HAS CONQUERED UNLIMITED SPACE TRAVEL.'* The urge to share such earth shocking knowledge with others is overwhelming. I can fully understand Joseph's need to share his accomplishment with someone and at this point in time I am fully aware of the importance of what lies ahead. During the class Robert brought up the poem that had been printed in the paper and asked that we discuss it's significance. Several of the class mentioned how moving it was and Robert mentioned that his uncle had been asked to study it and see if there was a hidden agenda in it. He said his uncle had mentioned the ramifications of the lines about not letting the draft board get you and for God's sake don't enlist. "Dr. Graham, he told me that the military was particularly concerned about that part of the poem but he had told them after examining it that it would not carry any weight with young people in case of a national emergency. Frankly, I think it should as I for one totally agree with that section of the poem. I think it is so profound and the author was highly intelligent to reflect on the horrors of conflict no matter where or under what circumstances. I would like to know the feelings of others in the class concerning it and the last line about four on the fourth at the eagle. My uncle said that really had him stumped. He finally dismissed the entire poem as profound but of no interest to any government agency.

Several other members of the class spoke up and agreed with Robert's assessment of the poem; particularly the section concerning draft boards and enlistment. Gail asked me my opinion and I could hardly contain myself. I chose my words carefully. "We have discussed on more than one occasion the evils of war and constant conflicts between nations, religions or for any other inconceivable reason. I believe you all know where I stand on such issues. As I have mentioned, I totally agree with Albert Einstein's assessment of mankind, *'ONLY TWO THINGS ARE INFINITE, THE UNIVERSE AND MAN'S STUPIDITY AND I'M STILL NOT SURE ABOUT THE FORMER.'* I believe the author of this poem was of the same opinion as the most brilliant mind to ever occupy this Earth. What prevents man from finding peaceful solutions to his differences? Is it ego; is it a quest for power, or just plain ignorance? What ever it is, a steady supply of manpower to fight the world's leaders constant wars is and has always been a factor. Maybe if the average person, who is usually much brighter than the politicians that get mankind into these wars, said no to fighting someone else's battles for them the leaders would be forced to find alternative means of settling differences. The author of this poem speaks with eloquence and wisdom." Robert was the first to respond.

"Doctor, I think we all agree with your assessment and pray that none of us will be put in the position of having to decide whether we will fight in the future, however, with man's past record I am not optimistic. I, for one, particularly since my uncle shares so much with me of his contempt for world politicians and leaders and their utter disregard for their fellow man, feel strongly about this issue. If we cannot find peace on this planet Earth maybe we will someday be fortunate to find it on a more peaceful planet in a far off galaxy."

"Thank you Robert, and all of you for your input. That was an interesting discussion we had today and please come prepared next week for more of the same." I left it there, and as they filed out I thought to myself that just maybe some of these wonderful inquiring minds might someday also be able to fly off to distant galaxies. There they would be able to marvel at the wonders of the Universe and the beauty that God placed there for all to see someday.

I left for our meeting with Rick and the three of us early the next morning. We met at our agreed upon location, as Rick had mentioned the more public the place to meet the better. Sally had filled him in on the latest proof from Joseph. The four of us all agreed that what Joseph was claiming was in fact the truth; he had conquered unfettered space travel. I told everyone about the class discussion and especially Robert's comments about the interest the poem had generated with some avenues of government and the involvement of his uncle. Rick dismissed that and said there were entire departments in many branches of government involved solely in trying to interpret any suspicious Internet traffic, print material, etc. He said the present government was paranoid about plots against them and was spending a fortune to attempt to uncover anything threatening. "I also feel we are fortunate to have some persons of common sense, such as Robert's uncle involved, to act as a counterweight to the extremists on the opposite side.

Rick asked me if I wanted he and some of his crack staff to cover me when I meet Joseph at the space museum on the fourth.

"Rick, Joseph mentioned one time that he was familiar with you and your agency and very comfortable with your expertise and honesty. As I have shared with all of you, I promised to accompany Joseph on a space exploration, if he in fact brought back proof. I have every intention of keeping that pledge and I cannot wait for that day to come. I assume that is one of the things Joseph wants to discuss with me when we meet. From what Joseph said about you and your firm I would feel more comfortable if you and some of your staff were watching our backs at the upcoming meeting. I'm not sure what the arrangements will be for my meeting Joseph for our much anticipated rendezvous in space, but with that on the horizon the more security from prying eyes the better.

Rick agreed and said he would make sure he was there, and several of the key members of his staff discreetly in the background. "The safety of all of you is my paramount concern at this time. This achievement is earth shattering and I am convinced that events from this point on will move rapidly. We must protect all of you, and especially protect Joseph's unbelievable accomplishments. If this ever becomes generally known there will be no place to hide, especially for Joseph and Kait. I believe you mentioned that he has always headquartered his craft in a secret location in Kansas. I am surprised with so many government drones now intruding in people's lives, that he can discreetly come and go from anywhere in this country. Doctor Graham, plan on meeting Joseph at the eagle at the appointed time and we will make sure all is secure. Would you like me to send two of my top security personnel home with you for your personal protection between now and the fourth?"

"Rick, I realize we are dealing with the event of all times but I feel fairly confident the knowledge is contained amongst the four of us and Joseph. I have my necklace, which I can activate if necessary. I enjoy my privacy and I am willing to take my chances. I realize I am much more trusting than you, and I also readily admit you are much more knowledgeable of the dangers lurking around us, but I will take my chances. I'll be at the eagle at four on the fourth and we shall see where this leads us in the future. I cannot contain myself thinking about an adventure into the depths of the Universe. Just thinking about seeing what God created in all its beauty and brilliance is beyond my comprehension. I appreciate your being on our side Rick, but at this point please watch over Sally and Debbie as they desire, and I am sure I will be all right."

"Doctor, I will respect your privacy and admire you for your inner strength. Believe me when I say Sally will be in good hands and I will provide Debbie any security she deems necessary." We all smiled at Rick's remark about Sally being in good hands and Debbie said she would talk it over with Sally and let Rick know. At that point I was totally exhausted from the events of the past days and excused myself and headed home. I kept checking my rear view mirror but nothing showed that made me suspicious. When I got home I quickly went to bed and took some Advil to help me sleep, as I knew sleep would be long in coming. I finally dozed off to daydreams of flying unencumbered with Joseph to the far reaches of the Universe.

There were a few days left until the fourth and I tried to remain calm and go about the routine of the life of a professor. Mark mentioned to me that I seemed uptight and wondered what was bothering me. I avoided a direct answer and just mentioned that I was tired and that nothing particular was of concern. "Doctor, you cannot hide it from me as I know you too well. Has your secret admirer made contact with you again? You certainly act like a young girl who has just found love in her life."

"Mark, for the final time I am not falling in love, and as far as who you refer to as my secret admirer I am not sure where that all stands at present." I thought under the circumstances a little white lie would serve its purpose. Sometimes I become concerned that Mark is just too inquisitive, especially when it comes to Joseph and his adventures. I think I can trust Mark, but I am never sure what he might be likely to let slip when he is with one of his lovers and they are indulging in one too many drinks. At this point in my adventure the fewer folks involved the better.

Mark left the office a little downhearted since I wouldn't divulge more, but I thought things had gone far enough for the time being. If I eventually travel into the far reaches of the Universe with Joseph, I will most likely have to give Mark a heads up, since I may well be gone for an extended amount of time. In fact I have spoken to the dean of this curriculum area and told her that I may have to apply for a sabbatical. I told her it was due to some health issues, another white lie to add to my record on this Earth. If I keep up with these little white lies I may well end up on the Hell side of the Heaven and Hell planets. Hopefully God will still look kindly upon me, especially since I soon may be blessed to see first hand the splendor of His majesty in space.

The fourth came around none to soon, as I wasn't sure I could wait any longer. I was not sleeping with so much anticipation and excitement building up. I just hoped and prayed everything would go smoothly and I would not appear too anxious and turn Joseph off. He had said on more than one occasion he admired my independence and inner strength and I am worried I may come across as a high school girl going out on her first date. What awaited me could be the adventure of all times and I wanted to maintain my firm personality on the surface, even though I was a caldron within. I headed out for the rendezvous shortly after three thirty and when I parked and was walking towards the eagle I looked around nervously to see if Rick and his security personnel were present. I didn't see Rick anywhere and everyone else looked like a tourist in the area. I thought either Rick and the ladies decided I could handle things alone, or he and his staff were so professional they could blend in anywhere. Four o'clock came and went and still no sign of Joseph. I was becoming frantic when this older gentleman came towards me with his collar pulled up around his neck and wearing a white beard. I thought for a minute it was Joseph in disguise but as I looked closer I knew it wasn't him. As the man walked by me he reached out and handed me a piece of paper and then headed back in the direction he had come from. I opened the paper and noticed my hands were trembling as I unfolded it.

"My dearest Kait,

I knew you would interpret my coded message below the poem in the newspaper and be here as I asked. I am nervous about certain persons I see in strategic locations around the plaza and so I asked that gentleman to give you this note. He is an innocent bystander and seemed anxious to deliver it. Another soul looking for something to fill his many lonely hours with. I wasn't sure if some of those individuals that appear suspicious were watching out for you, or might be unscrupulous characters who decided to be here to see what unfolded on the fourth at four PM by the eagle. If in fact they are from Rick's security firm, that we have previously talked about, then please run your hand through your beautiful hair as a signal to me that all is secure."

I looked around frantically to see where he was and could not spot him amongst the persons in the plaza. I hesitated a moment and then ran my hand through my hair as instructed. As I turned I saw this distant figure edging his way through a group of tourists and moving in my direction. I almost lost it right there and was going to run to him and throw my arms around him when my years of being Professor Kaitlin Graham kicked in and I restrained myself. As he came nearer I was somewhat shocked by his appearance as he looked disheveled and extremely tired. He came up to me, stood for a moment staring into my eyes, and then all of a sudden threw his arms around me like we had been lovers for years. I stood there numbed, and almost as an automatic reaction embraced him also. He whispered in my ear, "Kait, I have waited for this moment it seems like forever, I so need you and yearn to be with you." He slowly released me from his strong arms and again looked deep into my eyes.

"Joseph, are you alright? You look so tired and disheveled from the last time I saw you. What is going on? You retrieved the note that Debbie's father had in his coat pocket when he was laid to rest and you were obviously successful in your mission. What has happened to you since?"

"Kait, it is a long story and a long road I have traveled to return to you. For weeks I have not been able to get you out of my mind and my mission to prove to you my accomplishments has taken its toll. I will explain it all to you when we are alone, without any prying eyes. You signaled me that the persons I thought looked out of place were in fact from the security firm and are watching over you, and now myself, but I still feel uncomfortable out in a public place like this. I shouldn't ask this, but could we spend some time together at your place where we would have some privacy? Forgive me for being so bold."

"Joseph, you are more than welcome to come home with me. You look like you could use a shower, a razor and a good nights sleep and I can provide all three. I cannot wait to hear the rest of the story, so let us be off immediately. Take my arm for support and let's head for my car." It took us about five minutes to walk to the car and again I spotted no one that looked like they might be from Rick's firm. When I helped Joseph into the car he immediately pointed out two people from the spectators in the plaza that he said were most likely looking out for us. He suggested that they or others of the organization would follow us and not to be concerned about it. I was amazed how observant he was and could pick these persons out of the crowd as he did. I asked him how he knew who they represented and he said when someone has literally been on the run as long as he has it becomes a second nature to spot someone out of place. We had not driven more than about three miles when I glanced over at this handsome man, that it seemed I was falling in love with, and he was sound asleep. I did notice a car behind us that seems to be following us, but dismissed it as Rick's people.

We arrived at the apartment and I literally had to shake Joseph to awaken him. He awoke with a start and seemed somewhat out of touch for a moment. I asked him where he had been staying for the past days and he shockingly said he had been sleeping on a park bench for several nights. "I am anxious to return to my home in Kansas but at this point in time I have more pressing items to attend to."

"Joseph, take my arm and I will help you up the steps. Do you want to take a shower and then get some rest?"

"My dear, I hope you don't mind my calling you dear, as it seems we have known each other for a lifetime. If you would be so kind I would just like to lie down on the floor in your family room if I could use one of your pillows. I am so tired I cannot think straight."

"There is no reason you need to sleep on the floor. The couch is large and comfortable and I will get you a pillow and a blanket. Do you want something to eat before you rest? He never answered me. He sat down on the couch, slowly leaned over, and even before I could fetch him a pillow and a blanket he was asleep. I went in the closet and got both and lifted his handsome head up and placed the pillow under it and covered him with a blanket. I stood there looking down on this man that had so mysteriously entered my life, and wondered what the future held for us.

After a few minutes I wandered over to the window and glanced out and there was a black SUV sitting outside in the street with what appeared to be two gentlemen inside. I knew they were from Rick's agency and felt relief to know they were watching over us. I quietly entered my bedroom and slipped on my bed cloths. Not for an instant was I concerned that this recent addition to my life was sleeping outside the bedroom on the couch. I thought to myself how I was becoming more and more attracted to Joseph. I wondered if it was his offer to fly me to the far reaches of God's great Universe or was it the anticipation of intimacy with this lover, or possible a little of both. Whatever it was, I felt secure and at ease in his presence.

When I awoke I could not believe how long and soundly I had slept. I arose and glanced out into the room where Joseph was sleeping and the couch was empty. The blanket was neatly folded and laid over the back of the couch, and the pillow was returned to its resting place. I wondered how he had remembered where the pillow had been since he was so totally out of it when we arrived here last night, but he continues to amaze me.

I heard the shower going in the other bathroom and so I retired to my bedroom and freshened up. I went out when ready and put the coffee pot on and wondered why Joseph was taking so long in the shower. I then thought to myself if I had been living on the street for some time, and finally had a chance to shower, I wouldn't want to get out quickly either.

I was enjoying my second cup of coffee when around the corner walked in a clean-shaven and looking well-rested Joseph. He walked up to me and leaned down and gave me a kiss on the cheek. I thought to myself here is a perfect gentleman as I fully expected he might embrace me again but he thought better of it as I had literally taken him in. "Kait, thank you so much for your hospitality. I look forward to repaying it many times over as we explore the stunning beauty of the Universe. You have been so kind, and if I may be totally honest you look as beautiful as ever this morning."

"Joseph, before I begin my in depth interrogation of you and what is going on, and why you were living on the street, let me offer you a cup of coffee and some breakfast. You look very handsome all shaven and cleaned up, if I may also be totally honest. When you feel up to it please tell me." He laughed good naturally at the compliment and said he was starving so I fixed him a full breakfast while we talked. In between his enjoying the breakfast he relayed to me his incredible story.

"Let me first say Kaitlin that Debbie's father sends his love to her and her siblings, and most of all his beloved wife. With the in depth information that she furnished me I was fortunate to have found him rather easily. It was not surprising, as the history of his life that I received was so complete, that I found him on one of the planets reserved for the most deserving of mankind. Not the most coveted planet, but certainly near the top as he had led a worthy life, thinking and acting for others, before himself. Wouldn't it be wonderful if more humans acted in such a manner rather than this constant fighting and threats of wars, and so many other evils that constantly walk this planet we call home? You would be amazed, and I pray I can show you first hand, the many populated planets of various life forms that actually live in peace and harmony with one another. This planet Earth, and those of us that inhabit it, I fear is one of the Lord's great disappointments. I apologize Kait, as I get carried away when I have seen so much of the best of life forms and then have to return to Earth and read the depressing news and watch such agony as man brings upon himself.

I finished, as you are well aware, the assignment you gave me. Afterwards I headed back to my home base in Kansas, and from the depths of the outer limits of my capacity to observe the surroundings I saw so many drones in the air that it was impossible to go any further. As I mentioned before, our government in Washington is utilizing drones to literally spy on its own people in greater and greater numbers, as they are so paranoid about subversion amongst the common folks. Having no place to land, without being observed in this country, I decided to take a chance and headed for the far northern reaches of Canada. The problem I faced was not so much finding a safe and secure spot, away from prying eyes to land, but how I would then find my way back to this country and especially to you. I did land, finally, in a location that

I doubt has been seen by human eyes for centuries, and initiated the automatic camouflage system so my space vessel wouldn't be spotted from the air. I also have an automatic self-destruction device built into the craft if the wrong people try to enter it. I also activated that."

"Joseph, you seem to have covered all the bases. I am amazed at your accomplishments. How was it possible to master unlimited travel in space. Are you the absolute genius I suspect you are?"

"I honestly sort of stumbled upon the key to unencumbered travel throughout the Universe. After I mastered it, and made contact with those occupying other worlds, it seems that what I came across is basically what these other life forms have been using for centuries to explore space. We have experienced UFO sightings here on Earth and frankly they are craft from many other worlds, some of which I have visited. The simplicity of it all is amazing, but then again once one masters any mystery it seems it is effortlessness once you learn its secrets.

Getting back to my landing in Northern Canada, I did observe as I was making my approach a dirt road, which turned out to be a logging road, about ten miles from where I put down. My problem then was threefold. Could I walk the ten miles through dense forest to the road, could I then find transportation and finally, what would I tell whoever picked me up that sounded plausible. As far as the ten-mile hike, it was a good thing that I am in pretty good shape, as it was not easy through such thick forest. It took me several days and by the time I reached the road I looked like I had been living in the woods for months. I started to walk south and the second day a logging truck came lumbering down the road. I waved it down and it stopped for me. The driver was a great fellow and asked me what in the devil I was doing out here in the middle of nowhere. I had made up a story that I was hiking across Canada and had become disoriented and was trying to get back to the United States. I'm not sure he bought the story, but being the down to earth chap he was he didn't question me. He agreed I could ride along to his destination and he said that when we got there he would talk to some other truck drivers who were going further south and see if he could hook me up with one of them. Fortunately that worked and I finally arrived back in the states. It took me a few days to find my way here, and when I did I was so disoriented and exhausted I just slept on a park bench for a couple of nights while I tried to re-orient myself. I finally feel like my old self, especially in your presence. Thank you so much for your kindness and for being there for me Kait."

"Joseph, I'm happy you are feeling one-hundred percent again. I was concerned about you, especially last night, as you were so out of it. After living on the street for a few days I am not surprised. Didn't you have any money so you could get a room for a few nights?"

"I had only a few dollars with me and just credit cards. I am so paranoid about the inquisitive eyes in the government intelligence services or whatever branch these people work for that I didn't want my credit card to be able to be tracked. Whatever the case all is well now, thanks to your kindness. I am going to hold you to your promise Kait, to travel into the absolute beauty and mystifying depths of the Universe. You will be only the second human to ever experience such a magnificent journey, and I can assure you it will be the experience of a lifetime, if not many lifetimes. The only problem we have is how we are going to travel to the far reaches of Northern Canada in order to begin our journey. I don't believe we want to hitch a ride on a couple of logging trucks going north and then walk the last ten miles through dense forest. We could rent a car but we still have the final ten miles to travel, which would be almost insurmountable. I would be the last person to subject you to such torment. We will have to put our collective heads together and come up with a plan, whatever that may be."

Joseph, I cannot wait to experience what only you have seen many times before. I firmly believe this planet we call Earth has been visited in the past by beings from outer space but to be from this Earth and visit their planets is beyond my wildest dreams. My thoughts on how we will be able to reach your spacecraft are limited. Since you are the genius who has unlocked this secret I would leave that up to you. I'm sorry I have no suggestions, however, come to think about it I wonder if we could utilize Rick and his organization to figure out how to get us there?"

"I was thinking along the same lines Kait. I am, as I have said, familiar with he and his group and I have complete confidence in their abilities and trustworthiness. Their loyalty, along with their anti-government mindset might well be our answer. The personnel in his group are made up of ex-military Seals and Rangers and are totally trustworthy. I think we should set up a meeting with Rick, as I would like to meet him and bring him into the circle of those in the know. My only concern with he and your two close friends, Sally and Debbie, is that they may want us to draw lots to see who goes on the first space voyage with me. That issue is non- negotiable Kait, as you are the one and only and my love and devotion for you are as deep as the Universe itself."

"I am not sure Joseph that I share that deep love and devotion that you mention. Please don't misunderstand me, I am extremely attracted to you and becoming more so every day, however, I really know little about you and I am by nature an extremely guarded person. I appreciate your agreeing to take me first and if everything works out maybe in the future my friends could also experience what I cannot wait to see. Let me call Sally and set up a meeting with Rick as soon as possible. Please make yourself at home in my humble abode and if you need anything let me know." I went into the next room and was about to call Sally when there was a knock on the door. When I looked through the security eye it was Debbie, Sally and Rick. I thought they must be mind readers to realize I was about to call them.

"What is the occasion that brings the three of you here so early this morning? By the way, I would like you all to meet formally my space chauffeur, Joseph. Joseph, this is Sally and Debbie, whom you saw briefly at the Cape, and I believe you are well aware of this gentleman who leads the security firm we have often spoken about. Rick, I would like you to meet the man of many mysteries, Joseph. I hope your being here is not due to some disturbing news related to this best kept secret." Rick spoke up first.

"I'm delighted to finally meet Kait's man of mystery. I am having a great deal of difficulty, being the cautions person that I am, getting my mind around what the ladies have told me you have accomplished. Believe it or not, like these three scholars, I have also always been fascinated with what lies beyond the limits of mankind to visualize in space. The ladies have convinced me that you have in fact conquered unlimited travel throughout the

Universe. Surprising, as it seems I also, especially in my younger days, studied extensively those clues that were left in ancient times of travelers visiting this planet from outer space. I have always been a believer that we are not the only life form to occupy the vastness of space and that many of those other life forms are much more advanced than mankind. Enough of my spouting off about my beliefs. Joseph, let me just sum it up by saying, I believe you and also hope someday that you might show me first hand what only you have seen. The reason we are here is that my ear to the communications division, that we like to refer to them as, has picked up some government chatter about a strange sighting recently in Northwest Canada. It supposedly was relayed to our government from the Canadian government that a commercial aircraft spotted something some time ago in the skies in that area. It was spotted near Hay River in Northwest Canada, could that have been you?"

"Frankly Rick I saw no aircraft of any kind on my approach to that area. As you my be well aware, that area is certainly well off the beaten track of commercial aircraft although there might be an occasional charter flight taking persons on fishing or hunting trips to that part of Canada. My guess is it is a coincidence. Now that we are all together I would like to have your input on how best to retrace my steps to the Hay River area so that Kait and I might experience the thrill of many lifetimes. As you may already know, I have for a number of years housed my craft in a barn with a retractable roof structure in a remote area of Kansas. For the first few years, after having acquired the wisdom of such flight, I was never observed taking off or returning to that area as long as I did it within the hours of darkness. Only lately, with such increased use of drones by the government to spy on its own people, has my location there been put in jeopardy. As I am sure you realize, it has made it much more difficult to fulfill my dreams of additional travel throughout God's vast Universe. Does anyone have any ideas how Kait and I can travel to the Hay River area so that we can begin our epic journey together?"

"My firm does own a number of helicopters, as you are well aware, and the very experienced pilots that I employ I have complete trust in. The problem we are facing however is that from my preliminary calculations we are looking at a distance of over three thousand miles from here to that area of Canada. Since even our largest and newest helicopter has a maximum range of four hundred miles before refueling, that is going to be a problem. I think what we should look at is the six of us, one of my more handsome agents will be Debbie's companion, take a sight seeing trip via one of my larger SUV's to that part of Canada. When we arrive in the Hay River area we will then go to plan B, whatever that may be, to figure out how we are going to get you two the last ten miles to your craft. You mentioned that the area in which you landed was very dense, would it lend itself to a smaller helicopter landing area? I was thinking after we arrive in the general area we could then rent a helicopter and fly the two of you there." Debbie spoke up and questioned Rick at that point and brought a little relief into the conversation.

"If the six of us are going on a sight seeing adventure to the far reaches of Canada, I think I should at least get to pick the one of your staff that will be my partner and, of course, lover for the trip. I hardly think it is fair that the four of you are matched up happily and I might well get someone with whom I have nothing in common. Why don't you line up about ten of your most handsome and desirable ex-military types and let me choose." I couldn't wait to respond to my very conservative and proper friend, that I had known all these years, as the reserved one.

"Debbie, what has gotten into you? You have been so reserved all these years and all of a sudden the new you is emerging. Just remember this trip is all business and in our layovers we will reserve two rooms, one for the three ladies and one for the three gentlemen. I don't see therefore what difference it makes whom your partner for the trip is. Anyway I am sure Rick will provide you with one of his key people that would be much more than you could handle anyway." We all enjoyed a laugh over the exchange between Debbie and I and it tended to relieve the tension of that which lay ahead of us. Joseph brought us all back down to Earth, so to speak, at this point.

"Rick, I think there was a small clearing about a quarter of a mile from where I landed that we should be able to land a helicopter on. From that point to the craft would be an easy walk for Kait and I. If it is ok with everyone let us plan on leaving day after tomorrow. Hopefully nothing untold will happen between now and then." Everyone agreed and we decided to meet for supper later this evening and Rick said he would bring along the secret partner for Debbie. From the look on her face I think we may well have a problem if she is not happy with his selection. I told Joseph to make himself at home and that I needed to return to my office to wrap up a few loose ends before we embark on our adventure.

I arrived and found Mark in almost panic mode. He said everyone had been asking where I had been and the word was out that I had applied for a sabbatical and everyone was shocked and wondered what my health problems were. The dean had let slip that I needed time off for my well-being and so everyone was speculating what was wrong. Mark asked me point blank if I was pregnant, to my shock.

He even asked me if Joseph and I had conceived a baby in deep space and he was so anxious to find out what such a creature would resemble.

"Mark, frankly that is none of your business. I can assure you that no baby has been conceived either here on Earth or in the far reaches of the Universe. I cannot understand why you keep suggesting that travel to the far reaches of space is possible. As far as I am aware no such feat has ever been accomplished." I thought a little white lie was well justified here, as I certainly didn't want Mark, or for that matter, anyone else to possess even remote knowledge of Joseph's exploits. There was still the ever-present danger of unscrupulous government agents nosing around and Mark would be an easy target, especially when he was at his favorite watering hole with his lover. At that point I dismissed him and told him he would be holding the fort for a month or so and that my substitute teacher would need his expertise to carry on the classes that I would be missing. He left somewhat downhearted, but nevertheless left.

I stopped by the apartment and picked up Joseph and we headed out to our dinner get together with the others. When we got there Debbie, Sally and Rick were there and as we were ordering our first round of drinks this extremely handsome, very solid looking fellow walked in and came over to the table. Rick introduced him to the rest of us while I noticed Debbie couldn't take her eyes off of him.

"Folks I would like you all to meet Dale. Dale is an ex-marine who is one of my most trusted employees. With everyone's permission he will be accompanying us on our so-called sight seeing trip to Northern Canada. Debbie, I trust Dale meets with your approval." With that Dale bent down and gave Debbie a slight peck on the cheek, much to her astonishment. The rest of us just smiled as we looked at Debbie. The look on her face said it all. When she recovered her voice she quivering.

"Rick, I don't think you will need to line up any of your other fellows as this one looks like about as much as I can handle."

We all had a good laugh over Debbie's reaction and from that point on most of the talk centered on the adventures that Joseph had experienced and that which I hoped to experience soon. As Joseph explained what he has seen and witnessed in outer space we all sat there speechless, as I don't think any of us could actually comprehend the enormity of it all. Here sat three college professors, whose specialty is the vast Universe, and we still could not absorb what Joseph was telling us.

"I cannot wait to take Kait on her first trip into the far reaches of space. As part of the trip I plan on trying to find her parents and be able to give Kait the opportunity to speak to them again. From what she has told me they should be relatively easy to find as they were very admirable people and built up enviable records while on this Earth. I also want her to see first hand the beauty that God created when He created the Universe, it is beyond description."

With that we finished the meal and our drinks and said goodnight with Rick and Sally heading out together and Joseph and I headed for my place. Debbie looked at Dale as if she wanted to go with him and then must have thought better of it. He did lean over again, however, and give her a little peek on the cheek and she blushed but seemed to thoroughly enjoy it. We all smiled again as we said our goodbyes. I wasn't convinced they wouldn't still end up together but we will let time and nature take its course. We planned on leaving in a couple of days for our so-called vacation to reach Joseph's spacecraft and I was looking forward to that trip immensely.

The day came around and we all met at my Townhouse to head out. Rick had a vehicle large enough to easily accommodate all of us and we settled in with Rick at the wheel and Sally sitting next to him. Joseph and I took up the middle seat and Debbie and Dale ended up in the caboose, so to speak. We had a grand time as the six of us were so compatible and one would have thought we had been three happy, friendly couples for a lifetime. Anyone seeing us interact with one another would have never guessed our goals.

We stopped in Niagara Falls the first night and had supper at a fine restaurant overlooking the Falls. Finally, about half way through the meal, Sally raised the issue of our sleeping arrangements as we had yet to reserve some motel rooms. "I will be frank with all of you and say that Rick and I plan on sharing a room together on all our stopovers on this trip. The four of you will have to decide what the arrangements will be for you folks. There, I have said it and I am glad I did." The next few moments were the most silent that one could imagine, especially amongst the other four of us. You would have thought we were four school kids just returning from our Senior Prom the way we all danced around the subject. Finally Sally spoke up again. "Ladies, let me put this as blunt as I can, you frankly don't know what you are missing and believe me when I say none of us are getting any younger." I decided it was time for someone to make a decision so I threw my two cents in.

"Since I am the oldest of the three ladies here I will make a decision for the four of us. Rick and Sally of course are free to pursue their dreams, but Debbie and I will share a room and Joseph and Dale will share the other room, period." When I glanced at Debbie there was this look on her face of such confusion I was actually for a moment concerned. When I looked at Joseph and Dale they both appeared to be on the verge of tears. They both acted as if they had just found out their lottery tickets were null and void and both burst our laughing. Dale was the first to speak.

"It looks, Joseph, that the decision has been made for us. I won't say I entirely agree with it but I will certainly live by it. I might be so bold as to say I will be working throughout this trip, however, to change Kait's mind but for now Joseph and I will keep each other company for at least this night." Believe me Debbie, I will be dreaming of you for the next hours however." We all broke out in a nervous laughter over this and slowly arose and headed next door for the motel and our various rooms. When Debbie and I settled in for the night she curled up in her bed and just before turning the light off she looked at me, winked and said, 'we shall see.' The light went off and I sat there wondering what she was thinking. It didn't take me long to figure it out and I, all of a sudden, thought of Joseph next door with Dale and wondered also how long this arrangement would last. Am I finally budding out?

Morning came and we again met at the restaurant overlooking the Falls. Rick and Sally did not look as rested as the other four of us but they did both have a smile on their faces. After breakfast we headed out for the border check point. We had our passports and the passing through went smoothly as we expected. The border guard that checked us through thought we were just six friends headed for a vacation trip and nothing more. We all breathed a sigh of relief even though we had not expected any trouble. Coming back might be slightly more complicated however, since six of us entered and only four would be returning. Joseph and I, hopefully, will be going to mysterious places without any borders to cross. I'm sure Rick will come up with an explanation, which will satisfy the guards.

We had an uneventful day, with Rick checking in with his computer genius department several times to find out what the latest secret government chatter was concerning UFO's and any official or unofficial communications about them. Rick said all was quiet so we breathed a sigh of relief and settled back for the trip. The scenery was beautiful and we enjoyed ourselves tremendously.

It took several more days, and several nights of questioning our sleeping arrangements much to everyone's delight, before we reached our destination. We set up our headquarters, so to speak, at a local hotel and Rick said he was going to make inquiries as to renting a helicopter, supposedly for a sight seeing tour of this beautiful area.

Rick met us for supper at a local restaurant, which provided a beautiful view of the countryside. "Folks, I have some mixed news, I did find a fellow who rents out his chopper for sight seeing tours and it accommodates four people besides the pilot. The problem is that he would not rent it out for someone else to fly. I told him one of us was a licensed, competent helicopter pilot, but he was insistent that if it goes he is flying it. I'm not sure what plan B is but we need to talk about it. If anyone has a suggestion I would be happy to hear it. By the way, the owner of the chopper did mention the area was extremely picturesque and had even recently experienced a UFO sighting. I think he was trying to peak my interest in reserving his craft for a sight seeing tour, to throw that in, but it does remind us to be on our guard." Joseph spoke up in response.

"Rick, I think we should rent it and let him fly a couple of us around the countryside. We can come up with an excuse to check the area where I landed so I can observe things from the air and make sure everything looks secure. After that we will need to go to plan B, whatever that is." It was my turn to speak up after that.

"I think it is time I put my two cents in here. Now that we are here and I look over the surrounding countryside, I agree with you Joseph that it is pretty rough. You may have noticed, however, that I am in pretty good shape and I think I could well make it through those ten miles of forest if I had to. I certainly have every reason to want to get there as soon as possible, since what awaits me is the adventure of many lifetimes. This will be plan B if we cannot come up with something else. Anyone else have any suggestions?" Dale spoke up and shocked us all.

"I think it would be relatively easy to 'borrow' that gentleman's helicopter for a few hours and drop Kait and Joseph off at the drop zone. We could even leave him a generous payment for the loan of the craft so, hopefully, he would not raise any alarms. With your permission Rick, I will set things up and we can work out a diversion, maybe involving Debbie." We all looked at Debbie and couldn't tell if she was going to hit Dale over the head or reach over and give him a kiss. They had become quite familiar with one another on our multi-thousand mile road trip, so either one was possible.

We decided to rent the craft tomorrow and that Joseph, Rick, Dale and I would take the trip and see what the lay of the land looked like. We could get an in-depth look at our owner/pilot and figure out the best way to divert him. When Rick and Dale went to set things up they reported to us later that they found the pilot fairly intoxicated at the local tavern. Dale didn't think it would be any problem to borrow the helicopter after he talked to the bar tender about the owner's drinking habits. He told Dale that the helicopter owner was at the bar most every evening and almost one-hundred percent of the time he was inebriated. Dale said that he felt comfortable that we could confiscate it some evening and fly Joseph and I to the site, even in the dark. Joseph agreed and said that would be preferable, as we would not linger on the ground but take off almost immediately once we reached the craft.

"I would also want to leave a substantial payment of some kind for the helicopter owner, maybe we could slip the bar owner enough to cover his drinks for the next year without revealing our identity. The cover of darkness to ascend into the heavens is exactly what we want, so then hopefully only friendly eyes will observe us. What we need to decide sometime before we take off is where we will attempt to land when we complete our journey of several weeks. I would prefer to land in Kansas, at my base of operations, if we can avoid the drones. Possibly, Rick, we could talk about a diversion at some point. Let's plan on my making contact via satellite phone once we decide on a landing date. I'm not sure what we could set up to divert attention as it would have to be relatively major to draw off the eyes in the skies."

"I'm sure, Joseph, that my organization could come up with some diversion in the area of Kansas you designate, that would briefly call the drones off their assigned areas of observation. I will ask several of my capable staff to think on it and we can work out the details later on. What say we all get a good night's rest and tomorrow we will go on our planned helicopter ride we contracted with the owner to take us on. Hopefully he will be completely sober when he flies us around the countryside."

We all retired to our respective rooms, with Debbie and I still sharing a room and Dale and Joseph sharing the other room. When I observed how happy Sally was all the time, with a smile on her beautiful face constantly, I continued to wonder what Debbie and I were doing wasting so many precious moments. I was positive that on their return trip to the states the sleeping arrangements would be much different than they had been on the trip up, with Dale and Debbie sharing a room, as certainly Sally and Rick are not going to change their arrangements as they seem to enjoy each other all the time. I envied them more so each day.

The morning couldn't come around any too soon as the night was long and lonely. We drove out to the fellow's helicopter pad and wondered if our pilot would be staggering when he showed up. We only had to wait a few minutes and up he drove. When he got out of his jeep we were amazed at how rested he looked, he seemed one-hundred percent alert. We climbed in, leaving Debbie and Sally to fend for themselves; they said they were going on a brief shopping trip, and off we went. The pilot may have wondered why we chose to leave the two ladies out, the helicopter only carried four passengers, but we dismissed it in the pilot's mind saying they decided to shop today and he said he could certainly understand the ladies wanting to do that.

We took off comfortably. Everyone relaxed as the pilot was in complete control and seemed to be without any after effects of his night of binge drinking. We had speculated that if he was an habitual drunk and usually they have a tendency to be completely sober the morning after, compared to someone who seldom drinks and becomes intoxicated rarely. Whatever the case we all breathed a sign of relief with his expertise and seemingly total self control.

Rick sat in the co-pilots seat and Joseph, Dale and myself sat behind them in the triple seat section. Joseph sat by the window and Dale was kind and gave me the other window seat. Dale's main interest was to observe the pilots operation of the plane, as he would be the one to fly it when they would be dropping Joseph and I off at the site after we 'barrow' the craft. We had already set it up that Rick would subtly direct the pilot to take us over the area where, hopefully, the craft was intact. We had no reason to believe anything had been disturbed in the area of Joseph's landing since it was so remote, but we wanted to be sure. The area in question was referred to, having done some research locally, as 'The Bend In The River'. It didn't take long to maneuver the miles of sightseeing and before we knew it we were flying over the area we were interested in. Joseph was intent on looking out the window and after a few seconds he gave us all a thumbs up, as everything looked secure to him. I tapped Rick on the shoulder to let him know we were comfortable with what we had seen and Rick directed the pilot to head further east for some other spectacular scenery. We also observed a small clearing next to the river where we could land the helicopter for our drop off. Everything seemed in place, but then again so often when things look like they are all falling in place something comes along to throw a monkey wrench in the plans.

We flew for another half hour; the area was truly beautiful and wild. I could see from my vantage point how difficult it would have been to walk the ten miles from the road through the woods to the site. Even though I was in fairly good shape, in looking at the countryside I really wondered if I could have ever made it. I was impressed thinking that Joseph had managed it and I was sure, even he, would not have relished the idea of repeating the adventure. When we landed we all stretched as we disembarked from the cramped seats and I think we all were comfortable having solid Earth under our feet. I looked around and caught Joseph staring at me, with a smile on his face, and at that moment I wanted to throw myself at him. My imagination was running wild as to what awaited us in our journey into space. He was my anchor that I so badly needed for what I felt awaited me.

At supper that night Rick laid out the plan for 'borrowing' the helicopter this coming Saturday night. We knew that the owner/pilot would definitely be at the local watering hole on Saturday so we felt comfortable planning our escape to the craft then. We decided that Debbie and Sally would accompany Dale, Joseph and I this time, even though it would be dark, since they had not had the pleasure of the helicopter ride on the sight seeing trip. A full moon was expected which would give them a good view of the area. The only problem with the full moon was that it increased our chances of the craft being spotted as we disappear into the heavens. Rick was going to stay behind and spend time at the bar keeping an eye on the owner of the helicopter to make sure he stayed put for the approximately two hours we would have it. Rick was also going to leave a fairly large sum anonymously, with the owner of the bar, and tell him it was for the pilot's drinks as long as it lasted. He had concocted a plausible story to tell the owner if he questioned why.

Saturday night came around soon and we headed for the helicopter pad. Dale checked out the area with Joseph. Everything looked clear so they motioned for us to get on board. We all climbed into our seats with the three of us ladies in the back and Dale flying and Joseph in front with him. It only seemed to take a very few minutes and we had covered the ten miles to our destination. Dale sat the chopper down smoothly in the clearing by the river and we climbed out. We headed immediately for Joseph's craft. He activated the device to remove the camouflage and deactivated the self-destruct mechanism and offered me a hand up into one of the two seats. I gave Sally and Debbie a tremendous embrace and told them that I loved them both deeply. I even gave Dale an enormous embrace while Joseph was embracing Debbie and Sally. For a moment I thought I might change my mind but then my adventurous spirit kicked in and I said to Joseph, "take me to the far ends of God's creation dear." With that we were in and buckled and he pushed a switch, the folks stepped back a suitable distance, and the next thing I remember I was looking at Earth from far out in space.

CHAPTER SIX

Unraveling the Mystery of the Universe

Never in my wildest dreams had I ever imagined what I was experiencing. Here in front of us was a panorama view of billions of stars, and the planets of our galaxy all up close. It seemed as if I could reach out and touch them. Tears came to my eyes as the realization of what we were doing and where we were going came crashing in upon me. "Joseph, this is amazing, I cannot believe I am experiencing what I am. The beauty of our galaxy is beyond description. What you have mastered is truly a gift from God. Where do you plan on taking us during this trip?"

"Kait, the beauty of the Universe is only surpassed by the beauty of my companion this day. You have so honored me to share this trip and be the first human, besides myself, to travel unencumbered throughout space. As you say, our galaxy, the Milky Way, is beyond description in its beauty but remember it is only a small part of the vast Universe. It has been estimated by scientists that there are between three hundred and five-hundred billion galaxies in the Universe and we will be visiting only several this trip. I have visited over twenty in my various travels so you can see, even though I have achieved unfettered space travel, my journey into the vastness of space is hardly more than a small moment in time. I cannot envision what still lies out there that I, and no human, has ever seen. In the twenty or so galaxies that I have visited there are many different life forms. Many of these creatures I have visited and communicated with.

On this trip I would like to take you to the planet of the burning rocks, one of which I brought back to you as my first attempt at proof of my accomplishments. The creatures on that planet are friendly and you will be welcomed as one of the breathtaking beauties from planet Earth. I also would like to attempt to find the planet that your parents reside on and, hopefully allow you a time to say again how much you love them. That may take a bit of searching but they should be near the top of the Heaven side of the Heaven and Hell planets from what you have told me about them. For now sit back, relax and enjoy the journey. Just think what you will be able to tell your class of gifted students once we return to mother Earth."

"Joseph, you are kidding aren't you? We have talked many times about how important it is to keep this all confidential and I have no intention of telling anyone about our adventure except for Sally and Debbie. The fact that we must keep such a wonderful accomplishment a secret just shows the utter failure of mankind. If man's evil side were not so prevalent just think what the future would hold for all persons to experience this, if this story could be told. To use such knowledge for peaceful purposes would be a giant step in the progress of mans ability to expand his knowledge of the origins of the Universe and of man itself. As we have often talked, however, the evil amongst us always seems to gain the upper hand. The Earth has surprisingly survived millions of years, but its long-term survival from here on out is questionable. There I go, getting on my soap box again about mankind's failings when I should be enjoying every moment of such absolute beauty."

"Kait, I share your passion and wish it was not so, to what you speak. I dread the thought of passing from this life and taking my secret to the grave with me, as I fear it might be centuries before anyone else ever achieves what God has entrusted to me. When you meet some of the creatures from just the planet of the burning rocks you will see how it could have been on Earth if man had followed God's teachings and lived in peace and harmony with one another. I fear, in the scheme of things, amongst all the various seeds of life of one type or another that God planted in this vast Universe, the humans on Mother Earth are one of His greatest disappointments. Albert Einstein, as you have often mentioned, seemed to sum it up the best with his remarks about mankind's idiocy and the Universe. Sad it is so, but the issue has been proven time and again over the many centuries of mans conflicts on our Earth."

"Joseph, I think we are dwelling too much on mankind's failings. Let's make a pact to put all of the negative thinking behind us and concentrate on the beauty surrounding us. I am almost speechless of what I am seeing and as you said this is only the fringe of what we will experience. Let us go to the planet you refer to as the one with the burning rocks. I cannot wait to see the creatures that live there in peace with one another.

Joseph was true to his word. Within another day of travels through such magnificence we arrived at our destination. As we approached, from well out in space, I saw a number of what I could only identify as UFO's. I wasn't sure what I was seeing and asked Joseph. "These creatures, for want of a better term, that occupy this planet long ago mastered unrestricted space travel. They have communicated with me that for centuries they have been free to move about this galaxy and many others. In my communications with them, I have been told that many of the UFO sightings on our Earth have been travelers from this planet."

As we made our approach, several of their craft came alongside us and they seemed to be observing us carefully. Joseph said they would have by now recognized his airship and the green light had been passed to their planet to let us land. We touched down gently and as Joseph opened our spaceship we were approached by what I could only describe as creatures that resembled nothing that I had ever imagined in my wildest dreams. They did not walk towards us but sort of floated and surrounded us as we moved towards what looked like a structure of some sort. We were motioned to enter and as we sat Joseph looked towards me and then towards who appeared to me to be a leader amongst them and they nodded in my direction. It was as if, through his hand signals, he was communicating with them and introducing me to them. Not knowing how to react I just sat there and nodded and Joseph and all the creatures seemed to break out in laughter. Joseph told me that with the sign language that he had perfected with these folks he had told them that I was his companion and lover. I just looked at him and all the others and shook my head, which brought on more laughter. These creatures seemed so friendly and peaceful. Joseph said that their leader had asked us to please spend at least one night here, which he had agreed we would do. He apologized for not first consulting with me but I told him whatever he wanted to do was fine with me.

We spent a restful night and in the morning we headed to our spacecraft. There were a great many of the creatures that inhabit this planet accompanying us and Joseph made some hand gestures towards them as we boarded his craft. Not knowing the hand signals I only nodded again and that was returned with what seemed to be light laughter. Joseph filled in the blanks for me. "Kait, they genuinely liked you and showed it with their laughter and the hand signals they presented to me. Through my many visits here I have learned to communicate with them using hand signals and they are such peaceful creatures that, as I said, have lived in total harmony with one another for centuries. God must have seeded many such planets in His vast Universe of hundreds of billions of galaxies with many different life forms, and I am sure He is smiling when He sees the success these creatures have achieved in harmonious living. It is so sad that man on Earth did not manage the same feat. It seems like it would have taken much less effort than the endless conflicts the Earth has seen of its people's over the centuries. Whatever the case, this planet of the burning rocks and it's inhabitants would be an offsetting factor to Earth and bring a smile I am sure to the face of God."

With that we again took off and headed into space, with an escort of about twenty of this planets UFO's seeing us off. Joseph said he wanted to move on to another galaxy, where the beauties of the Universe are unsurpassed, and then in a few days he said we would head to the Heaven and Hell planets to attempt to find my folks. It seemed to take us a very short time to reach the other galaxy that Joseph had mentioned. I never figured out how we were moving so freely in space and I wasn't about to ask him. It was his secret, his accomplishment, and when he was ready to share it with me I was sure he would.

We arrived and Joseph, as always, was true to his word. I could not believe what I was seeing. Nothing even close to this had ever been observed by the most powerful telescopes on Earth.

I had brought along a camera and spent about a half hour taking pictures of God's handiwork. Joseph and I had discussed taking pictures and what we would do with them to make sure they didn't fall into the wrong hands. He agreed I could take as many as I wanted, but we would only share them with our small group of those in the know.

We spent several days roaming around this beautiful area and even visited from space several planets that Joseph said were inhabited by living creatures. He said these creatures had not yet progressed to having mastered space travel. He told me he had actually set down on a couple of the planets and been welcomed by those that inhabited them. "Kait, I have visited various creatures on a number of planets, some of which are advanced far more then humans and some which are not yet. The one thing that impressed me the most about all of those that I have visited is that on all of them the inhabitants seem to be peacefully co-existing. I'm sure there are planets out there someplace in all this vastness where those living on them are hostile, but I have yet to encounter any. Earth is the only planet where I have found hostility. Very strange that so many of God's experiments were so successful compared to the seeding of Earth with humans. Hopefully someday that will change for the better on our Earth. If it is all right with you I would like now to head for the Heaven and Hell planets and see if we can locate your folks. Sit back and relax and dream pleasant dreams of a reunion with those you love.

I took Joseph's advice and rested for a while. I could hardly keep my eyes closed however with all the beauty surrounding us. I did finally doze off and when I awoke I could see out of the observation window a number of planets in the distance. I turned and looked at Joseph with this inquiring look on my face.

"Kait, you are looking at the final resting places for all of the humans that have at one time called the Earth their home. As we discussed, they are assigned a planet depending on the their record of good or evil they build up in God's eyes during their time on Earth. You will note that the planets on the Heaven side have brilliant sunshine and those on the Hell side are cast in dark shadows, which becomes much more dark and forbidding as one travels to the planet that houses the worst of the worst of mankind. On those planets it is in fact living torment, constantly, to atone for the evil they perpetuated while living on Earth. On the other end of the spectrum are many humans that have passed on living in absolute harmony with one another. As I mentioned, Mother Theresa lives on the most peaceful of the Heaven planets along with many other deserving people. I thought, from the description of the lives your parents led, we could start looking on the same planet that Debbie's father was on. He led a life of peace and tranquility and from your description your folks also did. You mentioned how caring for others they both were and the many hours they both volunteered at a hospice to comfort those folks who were near death. Hopefully we will find them here."

We landed on what appeared to be the second planet on the Heaven side. Joseph motioned for me to disembark, and stretching my legs was wonderful. Many people were mulling around in what I can only describe as a semi living trance. They all nodded and smiled to us and we both returned the hospitality. We entered a coliseum of sorts, where Joseph said was kept the record of all those that reside on this Heaven planet. He briefly communicated with what appeared to be a keeper of the books and turned to me and said, "your folks names do not appear in their Book of Life so we will have to look further. We have been asked to spend the night so we will move on to another planet in the morning. Joseph said the keeper of the books suggested we try the third planet on the Heaven side and he said he was surprised they were not here from my description of them. From what I could observe of those within our eyesight, these people were happy and content and living in total harmony with one another. As we were leaving the coliseum a man approached us and Joseph immediately spoke to him. It turned out to be Debbie's father that had written the poems and I could not wait to speak with him. Our conversation led me to believe we were back on Earth carrying on with a normal exchange between three people. Joseph introduced him to me, his name was Richard and he was a good-looking fellow.

"Richard, I read the poems that you had written during the time you served in the military during the Korean War. I was so moved by them. All of mankind should read them and absorb the true meaning of them as far as the futility of these endless wars. Possibly then, man would find peaceful ways to settle their differences. As I have often said, *MAN TO EASILY SETTLES*

CONFLICTS WITH WARS INSTEAD OF WORDS and has repeated this horror many times over the centuries of man on Earth. You experienced the hell up close and your words beautifully describe the tragedy of being in such devastating situations. I will ever be in your debt. Your daughter Debbie is one of my best friends and you should be very proud of her, as she is a wonderful person. I am so grateful that Joseph was able to prove his conquest of space by bringing back the second poem that you had written. Possibly, with Joseph's blessing, Debbie can someday visit this peaceful place and see the father she so adored."

"Kait is it, I think my daughter is blessed to have a beautiful, loving friend like yourself and I would cherish the moment I could see her again. She was a loving daughter and no man could have asked for so loving an offspring that was so attentive to the needs of her mother and father. Sadly, I did not live long enough to truly reap all the pleasures of spending time with her but, as you say, maybe with Joseph's blessing I can again see her and tell her in person how much she is loved and was loved. I understand you are looking for your parents and I am sorry you did not find them here on this peaceful planet. From what Joseph told me they deserved to be on one of the more blessed Heaven planets as they were caring, God loving people. I will be praying that you will be able to locate them on this trip in their final resting place."

I noticed a monument as we were bidding our farewell to Debbie's father. On it were inscribed the words, "***IT IS NOT WHAT YOU GATHER, BUT WHAT YOU SCATTER THAT TELLS WHAT KIND OF A LIFE YOU HAVE LIVED.***" I wondered where that had originated and thought for a moment possibly Richard had thought it up. After reading such moving poems that he wrote it would not surprise me if he were the author of it. Whatever the case it was very poignant, in my opinion. Joseph asked me if I was ready to continue our journey, and that I would be choosing which Heaven planet we would be visiting next in our quest for my parents.

We left this beautiful, tranquil planet and those who live within it in total harmony with one another. I was saddened to leave but so wanted to find my folks and be able once again to tell them how much they were and are loved. Joseph asked me which planet we should search next and also why I have chosen whichever one it is that I pick. I thought about it for a few minutes. "Joseph, I know my folks were very kind, caring people, and I fully expected they would be on the same planet with Debbie's father from what she had told us about him. I know they were deserving but I can't quite equate them with the likes of such God loving folks as Mother Teresa, so I think we should head for the third planet on this Heaven side. Maybe there is something that they did sometime, that I was never aware of, that lowered their record a couple of notches, but I certainly don't know what it could have been."

"Kait, there are many planets in the Heaven and Hell galaxy and it is not always easy to locate someone from what one knew about them when they walked the Earth. I am sure, as in any grading system, God draws a fine line and sometimes that means they were on the edge of acceptance on the planet we were on but didn't quite make it. Not to worry, however, as the top four or five planets accommodate the most worthy, and spending eternity on any one of them is a God given pleasure. Let's put down tomorrow on the third one and pray we find them there."

The time passed by quickly and in the early hours we landed on the planet I had chosen. After we landed we were approached by what appeared to be committee of possible leadership on this Heaven planet. Joseph explained to them why we were here and they all welcomed us. Their leader asked us to follow him to the building that contained their Book of Life to see if my parents were in fact on this tranquil planet of those that had passed on to a more peaceful place. After searching the records for us their leader said he was sorry but they did not appear to be assigned to this planet. Joseph explained to the leader that my parents had led exemplary lives of caring and giving and that we had already been to the second Heaven planet and could not find them there either. The leader mentioned that possibly they would have earned a place on the most coveted of all the Heaven planets, but he said they would have had to stand out from almost all other souls in their kindness and consideration of others to be worthy of spending eternity on that planet.

We spent the night on this tranquil planet with these wonderful caring folks. In the morning Joseph said on this trip we could visit only one more of these designated planets as we needed to return to Earth for certain upkeep of his space craft which was periodically necessary. "Kait, we can try one more before we head back. Again, I want you to choose, as you are most familiar with their lives. When we travel within satellite phone distance for communication, but outside the range of possible observation, I will contact Rick to see what diversion he has possibly come up with so we can redirect the drones and land undetected. He said he was sure his staff would be able to create some distraction, which would temporarily force the government to reroute their spy drones for the brief time necessary. Where are we headed next Kait?"

"Joseph, as I mentioned I loved my parents deeply and they were wonderful people, but even I don't think they could have earned a coveted spot on the top Heaven planet. I also firmly believe that they certainly deserved a place on one of the top two or three, so if it is all right with you may we please check the number one planet. I am going to be devastated if we don't find them there, after our searches on the other two planets. Thank you for being so patient with me, Joseph, in our search."

"Kait, you must know by now that I would do anything for you. I love you Kait, and your wish is my command. We are off to the most desirable of all the final resting places of mankind. This planet is not to heavily populated, as sadly not to many humans build up a record in the Lord's documentation book of being such a deserving being."

It took us but a short time to arrive and we landed and were greeted by none other than Mother Teresa herself. I bowed to this woman so deserving of praise. The sacrifice she had shown while tending to the less fortunate while on Mother Earth is almost beyond description. She was extremely gracious and asked us to join her and her other co-leaders to check the Book of Life available on this planet. She searched the book for the names I had given her and I almost lost it completely when she looked up with such a sad look on her face and announced that they were not here. Joseph, seeing how devastated I was reached over and took me in his arms and comforted me. At that moment I knew I was in love with this man amongst men, as I needed him so much. There is no greater love than the need for comfort and understanding of one's companion when they are in stress. I don't think I could have survived that moment without his strong arms around me and his whispering comforting words in my ear. Mother Teresa just looked on with tears in her eyes. She did offer some support however, which I clung to.

"Kait is it, there is one explanation which I am privileged to be aware of. You said you had visited the second and third final resting places for those deserving in your quest, and also did not locate them there. It is marvelous that Joseph has been granted by our Lord and Savior unlimited space travel, and all of those persons resting, on especially the Heaven side planets, welcome his contact with our past home on Earth. Our Father has many times answered my prayers. I am privileged to be aware that in certain circumstances couples that had been married for some time and had built up varying degrees of record while on Earth might well be assigned to different planets. If this were the case, they would in fact be separated for all eternity. Our Lord then would offer them the opportunity to remain as one forever, but they would have to accept residency on the pivotal planet between those most deserving and those destined for eternal damnation. Please don't be upset, Kait, as this particular planet, even though it is not one of the most coveted, is still peaceful and only those deserving end up there as couples. I am sure from what you have told me that your parents loved each other in their life on Earth so deeply that this was their choice. Joseph said you must return to Earth soon, but the next trip you are privileged to go on with him I would suggest visiting the pivotal planet and I am sure you will find them there. Bless you both."

"Thank you, Mother Teresa, for your insight and understanding. My only problem remaining is why, when they were so close to each other, they would have acquired different records of their lives in our Savior's sight. From all my years of being with them, and loving them both so dearly, I never saw any appreciable difference in their actions. They were giving souls, and kindness to others was their goal throughout their lives. I pray that if we are able to return we will find them living together in peace, as you say. Bless you Mother Teresa for your unwavering service to your fellow man and the example it set for others. If only more of us would follow your example what a wonderful, loving planet Earth would be.

"I must tend to other needs even here on this most coveted of all the Heaven planets, so I will bid my farewell. Do not be upset dear as the final record of all humans is often only separated by a fraction. That is why God in His infinite wisdom allowed couples whose lives of caring and giving were only separated by the width of a hair to choose to spend eternity together. Go with God and I hope to again see you in the future. The next time, if you choose to visit us again, I would like you to meet Albert Einstein, who we are privileged to have spending eternity with us here. His was the greatest mind to ever walk the Earth and would be enthralled that someone from Earth had finally conquered travel in the Universe that he so dearly loved. He is truly a fascinating figure, as are so many of those dwelling herein. Goodbye for now, and may God be with you both."

With that we bid our farewell and headed back to Joseph's ship and the trip back to Earth. I settled back for what one would have thought of as a never-ending trip but before we knew it we were in the outer space of Earth and Joseph was contacting Rick about the diversion. Rick, as usual, was on top of the issue and told us that his people, using very sophisticated communications equipment, were going to send an alert to the government. The alert would be that the dam on the Kansas River, which is about two hundred miles from our secret hanger, was going to be blown up, and even specify the day and the time, which of course would be after dark tomorrow night. He was sure the government would divert all of its drones from our landing area to the area of the dam for observation purposes. Joseph agreed it was a perfect diversion and agreed to the time.

We waited until the appointed hour and then headed in for our landing. We approached the area quietly and without any lights and said a silent prayer that no one would observe us, and that no commercial aircraft would be in the area. Rick had checked all commercial aircraft routes and none were scheduled to fly over that area at the time of our arrival so we were comfortable as far as that issue was concerned.

When we disembarked my dear friends Sally and Debbie were waiting for us along with Rick. Dale was also there as he had become second in command and the most trusted of all Rick's organization, and also it seemed he had become extremely close to

Debbie, which delighted me to no end. Rick filled us in. "Dale's plan of calling the drones off this location had worked flawlessly and they were sure our landing had gone undetected. We had several of our staff strategically located at observation points. All of them were in contact with one another and they said as soon as the threat was received by the government the drones were immediately diverted. The next time we want to come up with a distraction we may have to think up something else, but Dale said he already has some plans formulated for the next take off and landing." We thanked them all for their expertise and Joseph even mentioned he was certainly hoping a next time would come around soon. He excused himself, as he alone had some items to attend to on his ship while the rest of us headed into his home here on the plains of Kansas. Debbie and Sally could not wait for my revealing what I had seen and if I had found my parents.

"Ladies, I have some good news and some bad news. The good news is that the trip was indescribable. The beauty of God's creation of the Universe is beyond, way beyond, anything any of us ever dreamed it could be. I could easily spend eternity traveling in outer space with Joseph. The bad news is that we could not find my parents. Debbie, we did find your father, however, and he sends his love to his beautiful loving daughter. Since you are the fortunate one Sally, and your parents are still alive, we did not have to search for them. The disturbing news, after Joseph was kind enough to take the time to visit three planets on the Heaven side, was that we never located my parents. We first visited the second planet where Debbie's father is, and as I said, spoke to him. He is a fine man Debbie and you should be very proud of him. His wisdom runs deep on the failures of mankind and we were both very impressed with his depth of understanding.

I then choose the third planet on the Heaven side, again without any luck. I'm sure you would understand my sadness and frustration. Joseph suggested we visit the most coveted Heaven planet, even though he said they would have had to be almost saints to reside there. They were certainly good, caring people but most likely in God's eyes not qualified for sainthood status. You cannot imagine who greeted us there, none other than Mother Teresa herself. Truly a saint amongst saints she was. Without any success finding them there Mother Teresa told us that our Lord in

His infinite wisdom would allow partners who lived years together, but accumulated varying records, to make a choice. They could separately reside for eternity on the planet they were assigned to, or if they chose, they could be placed on the pivotal planet between the Heaven and Hell sides and spend eternity together there. She suggested this is what must have happened in my parent's case, and Joseph has promised to take me there in the future. He also has mentioned, if we are fortunate to remain outside the scrutiny of this intrusive government in its present form, that he would like eventually to take Debbie to visit her father and Sally to see the spender of space. I'm sure he would take you Rick, again depending on our remaining out of the awareness of our government. That's just about as brief a summary as I can mention at this point since I am falling asleep on my feet. I also have, it seems, a million pictures that will astound you. The only thing we will need to do is figure out some security arrangement for the pictures, as they would be a dead giveaway if any eyes but ours saw them. What say we hit the hay? Joseph said to pick any of the bedrooms we wanted and I am sure ready."

I looked at Sally for a hint of the sleeping arrangement. I didn't have to ask as Rick put his arm around her and they said goodnight and headed off. Dale and Debbie just nodded at me, and also hand in hand, headed off to bed and what I could only imagine as a night of pleasure between two lovers. I stood there for a moment and wondered what was ahead. Joseph was still working in the hanger and I had no idea how long he would be. I finally, since I have been living on the edge for a while now, wrote a brief note and left it on the table for him. 'Joseph, I trust everything went well with the work on your fantastic spacecraft. Everyone has retired. I will be in the front bedroom upstairs and I would be delighted to have you join me.' My hand shook a little as I set the note down where he would not miss it and I headed up to bed. I crawled in bed and almost immediately fell asleep, with great anticipation.

It was about an hour later that I heard the bedroom door open slightly and very quietly I heard footsteps across the room to the other side of the bed. He was so quiet and being Joseph, my man of many mysteries, he pulled the covers back just as quietly so as not to wake me. I lay there trembling slightly and I felt the back of his hand rub against my back softly. I thought to myself, 'here I am in my late thirties, an attractive, successful woman and this is the first time I have been in bed with a man. I thought briefly of Mark's concerns about my missing all the ecstasies of life and all of a sudden I found myself madly embarrassing Joseph. I think I totally surprised him and he whispered in my ear, "Kait, I love you deeply, please don't do anything you will regret." My response was short and to the point."

"Joseph, hush up, hold me tight and take me on that other journey I have long dreamed about, and I am not talking into space." I awoke in the morning to a memorable night of love making with this fabulous man. He gave me a warm embrace and a kiss as we headed for our separate showers. My head was still spinning as I again remembered what Mark had often said about life's pleasures that I was missing. I wasn't sure I would be able to keep a straight face the next time I see Mark, and especially keep from blushing.

Joseph and I finished our morning routine about the same time and went down to the kitchen. The other four just stared at us and Sally and Debbie had this look on their faces, which said it all. I said nothing at all except 'good morning.' Of course Sally could not help but put her two cents worth in. "It is a good morning and from the looks of things it was a very good night also"

"Sally, enough now, let's have a fabulous Kansas breakfast and talk about our next move. After breakfast I want to print out the pictures I took when we were in space and then we need to decide the security arrangements for them." Sally and the others just grinned wide at my attempt to change the subject as they looked at Joseph and I. After a few more minutes of teasing the three of us ladies went about fixing a hardy breakfast for everyone.

Rick announced that he needed to get back to his office in New York and would be flying back in his corporate jet this afternoon with Dale and Debbie. Sally agreed to go along as they both needed to get back to their teaching jobs. Joseph said he needed to stay here, as there were a number of other things he wanted to attend to on his craft prior to the next exploration into the heavens. I was the one left in limbo, not knowing whether to remain here with my lover of late, or return to the college and move back into my studies. The professor that was filling in for me had been brought out of retirement and told that the schedule was flexible and that I could be returning at any time. I was torn and Joseph, who was now closer to me than anyone had ever been, seemed to be able to read my mind. He told me he would be extremely busy with his upkeep, and not be able to spend much time with me, and suggested I return with the others until such time as he decides on the departure date for our next trip into the Universe. This trip will be for the express purpose of locating my parents, hopefully on the pivotal planet. I really didn't want to leave him, but he realized better than I how serious a person I was, and that deep down I wanted to resume my obligations. I suggested I remain here for at least a few more days and then fly back on a commercial jet. I sheepishly said I had a few things left unattended so I needed to stay. The looks on everyone's faces except Joseph, who had an enormous grin on his, said it all. No need for me to try and hide anything and I really didn't want to anyway. I have found love in my life beyond my wildest dreams ever, and I had no intention of ending it anytime soon. Joseph spoke up and said he would love to have me stay, as he embraced me, and he and I would return in a week or so together. Rick said we should all plan on meeting to discuss our future plans when we all returned to the city area.

"Why don't we leave it that when Joseph and Kait return we will let them make contact with us and set up a get together. I for one, and I know the rest of us all want to be here when you decide to depart on your next adventure. One problem we should discuss at some time is the future, for take off and landings from this spot, is what we can use next time for a distraction. Dale has been working on it but it will not be possible to use the same diversionary tactics more than once or twice or we will arouse suspicion beyond what already is apparent. This could be our major obstacle so we will need to put our collective minds in high gear to come up with a solution. Joseph, I know you mentioned taking Kait, as you said, on the next trip to hopefully find her parents. You also mentioned taking Debbie to see the beauty of space and see her father. Needless to say is the fact that Sally, Dale, and of course yours truly, would love to also be amongst the select few humans to ever experience seeing the beauty of God's creation, as we previously discussed. With that many possible times, diverting all these drones will be a major issue."

We agreed that when Joseph and I returned we would initiate a call and we would get together. The afternoon came around too soon and all of us headed for the airport. Many a tear was shed amongst the three of us ladies as we parted. Rick and Dale settled into the pilot's and co-pilot' seat in their magnificent corporate jet and the departure was routine. We had decided that Joseph and I would print out all the pictures and bring them with us to our next get together. Our fears of one or more of them falling into the wrong hands were relieved slightly when Joseph pointed out that many of them, but not all of them, would appear to a stranger to be pictures taken through a massive space telescope, such as the Hubble telescope. Joseph and I headed back to his home and he reached over and held my hand as we drove, which was such a loving gesture. This handsome, highly intelligent, loving man is now the most important person in my life, and, I pray forever.

While Joseph worked most of the week on his craft I spent the time converting the multiple pictures I had taken onto the computer and printing them out. They were breathtaking and I could not wait to share them with Sally, Rick, Debbie and Dale. We had agreed to share them when we returned to the city and also agreed to keep them confidential. We had quite a discussion about them and finally agreed each of us would be allowed to keep one of them and the remainder would be kept under lock and key. Joseph said he was going to exercise veto power over each person's one selection, as he was very concerned that if the wrong eyes saw them our cover would certainly be compromised. We had all agreed to that provision. The remainder of our time here at his ranch was spent in many an embrace, and intimate loving moments. I had never experienced such a week in my life. My life was completely turning around, for the better as far as I was concerned, and I never want it to stop. I wasn't aware in my wildest dreams, and some of them were pretty explicit over the years, that life could be so wonderful, especially when you have a caring lover to share it with.

The week wound down all too quickly and we packed our things and headed out. We secured the photos in a lock box in the corner of the trunk, well hidden from any possible inquiring eyes.

John Parsons

We didn't expect anyone to look in the trunk but one never can be too cautious, especially on the long drive to the city. We had chosen to drive rather than fly commercially since we both wanted to stretch out our time with just the two of us together prior to reuniting with the others. We stayed in some of the nicest motels and it was two lovers on their honeymoon. I'm sure anyone observing us must have thought the same thing.

I called the gals the day after we got back to my place and had settled in. It seemed like Joseph had been living here forever, as we settled in together as if we were an old married couple who still had passion for one another. We agreed to meet at our favorite restaurant the day after tomorrow and they reminded me to bring the pictures when we meet. Joseph was still somewhat reluctant about the pictures falling into the wrong hands but I assured him they would be well protected.

The day came around and it was so wonderful to again be with my sisters, in name only, but still sisters in my heart. Rick and Dale showed up also and we settled in for a fine lunch and took the time to study the pictures. Debbie asked again how come I had not taken any pictures on the Heaven planets we had visited and I reminder her that I was going to but no one showed up through the lens when I attempted it. Our only explanation was that those that had gone to their final place for eternity did not want to have their pictures recorded, or God had chosen that it would not be possible. Whatever the case, I was content with the magnificent pictures I had taken, as were the others. We were careful to conceal them from anyone else in the restaurant. Since it was not too busy that was relatively easy. As we had agreed, each of us picked out our favorite one and the remainder, we all approved, would be locked in my wall safe at the office.

Rick brought up the issue, when we finished admiring the pictures, of diversions for our departure and landing in the future. He said Dale had come up with using a laser from the mountain range again, about two hundred miles from Joseph's home base. "There have been so many instances of persons pointing lasers at commercial aircraft which of course is extremely dangerous. We would have to make sure there were no aircraft in the vicinity when we do it, but that is a given, as we do not want to depart or land with commercial aircraft anywhere nearby. The government,

117

rightly so, is starting to crack down on this illegal activity as it could cause an accident. Dale said if we point a laser into the sky in the area in question that the drones would be called off to investigate immediately. Other than that idea we have not been able to come up with any other diversions for future take off and landings. We are still trying to come up with other diversions but until we do we may have to use plan B, or go back to Hay River." Joseph was the first to respond.

"The laser idea that Dale came up with is brilliant and I would dare say we could use this idea more than once. We will need to think up several others however or, as you say, another plan as I certainly will keep my part of the bargain to see all of you accompany me into the beauty of God's Universe. I cannot envision sharing my accomplishment of unlimited space travel with anyone more deserving than the five of you. As Kait well realizes, when one possesses such knowledge the urge to share it with others is insurmountable. Of all those in this world I could have chosen to share this with I think I have again been blessed with such wonderful, intelligent and loyal friends as you have all been. Thank you from the bottom of my heart. If everyone is in agreement could we plan on returning to my home base a week from today and we will then commence Kait's and my latest voyage. I will pick up the tab for the commercial airways tickets if everyone is comfortable with the timing." Rick said it wasn't necessary to fly commercial as we could take one of his corporate jets to Kansas, especially since he had other company business to attend to out there.

We each picked out the special picture that we wanted to keep and I packaged up the remainder of them and intended to secure them in my safe at work, as we had all agreed. Joseph looked over each one that we had chosen and he felt comfortable that anyone glancing at them would think they came from a powerful space telescope. We did agree that several of the pictures that I was to secure would certainly raise eyebrows, especially those that I had taken on the planet of the burning rocks and the wonderful creatures that reside there. Joseph said most likely if anyone outside our circle saw one of them they would think it was taken at a Halloween party unless, they were someone as brilliant as Robert's uncle in interpreting such things.

The week went by quickly. I did return to the office, especially to lock up the pictures and I also wanted to touch base with Mark and the substitute teacher who was handling my classes. Mark was so excited to see me and couldn't wait to dwell into the past few weeks and if my love life had blossomed out. "Doctor, you have such a vibrant aura about you. Can I surmise that you have finally found another of life's great pleasures with your man of mystery? I have never seen you looking so happy and contented. I would love to have you share some of your most intimate moments with me about your experience."

"Mark, it seems we have been down this road before. My personal life is frankly none of your business. Let me just say that I am extremely content in having found happiness, and whatever you think that is I would let you use your imagination. I want to know where things stand around here with my substitute, the mail, and anything else I should be aware of. I also wanted to mention that I again will be absent for the next few weeks and that has already been cleared with the dean."

"You are really making up for lost time now that you have found love. I won't pry any further. Just let me say that I am so happy for you. You are a beautiful, intelligent woman and all you needed to fill out your life, beyond a successful career, was a handsome man in your life. Now you are complete. The mail, which I did not already handle, is on your desk and any notes of an importance are there also. I will leave you to your work and your dreams, Kaitlin."

I almost physically chased Mark out of the office, but when he left with a big smile on his face, and the door was closed, I just stood there for a minute and thought to myself, I should have listened to Mark years ago.' I was a slow learner when it came to matters of the heart, I thought to myself, but I am sure making up for those missed years now.

The mail was all-routine and everything seemed to be going along fine with the substitute. Not to well I hoped so they would decide to keep her rather than me, but I really thought to myself at this point do I really care anyway. Joseph has suggested we marry and move to his home in Kansas but I have been reluctant to commit to that, at least not yet. Joseph, being the fine gentleman that he is, has not pushed me and just said he hopes some day we may become man and wife. Time will tell.

Joseph and I spent a wonderful, fulfilling week together and as it turned out we only saw the others on one occasion for supper, as both Rick and Dale were extremely busy with company obligations and not surprising they took Sally and Debbie along with them. Each of those couples are becoming inseparable and that also delights me to no end. When we did meet we set the time to meet at the private airfield for our trip west, for Joseph and my second journey into the heavens. I could not contain myself, especially thinking I was hopefully going to find my parents this trip. Joseph had also said he wanted to travel to a completely different galaxy than we visited last trip, and introduce me to some amazing creatures that live on one of the planets in that galaxy.

Joseph said that the Universe must be filled with many planets with various life forms. He admitted he had only scratched the surface of visiting galaxies, since their were so many billions of them, but from what he had seen he was convinced that God had populated His Universe with many creatures.

We were scheduled to leave on Saturday around three PM and about nine in the morning I got a frantic call from Sally. "Kait, make sure you and Joseph are watching your backs. The same two scumbags that threatened me some months ago visited me this morning as I was leaving home to meet Rick. They approached me as I was about to get into my car and I almost fainted when I saw them. They said they had been following my travels and wanted to know why I had recently been in Canada and also in Kansas. I immediately pressed my security device and as I was arguing with them up pulled a local police officer within minutes. He asked them what they wanted with me and they said they were government agents and the local police had no authority to question them. The officer held his ground and within a couple more minutes, I was amazed how quickly, two of Rick's staff showed up. One was a fellow and the other was a woman. They immediately took over, thanking the officer for responding and after talking quietly with the policeman he seemed satisfied and left. I would not have wanted to tangle with either one of Rick's staff and the two so-called government agents decided it was time for a hasty retreat. As they were pulling away Rick drove up in his massive SUV and cut them off. He jumped out and yanked open the driver's door while his two staff members took up strategic positions away from their car. I couldn't hear what he was yelling at them but he told me later he told them if they ever bothered me again they would be history. From his expression and tone of voice there was no question they believed him. The two scumbags immediately drove off and I firmly believe I will never see them again. Rick calmed me down and all is well now but I wanted you and Debbie and your better halves to be aware. Seems the government agency, these low life's represent, is still suspicious of our activities and just what is going on."

"Sally, I am so relieved you are alright and that the security device that Rick set us up with worked as he said it would. I cannot imagine why these people are still interested in us. I would love to be able to talk with whomever it was that sent me the anonymous note some time ago warning me to be cautious. I still think it might have been my students Robert's uncle, but I have no way of knowing for sure. Since I don't think we were observed taking off from Hay River in Canada, or from the home base in Kansas, I cannot imagine why they are still paying attention. Just think what we would be facing if they actually observed our take off or return. I will see you folks at the airport this afternoon, I am so sorry this is happening to you, love you Sally."

"Love you too Kait, and remember we all are in this together, as we freely chose to be. See you later." With that we cut things off and I filled in Joseph on the happenings and he also couldn't believe there were still suspicious people in our so-called government. He mentioned they sure must not have much to do to be able to follow up such slim leads as this one. We both agree how things could become very intense if they actually had proof of Joseph's accomplishment.

We headed out for the airport and our flight on Rick's corporate jet to Kansas and my much-anticipated next flight into space. I was praying that I could see my parents on this trip. When we all arrived everyone it seemed, except Rick and Dale, were all abuzz about what had happened with Sally. Rick just said it was over and done with and not to worry about it. He said as long as they don't have direct proof we have little to worry about.

We took off on time, with Dale at the controls and Rick standing by. They kidded Joseph that they might need him to fill in and fly the jet, but Joseph just laughed and said he didn't think he was capable of flying it even though he could fly his craft unencumbered into the far reaches of the Universe. We all had a good laugh over this and it helped relieve the tension from the recent encounter. We arrived just about dark and after parking the jet Dale headed off in the direction of the mountain range to set up the laser diversion and the rest of us headed for Joseph's home base.

Joseph and I bid our farewells to the others and boarded the craft. At the prearranged time Rick gave us the thumbs up as the laser was searching the skies in the distance for commercial aircraft targets and already the drones were being pulled out of this area and headed towards the source of the laser light. Of course there were no commercial aircraft in the area but the controllers and officers behind the drone controls weren't aware of that immediately. Joseph pushed the control to open the roof of the hanger and gave me thumbs up and we were off.

We had agreed that we would first visit the galaxy that Joseph had earlier said had a planet within it where a beautiful group of living creatures reside. He had said he had once before spent some time there and was so impressed by their beauty and friendliness. We then would visit the pivotal planet, between the Heaven and Hell side of mankind's final resting places, to see if my parents reside there.

Everything went smoothly and we even came across some UFO's in our travels that Joseph said were from the planet with the burning rocks. As he had mentioned before, they were very peaceful creatures. They did, however, have an intense desire to remain so and were worried that someday creatures from a hostile planet, such as Earth, would attempt, when they unraveled the secrets of space travel, to invade such a peaceful place. They had previously told Joseph that they had visited many planets in the past and observed their inhabitants. Of those they were aware of Earth was by far inhabited by the most unstable, hostile creatures. Being a peaceful group amongst themselves however, had not precluded their developing very sophisticated space vehicles with very powerful weapons to use if threatened. Joseph told me that he was one-hundred percent positive they would never use them, except in defending themselves. "They are highly intelligent Kait, and very devoted creatures."

We arrived, after a few long days of travel, in the galaxy that Joseph had wanted me to visit, and soon were in the outer area of this planet which Joseph called the planet of absolute beauty. We made a pass over what appeared to be a landing area and a bright light came on. He said that was our clearance to land. Since he had visited here before he was recognized, and obviously welcomed.

We landed and were greeted by what I can only describe as the most beautiful, heavenly creatures any human would want to see. It seems that Joseph could communicate with them in what I can only explain as a universal language of the Universe. It was mostly sign language, and after a few minutes they all looked at me and nodded there heads and seemed to smile in agreement with his saying that he had brought the most beautiful human from Earth to meet them. I wanted to take some pictures but thought better of asking since he had told me before we landed that they were very private creatures and most likely would not want their pictures taken. As it turned out we spent a wonderful two days with them, and again I could only imagine if the Earth was inhabited by such gentle, peace loving people.

We reluctantly left on the third day and headed for the pivotal planet between the Heaven and Hell side of the final resting place of all humans. As we approached this planet I became so nervous. Joseph could see my anxiety and immediately calmed me down. "Kait, I am sure we will find them here, just take some deep breaths and let me do the communicating and find out who is overseeing the Book of Life records for this planet. Everything is going to work out, I promise you."

We approached from the Heaven side, and as I gazed into the distance I could see some of the Hell side planets that were lined up in the other direction from this planet, which is the half way point. Our approach was cast in beautiful sunlight, and as I gazed upon the Hell side they were increasingly darker the further down they went. Not only must those that have accumulated a miserable, failing record while on Earth share their space with other less than desirable people, but they must also spend eternity in ever increasingly inhospitable planets. Truly the Lord has found numerous ways to punish wrongdoers from planet Earth.

We landed and were greeted by the designated overseer of this planet. Joseph explained our quest to locate my dear departed parents and the gentleman was most cooperative. He said they had been visited on a number of occasions from creatures from other worlds that had long ago conquered space travel, so we were not the first or would we be the last. He led us into the beautiful building where the records were kept. He mentioned that the vast majority of persons spending eternity on this pivotal planet were couples that had varying records accumulated while on Earth and therefore were assigned to different planets on the Heaven side originally. They had all chosen to spend eternity together, therefore they ended up here. He mentioned the peace and tranquility that existed here and how blessed they all were that our Lord and Savior allowed couples this option. Joseph gave him the name of my parents and he immediately consulted the Book of Life. After a few minutes he looked up with a look of astonishment on his face. "You said you visited the most coveted of the Heaven side planets and also the additional three and still could not locate them? With what you have said about their kindness and generosity while on Earth, you should have by now located them. It is hard to believe they are not on either this planet or one of the other ones you visited. I am so sorry to disappoint you. You certainly seem like such a nice person, and such a wonderful couple. I'm sure your parents were what you have said they were, for having raised such a beautiful, loving daughter. By the way are you two married?" Joseph beat me to a response.

"Unfortunately as of this moment we are not but I intend to work on it very soon. In fact I was hoping Kait would say yes to my proposal and we could find a minister that is spending eternity on this planet, or one of the other Heaven planets, to perform the ceremony. The significance of such an occasion is earth cataclysmic. We would, at least I think we would, be the first two humans to not only travel unencumbered throughout the Universe but also to be married in space. Maybe then we could even think about conceiving the first human baby in space."

"Joseph, it is a good thing I know you so well, and frankly am in love with you, or I might end our relationship right here and now and leave without you. Enough of this foolish talk. If we ever choose to become husband and wife it will be carried out on Earth in a proper ceremony. The time and place will be at my choosing. You may be the only human to ever conquer space travel but that doesn't mean a thing to me when it comes to love and marriage." We all shared a laugh over the exchange and then Joseph's serious side came forth.

CHAPTER SEVEN

Detour + Four Future Space Voyages

"Kait, I am not sure how to raise this issue but since we have not been able to locate your parents on any of the planets they should be on, are you sure they are deceased? That had not crossed my mind before now, since I was sure we would find them here but now, I am beginning to wonder. What were the circumstances of their passing? You told me one time that it was a tragic sudden accident?"

"Joseph, it was several years ago and they were on a small cruise ship off the coast of Italy and the ship hit a reef and floundered. I was told a number of persons were rescued but that many went down with the ship? When I heard about the sinking and knew they were on it I immediately called the cruise line to inquire of them. They initially told me they were trying to gather together the records of who had survived but it was difficult as the ships accounts went to the bottom of the Mediterranean Sea. They further said, which I found very strange, that their computers had crashed and they had no official records of who perished and who survived. I always thought it was a convenience that their computers had crashed so they might not be so libel if someone couldn't prove that their loved ones were on the ship when it went aground and sank. The official word I finally got from the Italian authorities after the inquiry was completed was that my parents had in fact perished. I was told by some other relatives of victims, when I visited Italy, that some persons were pulled from the waters and survived, but in a comatose state. These relatives said the records were so poorly kept that no one knew for sure all of the circumstances of the survivors or those that perished. All the official information I was given was that they had in fact gone down with the ship and that their bodies were never found. Do you honestly think, after our failure to locate them on the Heaven planets, that they in fact might have been amongst the survivors?"

"Kait, I think our travels in space are going to be interrupted by travels to Italy to try to get the authorities to tell us exactly what they know. It seems inconceivable that if they survived they have never been identified, or anyone has tried to contact you. If in fact they survived in a comatose state they could well be institutionalized without those attending to them knowing who they are, or being able to communicate themselves with those watching over them. I hesitate to say stranger things have happened, but we will never know unless we pursue the issue when we return from this trip. Let us spend the night here and head back to Kansas in the morning. We can, when we get within satellite phone range, contact Rick and have him alert Dale to set up the same laser diversion for our night landing. We all had agreed we could use this diversion at least once more before trying to come up with another."

"I can't believe this is happening, Joseph. After seeing the peace and tranquility those that have gone before are enjoying on the Heaven side planets, I would prefer that to my parents being kept alive artificially, if in fact that is what is happening.

"Kait, I think you have to prepare yourself for any possibilities. I realize I promised to take Debbie, Sally, Dale and Rick on a space voyage, but this comes before everything. I know how much you loved your parents, and to be left not knowing what happened to them, or even worse to have the cruise line intentionally cover up the fact that they survived and are in a vegetative state, is even more unthinkable. There will be plenty of time for our future space travels and it might be to our advantage to cool it for awhile so the government doesn't get any more suspicions of something unusual going on. Whatever the case I am here for you Kait, and your quest to find the answers is also my quest. Let us rest this night and leave this tranquil place in the morning."

Our host was most gracious and wished us luck in our search for the truth. We left in the early morning hours so that we could time our return after dark when less inquiring eyes might be up and about. We got within the satellite phone distance and dialed up Rick. He answered almost immediately and said he would alert Dale and Debbie, who just happened to be with him, and assured us that everything would be set up for our landing at the appointed hour.

It went very smoothly and we could see the laser in the distance and also see all the drones being directed away from our landing area to investigate the laser. Dale had to be careful, as the drone operators would most likely call in ground support, but we were confident they would be several steps ahead of any authority that was called in to investigate. This would most likely be the last time we could use this diversion, as the government will certainly become suspicious if we were to use it too many times. We are all trying to think of other ideas to call the drones off, or move our base of operations elsewhere, but so far nothing concrete has been put forth. As Joseph had said, maybe it is good that we are being diverted to other concerns to let things cool down. Our landing went smoothly and Rick and Sally were there to greet us. Sally couldn't wait to find out if we had located my parents.

"Were you able to find your beloved parents on the pivotal planet as you were led to believe, and what other fascinating adventures did you experience?"

"Again, Sally, I have good news and bad news. The bad news is that they were not on that planet within the series of Heaven and Hell planets either. The caretaker that we met was also very surprised after we told him all the details of our quest, and the fact that we had already visited the top three most coveted Heaven planets. Joseph raised an interesting thought, concerning my quest, that maybe my parents did not die a few years ago when their cruise ship went down. He thinks they might have been pulled from the icy waters without any identification and in a comatose state of mind. As I told you before, when I went to Italy after it happened, things were inconclusive and the authorities there were evasive at the time. All I could find out was that they were assumed to have gone down with the ship. What an irony that several years later, when I have been honored to be selected by Joseph to explore the heavens with him, that I finally might have found out that they are actually still alive. Whatever the case, Joseph has agreed to accompany me to Italy again to, hopefully, finally find out the truth. I realize this means delaying the trips into space for the four of you but I am sure you understand.

The good news is that we visited a planet, which is inhabited by the most beautiful creatures you will ever be honored to lay yours eyes upon. Not only were they absolutely the most gorgeous creatures, they were also, as have been all those planets we have visited, the most peace loving of each other. I still cannot understand what went wrong with God's plan to populate our Earth with peaceful creatures, as we have discussed. He certainly must be disappointed in this experiment. I sometimes wonder how many millions, or possibly even billions, of other planets in the vastness of the Universe might have also turned out to be a disappointment to Him. Maybe Earthlings are His only failure. Enough of my preaching, what say you Rick?"

"The longer I live the more I find that anything is possible. As you know my organization is mainly concentrated in the United States but I do have many contacts around the world, including Italy. Most of those contacts are in a similar business as I am, in providing security, etc., to citizens of their country who are in jeopardy from individuals, or even today more so from their own governments. I do personally know the top person, who happens to be a woman, in the largest private security firm in Italy and I would be happy to contact her on your behalf. I, of course, have no idea if she is aware of anything untold as connects to the cruise line and the possible cover up of survivors, but I would be happy to consult with her. She is one of the best in the business, has little love for the government, and has also surrounded herself with ex-military and retired police personnel who are most loyal. As you mentioned, it is strange how things turn out. Having believed all these years that your parents perished, and having met your genius, Joseph, who took you into the far reaches of space only to find out that possibly your parents are still alive. If we do locate them the authorities are going to be very inquisitive as to how you became suspicious of their survival, so we will need to be extra cautious when discussing the events surrounding the past many months. I think it would be well if we invented some story that we could all agree upon as to why after all this time you are re-opening the case. As it turns out I have business in Europe later this month so I will move things up and we can all go in my corporate jet. When I am there I will check with the security chief I mentioned for any information she may have. I will send her a secure message prior to our quest, to give her a heads up, and then she will have time to send out some feelers." Joseph and I concurred for a minute and then Joseph spoke up.

"Rick, we appreciate the offer but I also insist on paying the expense of the trip and especially the use of your jet. I agree that it is prudent that we let things settle down here on this end for a while, so any suspicion that the government has of my accomplishments will have time to cool down. Kait said she had an urgent message to call Mark at her office about some visitors that were there, but as yet she has not been able to reach him. We are concerned but decided to give it another day since we don't think he is in any danger as he has not been privy to any of the actual goings on. He has been suspicious, as Kait said, but nothing concrete. We will fill you in when Kait finally makes contact with him. In the meantime can we plan on leaving in the next few days as I am as anxious as Kait to find the answers to this latest puzzle?"

Rick agreed, and said that again the six of us would go as sightseers so Dale and Debbie can also tag along. He specifically wanted Dale as he is his right hand man and he was sure that Dale would not go without Debbie. It sure sounded like a plan to me so I didn't argue with it at all. I had left several messages for Mark to call me back, but so far nothing; I was becoming more and more concerned about his safety. As it turned out he finally called my cell phone later on in the evening. When he did call he was frantic to fill me in on the latest happenings.

"Doctor, those same two unscrupulous characters who were here before were back a few days ago. They insisted that I tell them where you were and they questioned me as to what you had been up to. They also wanted to get into the wall safe in your office and when I told them where they could go they said they would get a court order and be back. I told them if they wanted to get rough with me I would most likely not resist too much and that seemed to turn them off and they left. I am sure they have no grounds to get a court order but under this present government nothing would surprise me. Since I had no idea what you had in the safe, and I was afraid they might just find a corrupt judge to issue such an order, I took the liberty to empty the safe and have your pictures tucked away in a safe place. Kait, I can't believe what I saw in those pictures. Is what I think happened actually what you and your mysterious lover did? That would be earth-shattering and prove that UFO's actually existed in the past from other planets and that at least one human has unlocked the mystery of space travel. Tell me, please Kait, is what I think happened actually what did take place?"

"Mark, I am only going to say this once. Wherever you have hidden those pictures I want you to take them immediately and burn them, without hesitation. I am not going to confide in you what is going on, or what has gone on, but I am sure you have a pretty good idea from looking at those pictures. Please burn them immediately. If those two devious characters call on you again and you need any help call the local police without delay and also call my cell phone right away and I will have a friend send help to you. Frankly, Mark, the less you know at this moment the better. I will be traveling to Europe with several friends in the next week or so. Don't hesitate to get in touch with me immediately if you need to. Take care of yourself, Mark, and please don't share our conversation with anyone, including your boyfriend. The less persons in the know about what is going on the safer we will all be. Need I say more?"

"God bless you Kait, and stay safe."

When Mark hung up I turned to fill in Joseph and the others. They were as concerned and shocked as I was. Rick said he was not at all surprised, as the government agency, which is behind those questionable characters, will never give up their investigation whatever the issue might be if they think there might be a thread of truth in the accusation.

"This is particularly true in a case such as this one which, if they could ever prove it being true, has such stunning implications. Even if they have no concrete evidence of such an undertaking as Joseph has accomplished they will still keep the case alive just to be on the safe side, so to speak. They have literally hundreds of such uncertainties they constantly investigate, from speculation about someone having developed a substitute for fuel to such as we see here involving unfettered space travel. Don't ever be surprised at what lengths they will go to provide answers to their suspicions. Keeping an open mind on their activities and what they are capable of undertaking is what we do at our agency, so we hopefully can stay one step ahead of them. Be assured this is not the last time someone within our inner circle will be visited and questioned in the future. Our job, or I should say Dale and his staff and my job, is to make sure they never get too close to the truth, as the outcome would be disastrous. So far we have managed to stay ahead of them and keep this secret of Joseph's tightly within a small group, but we should never let our guard down."

As we went about our business the next few days I think we all were looking over our shoulder slightly more than normal. The days went by rapidly and before we knew it we were winging our way across the seas towards Italy. Rick had put out some feelers, especially to the head of the agency similar to his in Italy. She had responded that she would see what some of her agents, especially the ones that had in any way been involved after the sinking of the cruise ship, had heard about any survivors and their fate. He had set up an appointment with her for soon after we were scheduled to arrive.

We landed in Rome and took a couple of taxis to the beautiful hotel where we had reserved our rooms for our stay. We had reservations for two weeks and I prayed that would be enough time to find some answers. The next day after breakfast Rick said that he alone was going to meet with Elma, the head of the largest investigative and security firm in Italy. He felt he would be able to speak more freely with her without the others of us there. He said she might ask to meet me since it was my folks that supposedly had been lost in the disaster, but he thought this initial meeting should be just between the two of them. None of us took issue with this, especially since it was Rick who would be the most able to find the truth here.

We all settled in. The sleeping arrangements had progressed greatly since our road trip to Canada. We were all comfortable with the arrangements and I wondered again why I had waited so long to enjoy the many pleasures of a loving relationship with my man of mystery. Rick left shortly after breakfast for his meeting with Elma and I became so anxious while he was gone to see what he would find out. He was gone some time and when he returned the other five of us were having a light lunch in the hotel dining room. I immediately began the interrogation of him, even before he had a chance to order his meal.

"Kait, Elma was most gracious and sympathized with your plight concerning your missing parents. She said she would like to meet you, if time allows, while we are still in Rome. As far as why we were reopening this case after several years she did not question. I am sure she was curious what had prompted our questioning the Italian governments original notice that your parents went down with the ship and their bodies were never found. The only information that she picked up from her staff that had been involved in some investigations for surviving family members after the sinking, was that there were rumors of some survivors who were totally comatose. She said the rumors were that these few individuals might have been taken to a Catholic home on the outskirts of the city where the nuns were currently caring for them as they were on life support. She gave me the name of the facility and I plan on our going there tomorrow. I want to wait until tomorrow since I have another contact person I wish to consult with. This person happens to be in the Italian government and is totally trustworthy. I asked Elma why the government of Italy, or the cruise line, had not contacted all the passengers' families to possible identify anyone who might have survived and be in a vegetative condition. She only said it might have to do with potential lawsuits and liability, that there was a great deal of intrigue surrounding the events after the sinking and much speculation of a massive cover-up of responsibility. Tomorrow we shall see what turns up at the Catholic care center."

Tomorrow could not come around too soon and after a very restless night the six of us headed out for the rest home. I could hardly contain myself and I was shaking as we entered. Rick took charge and asked to speak with the nun who was in charge of the operation here. She was very elderly and looked extremely tired and when she spoke it was with a great deal of effort. Rick said that I was a daughter of parents that allegedly had been lost when the cruise ship went down several years ago. He told her that I had been notified by the Italian government that they had perished and their bodies had never been recovered. The nun asked why then were we still perusing the case, after we had official word of their passing. I thought it was my turn to enter the discussion and could not contain myself. "Mother, I was always somewhat suspicious that what I was being told at the time was not the entire truth of the affair. The fact that the cruise line claimed their passenger manifest had gone down with the ship, and their computer backup files had all crashed at the same time, seemed too much of a coincidence. I have always been suspicious that there had been a government-backed cover-up to avoid or limit liability. Recently it has come to my attention that there may have been some survivors that had been so mentally damaged that they were in a comatose state and being cared for somewhat secretly. Believe me Mother; I am not accusing you of any wrongdoing, only trying to find the truth. As we discussed, amongst ourselves, if there were such survivors why weren't the relatives of all the passengers notified to come to Italy to try and identify them. All I am asking is a chance to see whom you are caring for here and make sure it is not my loving mother and father."

"Dear, I can fully understand your pursuit. If it had been relatives and loved ones of mine I also would have wanted to explore every opportunity to find the truth. Please understand that the role myself and the other sisters that live and work here is to provide aid and comfort to those poor folks that are terminally suffering, for whatever reason. We do have a few individuals here that were placed by the government and little, if any information was given to us at the time. We were only told they needed twenty-four hour care, were in a vegetative state, and nothing more. I questioned the authorities at the time they were brought here and, frankly, was told my job was to provide comfort and not to ask questions. As daughters of our Lord and Savior I did not question the authorities any more. These Catholic hospices are funded by the church and the Italian government and under those circumstances I could not argue with them. Our role of providing the needs of the sick and the dying is too important to jeopardize it with excessive questions. All of you might question my attitude and position in this case, but never the less until you walk in my shoes you would not understand completely my position."

"Mother, believe me when I say I for one, and all of us here would not in any way hold you personally responsible for any cover up or underhanded handling of the aftermath of the sinking of that ship. All we want is to be able to observe those who you are caring for that are in such a state to determine if any of them are my dear mother and father. Our combined faith in our Lord and Savior has brought us here and will continue to guide us. Can we please be shown those of which we speak?"

"You must understand that I am not the final authority in this matter and I must consult with the Father that oversees this institution before I could grant such a request. Whether or not he will feel comfortable in allowing it remains to be seen. My fear is he will feel obliged to consult with the central government, which in itself would delay your being able to see them, and at worst deny you admittance completely. Several of the patients we serve are very close to death so I will do my best to expedite the decision. Forgive me for my position, but again I must think of this institution and the need it serves before possibly putting it in jeopardy."

I was devastated that we had run up against this brick wall of government control of these institutions and that we might be denied access completely. After having come this far I could hardly contain myself. The thought of my mother or father, that I loved so dearly, lying within feet of me and not being able to communicate tore me apart. Joseph saw the look of astonishment on my face and put his strong arm around me. Rick was also very upset, as we all were, and chose his words carefully when he responded to the mother.

"Mother, I can understand your position and the fact that you have to answer not only to the higher ups in the faith but also to the central government. I do take issue with your position, however, as a servant of God in not at least allowing Dr.Graham to briefly observe, without disturbing anyone, your few patients that fall within the guidelines you describe. Must we always bow down to governments when humanity is at stake, or can we not sometimes serve our Lord directly with our compassion? It seems to me that if we agreed not to divulge anything we see here, or talk about it, you could make an exception. You realize that Kaitlin's Mother or father, or both, may be lying within feet of her and yet she is being denied the right to see them. Mother, do you honestly see that as the position that our Lord would take in this concern."

"I'm sorry you see it that way my son but I have no choice. I must think of the entire hospice and it's future and not dwell on this one incident. I promise to consult with the father tomorrow and hopefully he will allow access. Your other avenue is to contact the government Department of Heath and request admission from them. I will be completely honest with you, however, that such an approval would be highly unlikely, especially to non-citizens. Again, I apologize but I must ask you to leave now. If you will leave me your number where I can reach you I promise I will call as soon as a decision is made, go with God."

Joseph almost had to drag me out of the hospice. I was ready to push the Mother out of the way and search the hospice on my own. I told Joseph that I would not leave without seeing if my beloved folks were here but he gently took me by the arm and led me out. Rick also saw how upset I was but assured me to be patient and everything would work out for the best. They literally had to almost carry me out as I was in tears. Rick said he would contact his connection in the Italian government and see if he could pull any strings to allow us access. I was an emotional wreck when we arrived back at the hotel and told the rest of our group I wanted to be alone and that they should go to supper without me. Joseph insisted on staying with me and I lay down on the couch with my head in his lap still weeping. I fell asleep almost immediately and finally he awakened me and said we should retire to the bedroom for a good night's sleep. He helped me into bed and again I think I fell into a deep sleep in a matter of seconds.

I felt as if I had re-gathered my senses in the morning when we met for breakfast. Rick said he had already put in a call to his connection in the government and was waiting for a reply. In the meantime he said we should just all relax and wait for the call from the good Mother, or from his connection. "I realize, Kait, that it is difficult to relax under the circumstances but please give it time and I promise you it will work out. I am confident either my government contact or the hierarchies in the church will allow us access soon. Dale is also working on plan B if all else fails. I'm not sure what that will be but knowing Dale's expertise in these matters I am sure it would be totally successful, if not totally legal." We all looked at Dale and he just had this shy smile on his face and we knew whatever his backup plan was it would be a good one that we could bank on. Dale was never one to trifle with in these circumstances and always was very original in his solutions. I felt a little better after Rick filled us all in.

The next morning the telephone rang in out hotel room and Joseph picked it up. All I heard from this end was. "Thank you Mother, we will pursue the approval of the government department that you mentioned. I understand your frustration and your concern that something is amiss here but you have your superiors to answer to and you have no choice in the matter. God be with you Mother and I hope we will be seeing you in the near future with the proper government approval." As Joseph turned towards me I could hardly keep from totally breaking down again. He told me that the hierarchies in the church had refused our request to visit the comatose patients. He went on to say he could not hold it against the good Mother as she also was frustrated and could not understand why such a humanitarian gesture was being denied. Joseph went on to say that in his opinion it was a massive cover-up of some kind and the church, receiving funds from the government, had no choice but to cooperate with them. Joseph suggested that we head out to meet up with the others before we discussed it further. He always seems to find a way to ease my anxiety and get my mind moving in a different direction.

When we arrived at the restaurant the others were already there. Sally could see the concern on my face and immediately asked if we had heard from the Mother. Joseph was kind enough to fill them all in since I was sure I would break down if I started to talk about it. Each of them was shocked, except Rick and Dale who as usual remained extremely calm. I wasn't sure if any momentous event would shake up either one of them, as if anything would. Rick reassured us as he had talked with his government connection and fully expected to hear back today.

As it turned out, after a day of sight seeing in this city so full of history we met for supper and Rick filled us in. "I have some bad news and some good news. The bad news is that my connection in the government was not able to pull any strings at the Department of Health. He told me that, from what he understood, the government preferred to let sleeping dogs lay and not reopen any cases involving the tragedy of the sinking of the cruise ship. It seems the government had some connection to the shipping line, which made it also potentially legally responsible for damages, and the many law suits that followed threatened to further bankrupt the Italian government. Since they are so far in debt, from years of irresponsible spending well beyond their means, they are trying to cover up any further liability. That is the bad news everyone, the good news is that Dale has firmed up plan B and is ready to set it in motion." I interrupted Rick at this point.

"I cannot understand the closed mindedness of both the Catholic management and government overseeing the hospice, and the utter contempt for human compassion of allowing a surviving family member to write closure to such a tragedy. As we have discussed I have no intention, and never did have any, to sue anyone over this untimely terrible event. I just want to see if my mother and father are in that hospice being kept alive artificially. Is that so much to ask? I guess in a way I can understand the position of the Catholic hierarchies in this case since so much of their funding comes from the central government, but the Department of Health's position is unconscionable. So what is plan B Dale?"

"The day we visited the hospice and talked with the Mother, Debbie and I stayed well in the background. I am positive that the good Mother paid no attention to us, as you and Joseph were in such close conversation with her. I purchased some attire for Debbie and I today and if I do say so we look fairly handsome in them. I will be dressed as Father Dale and Debbie will be outfitted as Sister Debbie. We will make an official phone call from the Vatican's line, thanks to Elma's staff's expertise, and set up an official inspection of the hospice for the day after tomorrow. Kait, you have shown us pictures of your parents and even though they may have changed somewhat, if in fact they are in the hospice I am sure Debbie and I would be able to recognize them. We will, I am convinced, be able to spell closure to whether they are in fact there." I couldn't contain myself and gave Dale and Debbie an enormous embrace.

"Dale, thanks so much for moving ahead with this plan. Debbie, I love you so much and appreciate your being a part of getting to the bottom of all this. If you find out that one or both of them are in fact there, how then do we deal with my being given access to them? As I said before, if they are there I have no intention of bringing any type of lawsuit or action, I just want finality to this nightmare. How would I find that from this point Rick?"

"Kait, I have talked with my government contact and he said if in fact we do prove that one or both are there then he will insist we be granted assess to them. He is one-hundred percent sure if we confirm that they are there he can open doors for us, both through the government and the Vatican. We will move along with Dale's plan, and through Elma and her expertise we will set the wheels in motion tomorrow with the so called official call. Let's all try and relax for the rest of the evening and we can move ahead after breakfast in the morning. I have some urgent business to take care of in the morning before the call is placed, as several issues are requiring my involvement back home with my organization. Seems the American government is becoming even more intrusive in individual's personal lives and I need to make several decisions on where my staff needs to move in a couple of issues. After that we will set the wheels in motion for Dale's plan. Rest easy Kait, as I am confident we are moving in the right direction."

We finished our supper and I was so anxious and exhausted I asked Joseph if he minded our going up to the room and just relaxing and he was in favor of doing that. He said he was also tired and wanted to try and see that we both got a good nights rest.

As it turned out I was surprised, as I fell asleep quickly in Joseph's strong arms, and slept like a baby until about six. We freshened up and met the others at eight for breakfast. Rick said he would be on a conference call for about an hour with his top staff in the states and then the call would be placed to the hospice through Elma's headquarters. It is amazing, I thought to myself, what can be accomplished nowadays with communications with the technology available. We decided to visit the Vatican in the afternoon and take in the sights of so much history. We went our separate ways and decided to meet for supper at the hotel dining room for an update.

When supper rolled around I couldn't contain myself and almost shouted at Rick to find out if the call went as planned. Everyone broke out in laughter, which lightened the moment for me and calmed me somewhat. Rick filled us in and said the call had been placed and the hospice was expecting Father Dale and Sister Debbie at seven AM in the morning to do the semi-annual inspection of the facility. The Mother had been most cooperative and was looking forward to their visit. I could hardly contain myself and Joseph comforted me as only this wonderful caring man could do. I have found love and am cherishing it. I wondered why I had waited so long, but then again maybe it was to connect with this fantastic lover and master of space that was pre-destined.

We decided rather than all of us drive Father Dale and Sister Debbie to the hospice they should go alone. As much as I wanted to be a part of it Rick suggested, or I should say insisted, that the rest of us remain in the background and wait for their report. I have never been so anxious in my life as I was when they left this morning for the hospice. Debbie gave me a warm embrace and told me to relax, as we were getting closer to the truth than at any time in this quest. Dale also embraced me and reassured me. Joseph held me tight and said we should just hang out in our room until we got the call from Dale that they were back.

It was the longest four hours of my life. Finally the phone rang and I almost knocked Joseph over reaching for it. It was Dale and he said to meet them in the dining room in thirty minutes. I wanted to scream into the phone to ask what they had found out but Dale hung up almost immediately. I asked Joseph if we could go without delay and he just quietly reassured me and said that they would not be there for a half hour so we should take our time. "Kait, I want you to be prepared for the worst as we have talked about it for the past few days. I honestly feel that there is a good chance one or both of your parents are there and in a comatose state of mind. I realize you have said you can accept this, but the reality will be much different than the speculation of just thinking they may be there. Try to stay calm, and we together will find closure to this entire sordid affair." I thanked Joseph and gave him a kiss and hug for being there for me, not just in this situation, but always. When we got to the dining room Father Dale and Sister

Debbie were back in their regular cloths and Rick and Sally were with them.

I approached the group with a great deal of trepidation, and as I did Debbie got up slowly and came up to me and put her arms around me. I knew then, immediately, that they had located one or both of my parents. Dale was the first to speak. "Kait, there is no question that your mother is a patient at the hospice. She is, as we surmised, in a vegetative state and according to the head nurse who cares for her has been so for the years since the tragedy. We visited all the patients and your father was not among them. The sister in charge of the actual care of the patients said that only one elderly man was brought in, shortly after the sinking of the cruise ship, and he had miraculously been discharged some time ago, fully recovered. She said he was from Ireland and after he was well enough he contacted his family and they came and took him home. The other five survivors, all in a comatose state, are women, your mother being one of them. The sister told us that none of them have suffered and all of them have been kept alive by artificial methods. She went on to offer the thought that she could not understand why more effort had not been made to locate their families so a decision could be properly made to humanly end their life support. She was a very gracious lady, as were all the attending sisters who cared for the patients. I believe Rick has already contacted his government connection and the wheels are turning to allow you free access to her. She appears to be at peace with her surroundings, both Debbie and I are convinced, and has not suffered, so rest easy Kait as she is in good hands. As far as the fate of your father is concerned we can only speculate that he perished along with so many others when the ship sank."

"Thank you Dale and Debbie, I cannot wait for permission to visit my mother whom I loved so dearly. I cannot understand Joseph why, if my father perished, we could not find him on one of the Heaven planets. I have to believe he has to be on the Heaven side of the Heaven and Hell planets as he was such a caring and loving individual. He was the best father anyone would ever wish to have and a very loving husband to my mother. When can we see her Rick?" Before Rick could answer his cell phone rang and he excused himself from the table. Joseph spoke up.

"Kait, there is no easy answer to the puzzle of why we did not find your father. Could he have been someone you really didn't know all the inner truths about or maybe we just didn't look on the right Heaven planet. Even though we visited several of them there were still others we didn't visit. There is a solution to all of this and I think after you visit your mother we should take a deep breath and discuss our next move. No matter where your beloved father is there is a way that he and your mother can be re-united on the pivot planet, but enough of that, lets see what Rick has found out."

"I have some good news everyone. My connection in the government has been successful in opening doors and we are all granted official access to the hospice starting tomorrow. Part of the agreement was that you would not initiate any type of legal action against the cruise line or the Italian government. I told him we all agreed with that, as you had made that point extremely clear from the beginning. Lets plan on leaving here after breakfast and heading out. Kait, you must try and relax, as difficult as that is at this point knowing tomorrow you will see your dear mother for the first time since the ship floundered and you thought she was lost. How mysteriously some things work out. If Joseph had never contacted you and subsequently taken you on the adventure of a lifetime, or the greatest adventure anyone could ever wish for, you would never have known your mother was still alive. I suggest we take in more of the sights of this magnificent city for the rest of the day, if you all agree. I took the liberty of hiring a tour guide for us. I am hoping and praying it will help you relax some Kait."

"Thank you Rick, I'm not sure anything would help me relax at this point but that is very thoughtful of you. It should help me keep my mind occupied until tomorrow and what I know will be a very emotional day for me."

The tour guide was excellent and was so knowledgeable of the times gone by of this fantastic city so full of history and the tour actually did help me relax. We finished off the day with a late meal at a fine restaurant and Rick even invited the tour guide to join us, as he was such a great fellow. He kept us all in stitches during the entire meal. Joseph and I retired early and only my head resting on Joseph's powerful shoulder allowed me to finally get some much-needed sleep.

As it turned out I fell into such a deep sleep of exhaustion that Joseph had to give me a light kiss on the forehead to awaken me as we were going to meet the others at eight for breakfast and then head out for the hospice. We freshened up and Joseph took me in his strong arms and we departed. Dale jumped in behind the wheel and we were off. Joseph held my hand tightly and Sally and Debbie hung close to me. When we arrived Joseph gently talked to me and helped me out of the SUV. I was shaking when we went in and met the good Mother whom we had spoken to the first visit here. She was gracious, even though now she realized the subterfuge we had initiated to gain access. We had previously decided that just Joseph and I would go into her room and the Mother led us down the hall. As we approached Joseph held me even tighter and finally we entered the room and my mother, whom I loved so deeply, lay in a peaceful sleep by a window streaming with sunlight. I slowly approached her and as I took her hand in mine I completely broke down. Joseph and the Mother were waiting quietly by the door and Joseph, seeing my anguish, came up to me and put his arm around my shoulder and comforted me. I stared deeply into my mother's unmoving eyes and prayed to God that I had been granted this moment to see her again. After a suitable time Joseph left and brought the others down from the waiting room and we all were in the room. As it turned out I don't think there was a dry eye amongst the six of us. I sat and held my beloved mother's hand for several hours while the others went for some lunch. Joseph insisted on staying with me, even though I had encouraged him to go with the others. They all finally came back and Sally suggested we should head back to the city. Joseph bent down and took me gently by the arm and I leaned down and kissed my mother lightly on the forehead. As I turned to walk, reluctantly, out of the room, I stopped at the door and turned and again looked at her lying peacefully there. It was then that I finally grasped the enormity of all the tubes and wires that they had hooked up to her, which of course were keeping her alive. Joseph led me down the hall and I was in tears as I left.

"Joseph, what am I to do, I love her so much and I know that she would not want to be kept alive in this fashion, but I can't bear to make a decision that she should be allowed to go in peace. Fortunately, through the grace of God and your genius I do realize she would spend eternity on one of the coveted Heaven planets. Do you honestly think there is a chance she could call on the Almighty to grant her and my father, wherever he may be, eternity on the pivotal planet?"

My love, we have been there and talked to some of those that spend eternity on the Heaven planets. There is no question in my mind that she would be more at peace, especially with your father there, than she is here in this condition. The Catholic Church, and its very devoted sisters, have been most caring for her, as well as the others, but frankly Kait it is time to let her go. Everything happens for a purpose, and I believe God has destined that you will make the right decision for yourself as well as for your beloved mother. She is not, and has not suffered, and it is time she was allowed to go to her reward. She had a good life, a loving husband, and a devoted beautiful daughter, let her go and rest in peace for eternity with you father, wherever he may be. I promise you dear, I will take you to visit both of them after I have taken the others on their promised adventures into space. I am convinced it is the right decision for you to make and I will stand with you solidly in the decision. Let me know when you have made up your mind and I will initiate a meeting with the director of the hospice."

"Joseph, you are sent by God, literally, as my lover and anchor. I want to see her again each day for the rest of the week and then I will make a decision. Thank you for being there for me, I could not face this without you and what I know is your love and affection for me. I love you so much, and am blessed you came into my life."

Rick had to return to the states on business and Sally, of course, decided to return with him. Debbie was hesitant to leave me here alone, except with Joseph, but Rick said he needed Dale and of course I told Debbie to feel free to go with him. I was more than comfortable with Joseph here with me. Each day we visited mom at the hospice and we talked with the sister about her condition and had a frank and open discussion about the decision I must make. Of course I didn't divulge to her what I was privileged to know about the afterlife, but we had an open and honest dialogue about the condition she was in and the ramifications of any decisions I would be making. It was the most difficult time of my life and I felt sorry for anyone who might have to make such a monumental decision as involved a love one. Joseph was a great comfort during the entire process and without him I don't think I could have ever survived this ordeal. At the end of the week the Mother Superior, the Doctor in charge, and a representative of the faith called us and said they wished to have a meeting to discuss my mother's future.

The doctor opened the meeting with a frank discussion about my mother's condition. He was very subdued and I am convinced he was feeling my terrible anxiety in what I was facing. He told us that there was absolutely no hope for any kind of recovery, that she was not suffering, and that the church was prepared to keep her on artificial life support indefinitely if I so desire that option. The Mother Superior was also very thoughtful and said she and her staff loved my mother almost as much as I did and were also more than willing to care for her for as long as I desired. The representative of the church apologized for the church's role in the so called cover-up and went on to explain that since the government provides so much needed funding for this critical care hospice the churches hands were tied.

Joseph and I had talked it over many times in the past few days and I was prepared to tell them to pull the plug and let her go to her reward in peace. I thought to myself, little did they know what that reward entailed, and that I would again be able to see her and talk with her and, hopefully, my father in the future. I signed the papers with tears in my eyes and with Joseph holding me tightly. Even the Mother Superior had tears in her eyes as she had grown close to all those they were caring for here. She said it would most likely take about ten hours and I told them I wanted to be with her all the time until the end.

It was again the most difficult time of my life to sit with the mother who had given me life, nurtured me through my adolescence, and prepared me for the many challenges life brings us all. She died peacefully and as she took her last breath all I could think of was her passing into the afterlife on one of the most coveted Heaven planets. I kissed her lightly on the cheek and said quietly to her that we would see each other shortly. Joseph held me tight as I left the room and the Mother Superior and her staff came in to move her body to prepare for burial. I had decided, along with Joseph's guidance, to lay her to rest here in the small cemetery by the church. As we had discussed, her final resting place would be on one of the Heaven planets so her earthly-resting place was not that significant. Even so, this was a beautiful spot and I was content that if as most people feel this would be her final home on Earth, it would be a magnificent one with the surrounding beauty of the countryside.

Rick, Sally, Dale and Debbie had returned and the priest performed a memorable service. Afterwards we said our farewells to the Mother Superior and her staff through many a tear. Rick again said he had urgent business in the states so we headed out the next morning. As I sat on the plane with Joseph's powerful arm around me I fell into a deep sleep dreaming of my mother on one of the Heaven planets reuniting with my father. I thought, wouldn't it be wonderful if the planet her record on Earth earned her a place on, happened to be the same one my father was on and they could spend eternity together in happiness as they had for so many years on Earth. Joseph had promised to try again when he and I visited space and see if we could find them on one of the Heaven planets we had yet to check. The other thought, of course, was that they would end up on the pivot planet as husband and wife who had accumulated slightly different records in God's eyes while on Earth. Either way I could not wait to see them again, I loved them so dearly.

We arrived back and landed near Joseph's ranch, as agreed upon. Rick said, and we all concurred, that the four of them, Rick, Sally, Dale and Debbie, would draw straws to see who was privileged next to accompany Joseph into the beauty and vastness of the mysteries of space. Debbie was anxious to go since we had found her father, of course, whom Joseph had brought the poem back from, and she could not wait to reunite with him. The other's parents were all living so they would be taken to other parts of the Universe to stare in awe at its majesty. As it turned out, Dale drew the winning straw and said he was honored and could not wait to be the third human to travel unencumbered throughout the Universe. He did offer his place to Debbie but she insisted he go next. He said he wanted to visit some of the peaceful planets and see first hand how creatures from other worlds could live in peace and harmony with one another, when that was yet to be achieved on Earth. The only immediate problem we had was setting up another diversion when they were scheduled to depart this Earth. We had yet to come up with an idea and everyone was concerned that we would need to change our base of operation out of this area of Kansas, least the authorities become more suspicious, if in fact we were sighted. We had used the laser distraction already twice so that was out, and the threat on the dam once, so we agreed we had better not use either one again. A take off or landing in the early dark hours of the morning would most likely avoid human exposure, but the dreaded drones that the government was assigning to the area were our biggest problem. Dale suggested we might want to shoot a couple of them down as some of the locals, especially the farmers, have threatened to do but he was joking, at least we thought so. Rick said maybe we should just take our chances and then if we are spotted move our base of operations around the world as needed.

With no effective diversion to use, Joseph decided that he and Dale would take their chances of not being spotted and we set it up for the next night for three in the morning. At the last minute, early that evening, Rick came running in the house and said his top notch computer staff had been able to crack the code that the government used to order the drones into their designated area. He instructed them to send out the proper interference signals starting around two AM that would cut off all communications with the central command and all the drones in this area. It was not likely any of them would crash, since they were programmed to just fly aimlessly if their signal from their headquarters was interrupted for some reason. The other advantage of interfering with the communications is that it would automatically turn off all cameras on the drones so there would be no record of our take off or landing. Rick felt we could most likely use this method several times as he was sure the government would feel some foreign power was behind the break down of direct communication with the drones. He said some of his other clients had already been asking him to come up with some way of negating the effectiveness of the drones in other parts of the country, so this latest achievement would prove useful in other ways also. Eventually the government will most likely be able to develop a wavelength to block the interference, but that should be some time from now. As we had discussed in the past, the next world wide conflict would most likely be a cyber war so no one in the government would be suspicious, at least at first, of interference by persons in this country.

The time rolled around and we could hardly contain Dale, as he was so anxious to begin this greatest adventure of his lifetime. Joseph and Dale took off as scheduled and with Rick's special night glasses we could see the drones flying aimlessly around without any patterns so the electronic diversion was working as we expected. They had planned to be gone a week so we headed back to our regular responsibilities until we were to meet up again to welcome them home. I headed back after Rick's jet dropped me off at the office to check in with Mark. I really wondered why I still kept ties with my job as a professor, since lately I certainly wasn't spending much time discharging those duties.

When I walked in the office Mark could not contain himself and came running up to me and threw his arms around me. "Kait, I have been so worried about you, where have you been all this time? Finally I managed to break from his embrace and he even had a tear in his eye when I could finally see his face.

"Mark, relax or you will have a coronary right here in the office. As I mentioned to you, I have been in Europe on business with some friends, and of course Joseph. Did you burn those pictures as I asked you to and have those two scumbags been around to harass you any more?"

"Doctor Graham, I could not believe the pictures that you had locked up in the safe. How those two creeps that wanted access to it had any idea what was in there is beyond me. You don't have to fill me in on Joseph's exploits, as one look at those pictures told me exactly what he has accomplished. Maybe some day you might put in a good word for me and I also could accompany him into the far reaches of the Universe. My lips are sealed, I have not mentioned it to anyone, not even my significant other."

"Mark, I am sure you can understand completely the ramifications of what is happening here and why the government is suspicious. As we have discussed before, they would literally kill to get their hands on such knowledge. Unfortunately, they would not use it for the betterment of mankind but to dominate mankind. We both know the evil rampant in today's government and therefore we could not trust them with such as Joseph is blessed to know. Make sure you continue to be tight lipped and I will put in a good word for you and maybe someday you and Joseph can take an adventure into space. I do want you to know that I will be gone for at least the next five weeks, and then possibly I will be returning to my classes here. Has there been many questions raised as to my absence, or is it still assumed it is for medical reasons?"

"Everyone assumes it is for medical reasons and they are all concerned about you. I have assured them not to worry, that whatever your problems are, or were, you are overcoming them. I think all of your students and colleagues generally accepted that explanation. The only one that has been asking many questions as to your whereabouts is that brilliant student of yours, Robert, who has been most inquisitive."

"Keep in mind, Mark, that Robert's uncle is an analyst for some of those covert government agencies. I have reason to believe he is a friend of mankind, so to speak, and not a threat to Joseph or his accomplishments, but even so, be cautious. I will, as I mentioned, be away for at least the next month, so carry on as usual. Remember what I said about needed help if those creeps visit again. Program this number into your cell phone and punch the send key, if you are ever threatened, and help will be here immediately. One of the members of our small group of those in the know runs a very tight security organization and they would be here in minutes if you summon them. I have already alerted Rick, the head of the firm, and he has agreed to the emergency connection for you. I know you said you would welcome those questionable characters getting rough with you, but believe me Mark use the security number if in any way they threaten you. I will contact you in a few weeks, and bless you as always."

I left Mark and headed out for my domicile. In the morning we were all scheduled to meet at the airport and head out to Kansas and the return of Joseph and Dale. I met up with Sally, Debbie, and of course Rick, and we headed out. None of us could wait to hear from Dale as to his experience in space. Having often seen the tough exterior that Dale exhibits I wondered how he might display his sensitive side, if in fact he has one, after such an experience as he has gone through. When we arrived and set up our base of operation Rick contacted his expert team at the technology department and gave them the word on the timing to activate the interference with the drones. He also instructed them to do the same thing in at least three other parts of the country so that the government agency in charge of overseeing the drones would not zero in on this part of the county as the source of the interference. The incident was set in motion. About the same time Joseph made contact with Rick and said if all was secure he and Dale were headed in. Rick gave him the green light, and within minutes the pair were landing and we secured the roof and all was quiet. Joseph disembarked first, follow by Dale. We could not wait to question Dale and headed into the house to settle in the living room, with Debbie holding on tight to Dale and Dale holding on to her even tighter. It seemed at first glance that Dale was very subdued and Joseph whispered in my ear that the questions should be unemotional and measured.

As we went into the living room Dale and Debbie were deep in conversation in the corner. We poured ourselves a drink and settled in. All of a sudden Dale spoke up and said he apologized, but was going to go immediately to bed. Debbie, of course, went with him and the rest of us sat there dumbfounded as we had expected Dale wouldn't be able to contain himself and want to share this monumental experience with us.

Joseph finally spoke up. "I think you should all give Dale time to sort things out and decide when it is best to share his thoughts with us all. As we all know, Dale is a no nonsense ex-Navy Seal and he has seen the worst of mankind in his battles over the years. We visited the planet of the burning rock and I also took him to three other planets that were inhabited by creatures in other galaxies. We didn't visit any of the Heaven and Hell planets as his parents are still living, as we had previously discussed. He didn't even share his thoughts completely with me but my guess is he was deeply affected and moved by the total peace and harmony that the creatures on these other planets are living under. On several occasions we talked about the dark side of mankind, which is so prevalent and, frankly, always has been and he could not understand why Earthlings could not coexist in peace with one another when so many other species on other planets, populated by our Lord and Savior, were living in total tranquility with each other. When one has seen the most evil that man can generate, and then sees that there is another pathway, it is difficult to cope with all of it. Most of us cannot even imagine what a Navy Seal has experienced, and I firmly believe seeing the other side, serenity amongst all creatures on a planet, has deeply affected him. Believe me Rick when I say he is no less an effective second in command for your operation, but he needs to have some space to come to grips with the fact that there is another way for man to live and it is not that hard to achieve. Frankly, I think he is a better man for you now than when we went into space with what he has experienced. In time he will share his thoughts."

We all found it hard to believe that this warrior amongst men could have been so deeply affected by his trip into the far reaches of the Universe. I thought to myself, wouldn't it be wonderful if some of our most evil, corrupt leaders in this world, including this nation we call America, could experience similar reawakening. The chances of that happening in my lifetime were nil, and like the others I couldn't wait to eventually discuss Dale's feelings. We did decide that Rick, Sally and Debbie would draw straws for the next candidate for travel with Joseph, and as it turned out Debbie's straw, that I drew for her since she had retired with Dale, was the winning one. I was so pleased as she would have an opportunity to visit the Heaven planet that her father resides on for eternity and be able to see him again. We were all exhausted and agreed it was the time to try and catch a few winks. Joseph held me tight, as we drifted off, and whispered in my ear many times how much he loved me. There is no greater peace to sleep by than having a lover hold you in his strong arms and whisper his love and devotion to you as you fall into slumber.

We agreed that the next trip would happen a week from today as Joseph needed some time to prepare his craft and we all needed a little down time. When we finally all arose, late in the morning, having gotten to bed around three thirty, Dale was still very quiet. He was in intense discussion with Rick over business and I heard Rick say to him, "You do whatever you think is necessary in that case and just keep me posted." During breakfast Dale was very quiet and, finally, Sally spoke up boldly and asked him what he thought of his trip into space. He looked at her a long time and finally answered her.

"I have never experienced such serenity in my life. The creatures that we visited were kind and considerate. All I keep asking myself is why, why mankind cannot live in peace with one another, when so many of these other occupied planets in various galaxies have certainly achieved it. The Lord in Heaven certainly populated many planets. I'm sure we have only visited a very few with so many varied life forms, why is our Earth so much different? Here on Earth man is endowed with such inflated egos in thinking we are God's chosen ones, but in reality we are the scum of the Universe, at least that which I have seen. Even Joseph, who has visited many more planets than we did, agrees with me on this. Since the beginning of time, when man first walked this Earth, has there ever been a time of true peace amongst men. I think not, and I have seen the darkest side of man, and frankly have seen more than enough. I firmly believe that sometime in the future, if man does not change his ways, that God will end his experiment on this planet in a massive cataclysmic event. Enough said, I have told you what I feel and I do not wish to talk about it any more. I am eternally grateful that Joseph was kind enough to take me with him into space. The beauty and majesty of the Universe is beyond description. That is the final word I have to ever speak on the subject."

With that we all just looked at each other and at Dale but no one was willing to challenge his closure of the issue. We finished breakfast in relative silence and Joseph headed for the hanger and the ladies and I headed for the pool area to relax. Rick and Dale were in a deep conversation concerning business and shortly thereafter they left for the airport. We had been given the option of flying back east with them, but chose to stay here for the week waiting for Debbie's much-anticipated trip. We were just three college professors on extended vacations, or leaves of absence, and we were thoroughly enjoying ourselves.

It was midweek and I received a frantic call from Mark. "Doctor Graham, I was sorting through your mail this morning and you have another one of those mysterious envelopes that has no return address or postmark, however, again it showed up in the regular mail. I thought you would want to know right away. What do you want me to do with it, since I have no idea where you are or if you can come in to retrieve it?"

"Mark, I'm afraid I am not in your vicinity so let me give this a little thought and I will call you back in a short time. In the meantime do not open it and put it safely away. I appreciate you alerting me to it right away. Please don't say anything to anyone else about its existence. I'll get back to you within the hour." After I hung up I shared with the ladies what Mark had called about. Both of them were concerned. Sally mentioned it could not have been sent by Joseph since that would make no sense, and of course the fact that we were here with him negated that possibility. Debbie said I should go and share the information with Joseph and see what he thinks we should do. I agreed and headed for the hanger.

Joseph, as usual, immediately grasped the significance of the situation and only had to think about it for a minute. "Kait, I am going to contact Rick and ask him to have someone in his organization stop by your office and pick it up from Mark and bring it with him, unopened, when they return at the end of the week. I don't think there is any way we should allow Mark to open it, as he already knows more than he should and, frankly, I am not sure how much he can be trusted. From what you have told me he is honest and loyal to you but also you mentioned his lose tongue, especially with his lover, might be a problem. I don't believe whatever is in the envelope cannot wait at least a few more days to be read." When Joseph contacted Rick he agreed with Joseph's decision and said he would send one of his staff to retrieve the envelope and I should alert Mark that someone would be stopping by. I should also give Mark a code word that Rick had suggested so that Mark would be comfortable that he was giving it to the right person. I called Mark and alerted him. He acted so excited with the intrigue of a code word and to be visited by a security agent. When I told him it might be one of Rick's female agents from his organization he seemed taken aback and mentioned he hoped it would be one of those strapping fellows that I had mentioned were ex Navy Seals, or similar, as he couldn't wait to meet them. I told him again, enough of that and just do what he had been instructed to do.

The end of the week came around rapidly and Rick and Dale flew in from the city. They had the envelope with them and asked me to read it and then share it with them, if appropriate. My hand was shaking as I opened it.

"Dear Doctor Graham,

Be assured we have communicated in the past and please consider me as a friend. I would sincerely appreciate it if this note is destroyed once you have read it. My position with the government would be in jeopardy if it ever fell into the wrong hands. Frankly, there are very few of us left in government circles that have the good of the average citizen at heart. Too many, as I am sure you are aware, are only concerned with expanding their own power and their grip on the people of this country. Sadly, America is going the way of so many other great nations over the history of time that have been destroyed from within. Those few of us that still stand between the people of this great nation and those tyrannical leaders are rapidly fading from the scene. Recently I have become aware of some top-secret communications between two agencies that are directed by the powers to be to use any means to uncover any subversive activity on the part of the people of this great nation. This includes, of course, uncovering any activity which would give these unscrupulous leaders an advantage over their fellow man, whether it be in this country or supremacy over other countries.

A recent report outlined the observations of an amateur astronomer someplace out west, it did not pinpoint where they had observed some kind of craft seemingly flying into space recently. It went on to mention that the drones operating in that area had been temporarily disabled at the time of the sighting. Please be forewarned that this entire issue is becoming a top priority item as they are becoming more and more suspicious that someone, or a number of people, have actually conquered travel in space. I heard some of these nameless so-called leaders, are almost salivating over the thought of controlling intergalactic space travel. Sadly, they would have no use for such an earth shattering accomplishment to better mankind, only to dominate it. I believe what they are suspicious of is that you, or someone of your acquaintance has actually accomplished such a feat. The ramifications of using such power to better mankind are indescribable, but sadly these so called leaders would have nothing to do with that. I strongly suggest you consider moving your base of operation elsewhere in the world, as areas in the west are being closely monitored. They still do not know positively what they suspect but they are getting closer to the truth. Remember, they will stop at nothing for such knowledge. Even murder and torture to obtain such world-shaking information would not be beyond them. Remember, I am your friend. I will try and alert you if they get any closer. Be safe and God be with you.

A friend"

We all just stared at each other and Rick was the first to speak. "Frankly, I am not at all surprised at what he is warning of us. I think, after this latest travel into the Universe for Debbie, we must come up with another base of operations. We have used one too many diversions here at this location and need to think of an alternative. My organization certainly has the manpower and the means and firepower to take on these agency's stooges that are sent to harass people, for whatever reason. The problem we face however is if they narrow down their search area we could be looking at a full scale military assault on our base of operation, no matter where that might be. We need to put our collective heads together and come up with another plan B I am afraid. What you have accomplished Joseph is much too important to ever have it fall in the hands of the wrong people. It sounds like your mysterious friend knows all too well that they would go to any lengths to be privileged to learn your secrets. None of us would be safe, especially you and Kait, from their evil reach. I suggest we all sleep on it and see where we go from here. I, for one, think Joseph and Debbie can safely depart once more from here but then we will need to decide where they will land for our new base. We have pushed our luck to the brink here in Kansas, I fear."

None of us could argue with Rick's summary of where we stand at present. We headed for bed and Joseph seemed a little downcast. When he and I reached our room he embraced me tightly. "Kait, you have no idea how much you mean to me. I would easily end my life than see you subjected to any danger. I love you dearly, but I am wondering if I should just disappear and leave you in peace. Will my love for you end in disaster for us and will we be able to survive these threats. I have a great deal of faith in Rick, and of course Dale, to find a plan of action for an alternate, safe area of operation, but I still am deeply concerned. Forgive me for drawing you into this danger."

"My precious Joseph, you did not draw me into anything. As you are well aware, I am a very independent woman and if I did not want to be involved I would have resisted your advances from the beginning. You must know by now that my love for you runs deep and we are in this together. Whatever happens will happen to both of us, and I am prepared for anything. I am sure there are alternatives, as the letter writer has suggested, and we just need to think of one. Maybe we should move our base of operation to the Hay River area of Canada. In Canada they at least have a sane, rational government and would certainly be more open to using your accomplishments to better mankind than to dominate it if they were to discover your secret. I'm sure among the six of us we will come up with a workable plan."

We retired for the night and Joseph was most restless. I tried to comfort him but he was carrying an enormous amount of guilt at the present time. I had told him that God would not have entrusted such knowledge to him if it wasn't for a greater purpose, and he should relax and we will find a way. I have come to love this man amongst men so deeply I would gladly sacrifice myself for him in an instant.

The day was upon us and Joseph was preparing his craft to take Debbie into space. She was so excited, as she knew she would be visiting her beloved father on the Heaven planet that he resides on for eternity. Joseph had also promised to take her to the planet of the burning rocks and several others to see and live with, if ever so briefly, some of the various creatures occupying the Universe. He had told her she would be visiting some of those that he took Dale to, as well as a couple of others. Rick summed up where we were at this point and said this departure must be the last take off or landing at this location. He and Dale were working on an alternate site for the time Joseph and Debbie return. When they come within satellite phone range he will give Joseph the coordinates for the new landing site. I gave Debbie an enormous embrace for her send off. Joseph and I embraced so long that finally Rick had to step in and tell us it was time to go. His people had already sent out the signals to interfere with the drone directives so we had a limited window of opportunity. After Debbie's trip we only had Sally and Rick yet to experience the thrill of many lifetimes and I prayed that we would be able to see that happen. Their take off was without incident and we all hoped that the armature astronomer was not awake and watching through his telescope.

As soon as they were off Rick was on his phone talking to someone and I heard him say something to the effect of being able to land the craft in that limited space. He also mentioned something about a below deck compartment, which peaked my interest. When he was finished he told Dale to make it happen and then he filled in Sally and myself. Dale has an uncle that runs a sea going barge, which has a deck large enough to accommodate Joseph's craft. Joseph is so proficient in operating the craft that we are sure he could land it on the deck of this barge well out to sea. It has sufficient lighting for loading and unloading so a night landing and take off should be without risk. Dale is contacting his uncle now and will try and firm it up soon. His uncle is completely trust worthy and, frankly, a typical New Englander, very independent and an anti government type, especially this government. He can be totally trusted and is also ex-military which fits our organization. We fully intend to bring him into our circle of those in the know, without reservation. The only thing he may ask is to be taken into space, but we will deal with that when the time comes. The only downside is he will have to furlough his crew and we will have to full in for them, so prepare to be a sailor for the next month or so."

Leave it to Rick and Dale to come up with a workable plan and to think outside the box. I couldn't wait to get out to sea and gather my sea legs under me. I also thought Joseph would be pleased with this arrangement and the challenge of landing on a moving deck. The fact that we would take off and land in international waters and there would be no drones was a major plus for us. All in all I thought this was a great plan and thanked Rick and Dale for coming up with it.

We arrived dockside a few days later and I was taken aback by the condition of this ocean going barge. It was certainly large enough for Joseph to land and take off from and had a large compartment accessible from the deck to store the spacecraft. The only downside, however, was it's condition which as I said was, in my opinion, questionable seaworthy. We met Dale's uncle and talk about a character. He was definitely the anti-government type and made no bones about it. He also was a heavy drinker and offered us all a round before we were to disembark. As it turned out we had a drink and Captain Ahab, as we were all calling him, had several drinks. Here was a character right out of the book, Moby Dick, and I also felt he was completely trustworthy as long as he didn't have a loose tongue when under the influence. We were amazed, however that, he could consume so much alcohol and still act perfectly sober. Whatever the case this was certainly a new chapter in this ongoing saga.

The time went by fast and before we knew it Joseph was calling and Rick filled him in. We were well out to sea and Rick gave him the coordinates. We all anxiously awaited and soon we were in visual contact with him. The barge was rolling pretty well in the sea, since we were experiencing a fifteen to twenty mile wind, which had riled up the water considerably. Some of us wondered if maybe they should abort the landing and wait for another day when it was calm, but I knew Joseph too well and I was certain he would successfully land. His craft was highly maneuverable so I was not worried. Even so we all held our breath as they came in, but it went smoothly and at the last moment Joseph made a quick movement to match the movement of the ships deck and landed successfully. We couldn't wait for them to leave the craft and tell us of their experience.

When Debbie disembarked she came running up to me in tears and for a moment I was worried something was seriously wrong. "Kait, I saw and talked with my beloved father she said through her tears. It was the most moving experience of my lifetime. Every one of us on this Earth that have lost loved ones should have the opportunity to do the same. If only mankind were more peaceful and could see the beauty in what Joseph has accomplished it would be possible. I would not have traded that time with my father for fame or fortune. I cannot wait to tell mother what he said. I realize she is not within the inner circle of those in the know but I have to share this with her and I know she will be tight lipped about it." Joseph stood in the background anxiously waiting for us to embrace but was polite, as usual, and gave Debbie all the time she needed with me. Debbie went on to tell us all about the other planet's she had visited and how impressed she was with the peacefulness of each planets inhabitants. The planet of the burning rocks especially impressed her, as it had Dale and myself. She said as they approached she saw many craft that she could only describe as UFO's and Joseph had said that civilization, as he had told me, was so far advanced they had long ago conquered intergalactic space travel. He also said they have very advanced weapons systems on their spacecraft just in case some other civilization, such as Earthlings, were to try and invade them. It seems Joseph had told them enough about mankind that even though they all live in peace with each other they were fully prepared to defend their planet. Heaven help anyone who mistook their tranquility internally on their planet with their resolve to keep it that way. Debbie was exhausted and she and Dale headed for their cabin so she could rest and it was my time with Joseph.

I could not wait his coming to me and ran to him to the amazement of the others, especially Captain Ahab. He could not control his laughter and said that embrace required a couple of drinks to fully appreciate. Rick introduced him to Joseph and the two hit it off immediately. After having a drink all around the guys retired to the captain's cabin for some business. Rick stated, before they went below, that Sally would have the next trip with Joseph and he, Rick, would wait till the last to finish the trips Joseph had promised everyone. Rick, as usual, was always the gentleman.

When the fellows returned from down below they filled us in. The good news was that Joseph had told them he could take one more trip off the barge but then he would have to return to his home base in Kansas for servicing his craft. Rick had asked, since this was such a secure location why we couldn't bring the necessary items to the barge so he wouldn't have to return there. Joseph said that was not possible, as one of the secrets of his unlimited space travel was imbedded within the soil at that location and could not be found elsewhere, or remain usable, if transported away from the site. They then all agreed Sally and he would take off from here in a couple of days and their return would again be to

Kansas and the risks would have to be taken. We would all try and think of another diversion to use.

When it came time for Sally and Joseph to leave she could hardly contain herself. She was torn between the excitement of what awaited her on the one hand, and the anxiety of such an experience on the other. We all embraced and Debbie, Sally and I held each other tight as we reassured Sally that what awaited her was earth shattering. They boarded the craft, and within a minute Joseph had it airborne and was almost immediately out of sight. Captain Ahab said we should all go to his cabin and tip one for their safe journey, which we did. The captain said he had considered asking Joseph to take him into space also but he didn't think he had room on the craft for all the booze he would have to travel with. "I have yet to see all there is to see on this Earth, so I think I will wait on a voyage into the Universe." What a lovable character he is. It has been such a pleasure to spend time with Dale's uncle and I feel comfortable our secret is safe with him. I sincerely hope we will spend time with him again in the future. Since Joseph and Sally will be landing at the home base in Kansas, at least at the present time, we will be leaving Ahab and his barge behind us.

We put into shore the next evening and boarded Rick's aircraft for the trip to Kansas. Rick and Dale had business on the west coast so they were going to drop Debbie and I off at Joseph's ranch on their way. When we flew into the Kansas airport, closest to the ranch, we were amazed at the number of drones in the air and on the ground. Seems that our esteemed government was certainly targeting this part of the country for surveillance. I was sure they were worried about possible discontent originating from here, as the folks that live in this area are fiercely independent and not afraid to let the government know it. I am surprised that no one has yet shot down one of these drones, but I would not be surprised if someone soon does. There are so many out here that our paranoid government has drones watching other drones. Talk about being obsessed.

Debbie and I settled into our routine for the week here at the ranch. I did touch base with Mark and he said everything had been quiet at the office and he hoped to see me back soon. I told him I would try and get back within the next couple of weeks, and

Debbie planned on returning to her classes at her institution of higher learning also. In the meantime I just wanted some downtime. Dale called Debbie a couple of days into our time here and said she and I should concentrate on a possible diversion for the time the craft would be returning. He said Rick's organization could no longer use the interruption of the electronic signals from the government operations headquarters as the government had figured out a way to override it. I talked to Debbie about it and reviewed what diversions we had already used, the threat on the dam, the laser interruption and the signal hijacking. Debbie suggested that maybe we could have them land during the day and set up a topless demonstration of a group of ladies a couple of hundred miles from here. Once the drone operators heard about it they would all zero in on it. I, frankly, thought it might work but a daylight landing carried too many other risks of exposure. I told her we would have to think up something else so we knocked around a few other ideas. "How about if we start a forest fire over in the dry area, but even before I mentioned it I thought better of such a drastic measure. Debbie said the government would not hesitate to use drastic measures against us, then why shouldn't we use drastic measures against them. I reminded her, and she agreed, that the risk to innocent lives and property was too great. We decided to sleep on it and see what might come to us during the night.

We both looked at each other when we arrived in the kitchen in the morning with a question on our faces, 'so what is the answer'? Debbie spoke up finally. "You know Kait, I think it is about time this country faced a revolution to overthrow this corrupt government. I am so sick of their constant intrusion into all our lives, their spending well beyond their means, and their obsession with power. We wouldn't need a diversion if we could overthrow the bastards. Thomas Jefferson said it best, 'every generation needs a new revolution.' Of course I would hope it would be a peaceful one, if in fact any revolutions are peaceful."

"Debbie, I think you are a genius. We were looking for another diversion and you just came up with the perfect one. I am sure Rick and Dale and their group can plant the seeds electronically for a revolt to start somewhere a few hundred miles from here on a particular night. Once we hear from Joseph it could be initiated immediately, which of course would be the best for the drones to be called off. In fact, to temper suspicion that it is centered only in this area of the country we could plant the seeds within an hour or so of an imminent uprising simultaneously in several sections of the country. Each section would contain a key government office building that was suspected of coming under attack shortly. We can bounce this off Rick and Dale when they return. With their vast network of staff, a few key phone calls from untraceable phones warning of impending action would set the stage for the redirecting of the drones. I think we have our action, thanks to you Debbie."

When Rick called I didn't go into details, since the phone might not be secure, but just told him a plan was in the works. He said great, as he and Dale had been so busy with other demands that they hadn't had time to think about it. He agreed to return day after tomorrow and then we would bring the two of them up to date. We relaxed the rest of the week and when the fellows returned we filled them in on Debbie's plan. They both agreed it was time for a revolution, even a fake one, to oust this corrupt government that was hell bent of not only the domination of Americans but also the entire world.

Everything was set for the distraction. The timing was perfect since we received communications from Joseph that he was due to land late this coming evening. Rick and Joseph set up the schedule and when the appointed time came Rick's organization set in motion the necessary calls to key government buildings that they would be under attack shortly. It worked like clockwork and it was actually exciting to watch all the drones be called off collectively. We knew it was happening in several chosen spots throughout the country, which was also part of the plan. Joseph's landing was successful, and certainly not observed by any government aircraft and, hopefully, no one from the surrounding area at three in the morning.

Joseph departed first and then helped Sally down. She was in tears and embraced Debbie and I so firmly that I was worried we would break something. I asked her why she was crying.

"I could not believe the utter beauty of the Universe and of the planets we visited and creatures that we encountered. There is such magnificence in God's creation and such peace amongst the inhabitants we were privileged to visit. I am so saddened by the record of those that inhabit this planet we call Earth. Enough of that, however, as we have talked that issue almost to death. It was a once in many lifetimes experience and I owe Joseph a deep debt of gratitude for allowing me the privilege of seeing first hand the beauty of what lies beyond our reach. If only all mankind could experience what I have seen and most of you have seen. I will ever be grateful." With this she gave Joseph a kiss and we all broke out in laughter. I wondered what might have gone on between them in deep space, but Joseph just winked at me and I smiled a knowing smile in return. We returned to the house where we decided, even at this early hour, to settle in for breakfast and had a wonderful, heart-warming talk about their experience. Joseph mentioned that we needed to schedule his and Rick's adventure soon after he serviced his craft.

We decided to use the diversion once more when they depart that we had used for this landing. We thought, making calls once more warning government buildings of impending assault would be successful, at least one last time. We also agreed that their landing would be far out to sea on Dale's uncle's barge and we set the date for ten days from now. That being decided we all looked at each other and without saying a word, even though it was five in the morning, we headed for our respective bedrooms to make up for lost time. Joseph and I slept until well after noon and when we came downstairs we found out we were the last ones to arise. They were having lunch and gave the two of us a strange look as Debbie gave us the thumbs up. All I said was that we had both been exhausted and needed our rest. Sally and the others just looked at us, and she said something to the effect of 'sure you did'. Everyone broke out in laughter and I caught myself blushing as Joseph threw his sturdy arms about me.

The rest of the days went by quickly. We all unwound and relaxed until it came time for them to leave on their grand adventure. Rick left Dale with last minute instructions on several key points his company was dealing with and said he would see us on the barge in ten days. Hugs, kisses and hand shakes completed, they boarded the craft. Dale called for the diversion to be initiated and they were off as we observed the last of the drones being called out of this area.

CHAPTER EIGHT

AAA

The ladies and I had decided to return to our classrooms for a few days and then to meet at Captain Ahab's barge for the trip out to sea and the return of Joseph and Rick at the end of their allotted time. Mark welcomed me back and said all had been quiet on the home front and wondered how my love life was progressing. I just told him it was none of his business and he just smiled as he caught me blushing. There had been no mysterious letters or visitors, which was good, so I breathed a little easier. I held classes and the advanced class with Robert was interesting, as several of the students talked about recent false alarms of insurrection and other happenings that had made the paper and they all speculated why these threats were happening. Robert even went so far as to mention he thought they were meant to be diversions for something else that was occurring someplace and mentioned that his uncle had been called upon to offer his opinion. He said his uncle had said he told the government agencies he works for that they should take the threats of attacks on some government buildings seriously, as the populous was becoming more and more unsettled. He went on to say that he told them the constant and increasing intrusion by the government, into everyday Americans lives, was making many folks extremely nervous and he said he told them it was just a matter of time before an actual insurrection began. He said the heads of the agencies he reports to, that have developed such a respect for his insight and opinion, were beside themselves with the news.

The days went by very quickly and we left for the port and our trip on the barge. Everything was arranged for the exact landing coordinates, and Dale's uncle said we were on schedule to be there several hours before the landing. It was interesting, as the television and newspapers currently were speculating a great deal about UFO sightings in several countries so we would have to be particularly careful. Dale and his uncle both assured us that the landing coordinates were well out to sea and away from any commercial aircraft routes. There also were no drones this far out to sea. The day finally arrived and we all gathered on deck hoping to catch an early glimpse of their return. Everyone felt comfortable with a daylight landing since we were well out to sea and there were no aircraft or other ships around. Dale had his satellite phone with him and was waiting anxiously to hear from Joseph. The time that we had previously agreed upon came and went with no word from them. We checked our watches to make sure we agreed on the predetermined time and were all of the same conclusion. Sally became somewhat unglued when they didn't make contact and I took her below and calmed her down. "Sally, many things can disrupt their time line when they are traveling in space. I'm sure everything is all right with them. Let's just give it a little while longer."

"Kait, I cannot bear the thought of anything happening to them. I have finally, at this stage of my life, found true love with Rick and I would be devastated if they did not return, as I am sure you would be if Joseph failed to return. Joseph is always so prompt and of course Rick is so organized I can't believe they would not be here as scheduled unless something has happened to them." I told Sally that we should give them another twenty-four hours before we started to worry and that I certainly shared her anxiety as to what is happening. I told her I was sure we would hear from them soon and to keep a stiff upper lip. It was easy for me to say, even though deep down inside I was slowly coming apart.

Twenty-four hours came and went and still no word from them. We were all beside ourselves when Dale asked everyone to meet in Captain Ahab's cabin. Dale wanted us to reach a consensus as to the time line we should follow before we give up the quest. As usual, Dale was all business and very practical. It was Dale's uncle that spoke up first. "As we are all aware, the unexpected can be the expected in many cases. I can remember back to a time when a friend of mine on a fishing boat he owned disappeared in the ocean and we all assumed he had perished. We even went so far as to hold a service at sea and pray for the soul of my dear departed companion and friend. None of those of us that were close to him could believe he had perished as he was an excellent seaman and never took chances with the weather. About ten days after the service, I happened to be just leaving the harbor early one morning when I glanced out to sea and could not believe my eyes. There on the horizon I spotted my friends boat and headed directly, full speed, towards him. When I got close I could see his boat was badly damaged and he and his crew were hardly able to make any headway at all. I pulled alongside and Gene waved to me, along with all his crew. We boarded his ship and connected several tow devises to it. When we finally got under way, he filled me in on what had happened. He said they had struck an old mine left in the water, he assumed, from World War Two and it had taken out completely his engine along with the control panel. All they had was a makeshift sail they were able to mount, which propelled them very slowly but did give them some headway. A miracle had happened when Gene returned to us and I firmly believe, having met and talked with Joseph and Rick that they to will find their way back somehow."

The story that Captain Ahab told us gave us moments to reflect. I did agree that if ever there were two individuals that could figure their way out of almost any situation it would be Joseph and Rick. Nevertheless I was still worried deep inside. "Dale, if everyone agrees I would like to give them at least another week while we wait in this position. I don't believe we have our signals mixed, but just maybe it is next Wednesday that we agreed upon rather than this Wednesday. I may be grasping at straws, but please consider at least one more week. I will be happy to cover your uncles boat expenses out of my savings and not ask any money of any of the rest of you if you will agree to this added time." Sally spoke up first and strongly supported my request for another week, at the minimum. Of course Sally and I both had the most to lose if they were literally lost in space as our companions and lovers were the ones missing. Everyone agreed to the one extra week as they could see the sadness in our eyes and the anxiety in our voices. Dale, being the practical overseer that he was, did say he was positive we had the correct Wednesday, but he would go along with the extra week. He mentioned obligations he had at the company and said after another week he would have to return to the harbor. We all agreed and retired to our respective cabins.

The week went by extremely slow as each day was filled with worry and anxiety. The second Wednesday rolled around and we all gathered on the deck clinging to what little hope we could garner. Dale had his satellite phone cleared and ready for any communication from either Rick or Joseph. He had instructed his management team not to call him at any time this day and to handle all business as if he and Rick were there running things. He was confident that everything was going smoothly with their operation.

I had never had a more upsetting day, as daylight became darkness. Captain Ahab, being the practical man that he was did not ask for any input but just told us flat out that he was pulling up the anchor and heading out. I, as did the others, headed for our cabins with heads hanging low and tears washing away the deck beneath our feet.

We arrived back in port in several days and I bid farewell to Debbie and Dale and hugged Sally tightly as we needed each other at this point so dearly. We all thanked the captain and told him we hoped to see him again some day. I reluctantly headed back to my university duties with a heavy heart. I had finally found love in my life, only to lose it again. I pledged to myself, never again, as the loss far outweighed the memories of so many passionate, wonderful moments together.

When I arrived back at the office Mark took one look at me and threw his hands over his face. "Doctor Graham, what in the world has happened to you? You look like you have been subjected to a most dreadful time. Lord, did those government monsters get to you. If they did I personally will hunt them down and see that each of them is subjected to a living hell on this Earth. Please tell me what has happened?"

"Mark, I think you are pretty much aware, having seen the pictures and other evidence, of what has transpired over these past many months. I have been reluctant to share the intimate details of Joseph's accomplishments with you for fear of getting you too involved, for your own safety. That concern is behind me and I want to tell you that, as you suspected, Joseph, who frankly had become my confidant and lover has completely conquered unfettered space travel. He can freely travel throughout our galaxy and well beyond into many other galaxies. He has himself visited many other planets with life forms living on them, as well as planets where all mankind spend eternity, depending on the record of good or evil that they build up while living on this Earth. You're most likely thinking, as I have, could Robert actually have known of the existence of said planets? We both know that Robert is an extremely gifted student but I dare say what he speculated about as mans final resting places was sheer conjecture on his part and not fact. If it were in fact actual knowledge of such destinations, then we can only assume more than Joseph have conquered space travel. Not only Joseph has visited these many planets, but he has shared the experience with myself, my dear friends, Sally and Debbie, as well as Rick and Dale from the security firm I have mentioned to you before. Debbie and I even visited a number of the so-called Heaven and Hell planets and spoken to loved ones, if you can believe it. Sadly, the last of our group that Joseph promised to take into space was Rick. They disembarked a couple of weeks ago from a barge well out to sea.

We had set up this landing area on the barge since it was becoming more and more difficult to take off and land at Joseph's base in Kansas due to all the intrusive drones our government is using to literally spy on its own people. All of our previous trips that Joseph took each of us on went very smoothly and we returned to Earth on schedule. Unfortunately, this time Rick and Joseph did not return as planned. We even waited an extra week at the site in the ocean and still no sign or word from them. As you envisioned I am devastated to think I have lost what I had only recently found, true love. Mark, I will admit you were always right when you encouraged me to become involved with someone. I certainly waited much too long and when I finally found Mr. Right it seems now I have lost him forever.

"Kait, you don't know for a fact that you have lost him. You have no proof that anything, other than an unavoidable delay, has happened. Please be optimistic and only think good thoughts, I for one think you will rest in his loving arms again. If ever there were two individuals, from what you have told me, that could find their way out of almost any situation it is those two. I will say a prayer for them as I feel strongly in my heart this is all going to turn out for the best. We do have some items about work to go over, do you want to do that now. I think it would be wise of you to immerse yourself in your duties here while we await some word about their return. There has been more and more in the paper lately about sightings of UFO's, so I believe you will be hearing from them presently."

"Mark, as usual you are the bedrock of my existence and I pray that your optimism is correct. I want so to cling to any hope that they are alive and will return to Sally and I. I'm not sure that I had mentioned to you that Rick and Sally had also become inseparable, so their being missing also devastates her. Thank you Mark for being there for me, not only being a gifted assistant, but a true friend. What do I need to know about things here at the university since I plan on resuming classes with my special class of gifted students this coming week." Mark and I went over where everything stood and I met with the substitute teacher and we reviewed things. I thanked her for doing a fine job and looked forward to picking up where I had left off here at my home away from home. My main concern at this point, besides being heartbroken over the possible loss of Joseph and Rick, is if I can restrain myself from divulging what I have seen and heard when the discussion in class may turn to the Heaven and Hell planets. And, of course, any other time of speculation about the Universe that I have actually visited.

Sally called me and said that she had talked with Debbie and Dale and they had heard nothing new. The only thing they mentioned was the same as Mark had said, that there were more and more sightings of UFO's noted in the world press and we had speculated why at this point. It seemed odd that with their missing all of a sudden these supposed sightings were increasing. We talked about it for some time and I also shared with her the fact that I had brought Mark completely into the circle and she was comfortable with that. I told her about Mark's optimism and she seemed to be encouraged by it. We agreed to keep in touch a couple of times a week and ended with a tearful goodbye.

The day came around soon for my meeting with my class of gifted students and frankly I was looking forward to it as a way to keep my mind occupied. I started the lecture by telling the class I wished to discuss a timeline for mankind to conquer unlimited space travel. As usual Robert spoke up and said he was positive it had already happened. "Professor Graham, we have discussed on many occasions the almost absolute proof that life forms from other planets have visited our Earth in the past. In fact, reading the papers and watching the news lately about all these UFO sightings certainly leads me to believe many creatures from outer space have mastered unfettered space travel. There is no reason to think man, at least somewhere on this Earth, has not done the same. As with all great advancements mankind has passed through over the centuries, unrestrictive space travel is just another goal which I am convinced is achievable, and most likely already has been accomplished. I have discussed it with my uncle, whom I have mentioned, and he feels strongly that it has already happened. If it has been mastered it is the triumph of all times that man has walked this Earth, and also a curse, as many governments, including and especially our own, would love to have this knowledge for total world nomination."

I asked others in the class for their input and most all of these talented students, somewhat surprising to me, agreed with Robert that space travel was already achieved but just not widely realized. One student went on to say that they thought this corrupt government had somehow mastered it but was keeping the knowledge from the general public until they could perfect it for military domination. The remainder of the class dwelled on Robert's theory of the existence of the Heaven and Hell planets. I could hardly contain myself, having actually been there and seen them first hand. We wrapped it up and I returned to the office only to find Mark glued to the television. It seems that not only a ship at sea, as well as a commercial aircraft, had reported seeing a UFO crash or land in the ocean and disappear. All the talk on the networks was about this and I also became glued to the TV. All I could think of, even though the area of the sighting was not in the area we had been in on the barge, was that Joseph and Rick had somehow returned but lost control of the correct longitude and latitude and ended up crashing into the ocean. Mark, again, was reassuring and told me with all the sightings lately it was not my lover and friend. He said he was convinced the craft had not actually crashed but landed in the ocean and could traverse the ocean depths as easy as it could the Universe. "Doctor, if these UFO's are from planets inhabited by creatures that are so advanced as to have mastered intergalactic space travel, they certainly can travel unencumbered throughout the ocean deaths. Who knows what they are looking for or what they are after, let's just accept it as a good sign." Again Mark was my rock and brought me back to reality.

There were no further sightings over the next months and I went about my duties with more enthusiasm as the time went on. I talked to Sally at least twice a week and to Debbie and Dale almost as often. Occasional sightings of UFO's had quieted down and the news media were concentrating, depending on their political leaning, on either supporting our corrupt and inept government leadership or condemning and criticizing them. The days of a non-bias press in America were past and most of the print and electronic news outlets were definitely prejudice towards one political movement or the other. Unfortunately, a free press totally disconnected from any political leaning, which should help to keep government leaders accountable, is a thing of the past in this once great country.

In my discussion with Sally this month I raised the issue, with tears in my eyes, of whether we should hold some type of memorial service for Joseph and Rick. I asked her, when she talks with Debbie to mention it to her and see what she and Dale think also. I told her, as devastated as I felt, I was at this point longing for some closure of this entire sad situation. I mentioned that I was wondering where we could have such a service and whether or not we could engage a clergyman to be part of it, or if that would be too dangerous. I wanted finality, as much as I wanted to cling to hope, but being as practical as I had always been I knew closure was where we were headed. I don't believe I will ever find another lover and confidant to replace Joseph. I've had my chance at love, a short time for certain as time is measured in one's life, but a memory that will stay with me until I pass hopefully onto one of the Heaven planets and my reward. I have even dreamed of someday, as time is measured as we pass into eternity, seeing Joseph again on the same Heaven planet.

Sally called me the following week and said that she had caught up with Debbie and Dale, as he was on business in California, and they both agreed that closure was fine with them. They said if we thought it would help end the agony of these many months of sleepless nights, and days of numerous memories of wonderful times that would never be repeated, they were all for it. Dale was now in charge of the company that Rick had started as that was the agreement they had if anything happened to either one of them. The only question, as well as if we should involve a clergyman, was where we should hold such a service. We all agreed to think about it and get back together in a conference call in three days.

When I returned to the office I mentioned to Mark that we had discussed some type of service which would hopefully spell closure, or at least a measure of it, to this devastating situation. I told Mark we had two questions to answer that we were struggling with, one about a clergyman and the other concerning the location for the service. Mark immediately spoke up and said he, as I was to some extent aware, belonged to a non-denominational church and was an assistant pastor and preached on a number of occasions. He said he would be more than happy to go with us wherever we decided to hold the service and officiate. He suggested it would be much safer to include his assistance than have an outsider brought into the picture. I could not disagree with him and said I would see what the others thought about it.

As it turned out, everyone else was totally comfortable with Mark's offer so all we had to decide was where we would hold the service. Debbie suggested we should contact Dale's uncle and arrange to go back out to sea and hold it there and lay two wreaths in the water to honor each of their memories. Frankly, I was not too enthusiastic about that suggestion and Sally agreed with me. Dale had suggested we hold the service at Joseph's farm in Kansas. I warmed to that idea as so many wonderful memories flowed over me when I thought about the quality, and especially passionate, times Joseph and I had spent there. Dale said he had to fly to the west coast soon on business, and Debbie was going with him, so why didn't we all plan on going and diverting for a short time to his farm base and holding the service. We all agreed and set the time for this coming week and I alerted Mark to the timeframe. He said he couldn't wait to go and had prepared appropriate remarks for the occasion.

The day arrived and we boarded one of Dale's corporate jets and settled in for the flight. After a short time I was beginning to wonder if selecting Mark to go with us as our clergyman was such a good idea. He was infatuated with Dale and couldn't stop talking to him and even making advances towards him. At one point I thought Dale, being the no nonsense ex-military Navy Seal, was going to toss Mark out at 32,000 feet. I finally corralled Mark and had a very frank talk with him. After our talk he promised me he would behave himself and only dream of being alone with Dale. All I could do was shake my head and wonder.

We arrived on time, rented a car and headed out to the ranch. I became more withdrawn and nostalgic the closer we got to our destination. When the ranch and the barn where we landed and launched from came into sight I broke down in tears. Sally was my Savior as she comforted me and seemed to be taking Rick's loss better than I was taken the loss of my lover. Time seemed to have eased her pain more than it eased mine. When Mark saw me crying he broke down also and the look on Dale's face when he saw Mark crying was one of total disgust. Dale certainly was not one to outwardly show his emotions no matter what the circumstances were. Finally I pulled myself together and when I did Mark also regained his composure. We arrived and settled in and decided we would hold the service this evening, just after dark, so it would coincide with the darkness we always cherished to leave and return in. We also decided to hold it in the barn where Joseph kept his marvelous spacecraft.

The time came and we solemnly proceeded to this beautiful old structure. Sally and I, the two that have suffered the greatest loss, moved slowly, hand in hand, as we followed the others. I did note that Mark stayed well away from Dale, as I had heard that they had a little talk here at the ranch and Dale had not minced words. Mark's fantasy of being alone with him was no longer; no one should ever attempt anything not suggested by Dale, which Mark found out the hard way. We entered the barn and proceeded to the launch pad. I noticed again, next to the launch pad, the excavation where Joseph used to say he dug up some special material that allowed him this freedom of movement about the Universe. Mark asked us to join hands and we all did. He then said a prayer for God to bless the souls of Joseph and Rick and asked us if anyone had anything to say before he wrapped things up with some words of praise. I was about to speak up when we heard a swishing noise outside the barn, which was followed within a couple of minutes with another similar noise. We all looked at one another with a questioning look on our faces. Dale was the first to move and drew his 357 magnum from his inside pocket and motioned to us to be still as he headed for the door. He slowly opened the door while standing to one side with the pistol ready and peered out. Not being able to believe what he was seeing he motioned for all of us to join him.

I peaked around the edge of the door and there on the lawn beside the barn were two UFO's, which I immediately recognized as from the planet of the burning rocks. Several of us had been on that planet and spent time with the creatures that lived there and there was no mistaking the craft. As we stood there, dumb struck, the hatches opened on the two UFO's and out floated two of the creatures many of us had spent time with on that particular planet. They sort of drifted towards us, each carrying a container of sorts. When they were just outside the door, just a few feet from us, they looked directly at me and in their own way seemed to acknowledge me. We stepped aside and they entered the barn. Within minutes they headed for the corner where Joseph supposedly dug up the material that he needed for his craft and the two began to fill their containers. I glanced around and Mark was standing as if he was in a trance as he watched what was going on. The rest of us, having been in space, were not that surprised at what we were seeing, only wondering why they were here and what was going on. Dale, being Dale, immediately stepped up and began to help them fill their containers and they seemed again to acknowledge his presence and his kindness. The containers once filled they headed for their individual craft, and closing the hatches they were within seconds departed and out of sight.

I did notice at the time they took off several cars and a tractor-trailer truck stopped on the road along side the property. I looked at Dale and he just motioned that we should all remain still until the vehicles left. Being dark enough I didn't believe they had seen us, only the streaking of the two UFO's as they left this Earth. The cars soon left but the truck lingered for a while longer and we noticed the driver was on his telephone. Dale suggested we quietly move into the house and get our stories straight on what had happened here. He said he most likely was calling 911 to report this unusual event and that we should expect at some point a visit from the local authorities. In a few minutes the truck driver pulled away and we breathed a sigh of relief. Dale called us all together and I looked over at Mark and he was literally shaking from all the excitement of the past hour or so. I took him to the couch, told him to sit down and poured him a strong scotch to calm his nerves while we concentrated on what Dale was saying.

"Does anyone have any suggestions as to what our story should be if and when the authorities show up here? I think we need to come up with a plausible account as I expect any report that the local police might file will eventually end up in some central government department's hands. Also if a drone happened to also photograph the departure it would ignite some suspicion of UFO activity at this location." I was the first to speak up.

"I think I have an idea that we can use to defuse the suspicion, if in fact we do get a visit. First of all, however, I want to know what these creatures from that planet we have visited were doing here, and especially why they wanted some of that special soil that Joseph uses in his spacecraft. I wouldn't think, and Joseph never mentioned, that they needed it to generate power to their space ships. What in this world is going on?" Mark had recovered somewhat and wanted to add to the discussion.

"Kait, you remember I told you and Sally not to lose faith. I told you to cling to hope that they were alive out in the Universe someplace, but for some reason they had been delayed. Could it be that they actually ran out of the necessary ingredient for their propellant and these creatures have come here to obtain it for them? Just keep in mind that they couldn't call AAA if they broke down. I realize it has been a long time that they have been missing, but whatever the case I think it is a sign that they are alive and will return." Sally and I looked at each other as Mark's words sank in and she rushed over and wrapped her arms around me.

"Kait, I am going to put my faith in what Mark says and I fully expect we shall see our friends and lovers shortly. I just have a strong feeling they are alive and well and missing us as much as we miss them. I think the only problem we have now is to try and figure out where Joseph will try to land. Will he look for the barge, land someplace in Northern Canada or attempt to land here?" Dale spoke up and brought Sally and the rest of us back to Earth.

"Let's not get ahead of ourselves here, I'm as anxious as anyone here for the safe return of Joseph and Rick, but what has transpired here, even though it casts a slight ray of hope on their being alive, doesn't really prove anything. If we assume they are alive then, as Sally has mentioned, we have no idea when they would return, where they would try to land and most important, if in fact they are alive and supposedly somehow stuck in space, can they still fly. I can remember Joseph saying he needed to use the propellant directly from the ground so would it still be suitable after the UFO pilots from the burning rock planet get it there. There is no way they would dare attempt a barge landing, as I am sure they would never expect the barge to still be at the longitude and latitude that we originally agreed they would land at. We have many issues to deal with, the least of these is when and where they would be returning. I, frankly, cannot afford to remain here indefinitely on the shear hope that they are alive and will return. Our company has never had so many demands on it with this ever-intrusive government becoming such a thorn in so many American's lives. Currently our personnel are stretched to the limit, and even though I want to believe they may return my services are needed elsewhere. If any of you choose to remain here indefinitely, that of course is up to you. I would be happy to leave my satellite phone with you and if you hear from them you could contact me immediately and I would attempt to set in place a diversion as soon as possible. There would be no guarantee however, on such short notice. Unfortunately, they would have to take their chances with commercial aircraft and or drones spotting their return. I will be heading back to New York tomorrow and anyone that wants a ride I would be happy to accommodate."

We all just sat there looking at each other and then finally Sally spoke up. "I, for one plan on staying here, even if alone, for the rest of this month. I have a substitute professor lined up during my absence and my personal days are almost unlimited so I do not have to worry about my position or the length of time I am absent. Please, all of you feel free to go with Dale and I will keep you posted as to any contact with them. I have faith they are alive and well and will return, and that faith is unbending." I looked at Sally, and with tears in my eyes I told her she would not be alone. Mark and Debbie both said they would stay, but we told them it wasn't necessary so finally they agreed to return with Dale. With that all settled we decided to go out for a hearty late, very late, Kansas supper. We needed to get our story straight, if the local authorities called on us, as to what had happened and I told Dale and the others we would discuss it at supper.

We arrived at one of the all night restaurants that were frequent around here, and after we had ordered our meal I filled them in on plan B. "Joseph and I had discussed, on several occasions, a plausible explanation if in fact any authorities ever came nosing around. He had purchased a number of fairly large rockets, which are sold to the general public as literally toys, and we had set some off a number of times. He even went so far as to build a launching pad outside the back of the barn and he planned to offer that as an explanation for anyone inquiring as to what was moving in the night sky around here on occasion. So far no one had become that curious so, if we are visited by any authority, this will be the first time to try out our story." Everyone agreed, with the exception of Mark, who thought that would not be enough to fool the truly inquisitive, but we all agreed we had no other choice but to depend on that.

After so much excitement we headed home for a good nights sleep, at least some of us. Debbie and Dale retired to their bedroom and Sally and I again, for what seemed like endless nights, retired to our rooms alone and lonely. Mark, seeing that again he was not going to get to spend the night with Dale, did not even suggest in a kidding way anything close to that, as he knew better now with Dale. He sheepishly headed off to his room also. It took only a few minutes to fall asleep from all the excitement of the past day. I was no exception and spent the night dreaming that I was in my lover's strong arms again.

We were having an early breakfast as Dale needed to leave shortly when Mark, looking out the window, announced we had company in the form of what appeared to be a local sheriff. I thought to myself, this is all we need with everything else that is going on. We had already agreed that I would carry the burden of an explanation and the others would only offer their input in case they saw an opening to score some points for our side's deception. I met the sheriff at the door. He was a handsome, middle-aged man and I could already see Mark looking at this good-looking fellow in his sharp uniform. I thought for a minute maybe I should have let Mark handle things, but then again the sheriff's reaction might well be similar to Dale's and complicate things even more. I introduced myself, and the rest to the officer. The sheriff said his name was Cameron and he was here inquiring about a 911 call they had received last night from a truck driver and a couple of tourists traveling through the area

"Doctor Graham is it, I was wondering if Joseph is around. He and I have known each other for years and these calls had to do with possible UFO sightings at this location. As you may be aware, our government in Washington requires investigation of any possible sightings by local authorities and subsequent reports must be sent to them. Frankly, I think it is a waste of my time and other law enforcement officer's time but then again, with the government directing more and more local enforcement, we have no choice. This supposedly happened last evening just after dark."

"I'm sorry sheriff, Joseph is in New York on business. He and I are very close, and myself and these other friends of mine decided to remain here until he returns and enjoy the beautiful countryside here in Kansas. As far as last evening, the only thing I can remember is that Dale gave us a demonstration of rocketry, since Joseph and I had sent some into the heavens and the others wanted to see how they worked. Dale wanted to show his sons how they worked when he got back home with Debbie. Do you want a demonstration sheriff, I think we still have a couple that are able to be propelled?"

"Doctor, the explanation might explain it but the observers all gave me the same story, that the objects which disappeared in a flash seemed much larger than a toy rocket. We have had other sightings around this area over the past years of strange movements in the sky, so naturally I had to follow up on these 911 calls. May I take a look at your launch site if you don't mind?"

No problem, sheriff, who wants to show the sheriff where we launched the rockets last evening?" Mark spoke up immediately and offered his services. I looked at Dale and he was rolling his eyes and said he would also go with them. I wasn't surprised as I, like the rest of us, didn't want Mark to complicate this inquiry any by putting some moves on this fine-looking law enforcement officer. I was sure Dale would take command of the situation and make sure Mark walked the line. The sheriff thanked us and said he would be sending his report to Washington and there was a slight chance someone from the central government would be contacting one or more of us, as well as Joseph. At the last minute, just as he was about to go to the launch pad with Mark and Dale, he turned and asked me if I might happen to have a cell phone number for Joseph in case he had to reach him to complete his report. Dale immediately spoke up.

"Sheriff, we both probably are familiar with our friend's cell phone habits. Even though we live in the age of instant communications Joseph never really has been enthusiastic about them. I've tried to reach him several times since he has been gone on business and he either ignores it or has it turned off. The number, and I wish you luck sheriff, is 585-644-7237. Anything else I can help you with sheriff, except showing you the launch pad? The sheriff was satisfied and I didn't feel he himself was very suspicious of the incident and pretty much had accepted the explanation. I was more worried that someone like Robert's uncle, if he came across the sheriff's report, would be able to read between the lines. The three of them headed for the rear of the barn after we had said our goodbyes. When Dale and Mark returned Dale filled us in.

"I'm comfortable that we have dodged a bullet at this point in time. I don't think his curiosity was raised beyond the explanation we gave him. He will of course have to file a report with the Feds and that makes me nervous. He did say he most likely will not get to it for a couple of weeks and he also mentioned his utter frustration with the central government's interference with local law endorsement, as well as his disgust with all these drones, he referred to them as spy planes, over this area of the country. He said you would think this is the middle of Afghanistan with all this intrusion. I'm going to keep him in mind for our company if and when he is looking for a change from his current job. Mark felt he bought our explanation, even though Mark and I both thought he might have had some misgivings. His loyalties lay with the locals and not this ever expanding and demanding central government. I firmly believe he will delay filing the report as long as he can to give us a window."

We all breathed a sigh of relief over Dale's explanation. Whether the sheriff was suspicious or not that there was more to the story than met the eye, he was very concerned about central authority interfering in everyone's lives so we all felt he would do everything in his power to ignore any further investigation. Dale said he had to leave in a short time so Mark and Debbie needed to get their things together and get on the road. He promised to contact us immediately if he heard from either Joseph or Rick. We briefly discussed that if we did, hopefully, hear from them, where we would advise them to put down. We didn't think that there would be, as we discussed before, any time to bring the barge into position so it was either here at his Kansas base of operation or someplace like the Hay River area. Mark spoke up at this point with what seemed like a far-fetched idea.

"Kait knows how much I enjoy my vacations in that wild town, where what goes on in Vegas stays in Vegas. Every chance I get, my significant other and I spend our time enjoying the mysteries and excitement of that city of so many lights. I have a suggestion, which may sound far out, but think about it for a minute. Landing here in Kansas is definitely out, especially at this time when this location is already under suspicion. I have seen so many wild things happen in Vegas that the landing of what looks like a UFO would not surprise anyone. Dale, you said you have offices in most of the major cities in this country and I'm sure you have one in Las Vegas. If in fact Joseph and Rick are returning and make contact with you, direct them to land in Vegas. The MGM parking lot would be ideal. I can guarantee you that anyone seeing firsthand the landing would totally think it is a publicity stunt or some kind of show. Have your Vegas staff alerted, with a tractor-trailer truck standing by to load the spacecraft into and head out towards this home base undetected. You could even fly

Cummings, my significant other, and myself there to supervise it all and then maybe he and I would spend an all expense paid week enjoying the sights, sounds and excitement of that great town. What say all of you?" Debbie was the first to speak up.

"Mark, I have heard some loony ideas in the past, but this one takes the cake. It is never dark in Vegas as there are so many lights it would hardly be an unobserved landing."

"That's the whole point, Debbie, and the rest of you. The more people that happen to see it the better. I can, as I said, from my many visits there assure you everyone who might catch a glimpse of it would not think anything of it but what I said. I can understand your immediate reaction Debbie, but give the idea a chance to sink in. Let's talk it over on our flight back east and Kait, you and Sally think it over and feed us your input when we next talk. I am convinced you will all agree on the brilliance of the idea. It would mean allowing a couple more of Dale's staff intimate knowledge of what is going on, but as you have often said you can trust them explicitly."

Dale added his input "Mark, I will admit this is thinking outside the box which is exactly what we need to do now, in case we hear from them. Too often our thoughts, or for that matter anyone else's, are confined to the obvious and never look beyond for solutions to a problem. I want to think it over and contact my Vegas supervisor, but frankly I think you have finally shown your worth. I'll keep you two here posted on what we decide. Of all the staff in this organization I have known the head of the Vegas operation for years, an ex-military special forces fellow, and I would trust him with my life. He is most likely one of my most verbal opponents to this massive, intrusive federal bureaucracy, so once I brought him into the circle he would be one-hundred percent behind us. It's time to leave everyone and we will keep in touch. Mark, for me and the others say a little prayer that Joseph and Rick are still alive and will return and if it happens, and a Vegas landing is successful, I might even consider a couple of days in Sin City with you. Remember I said days, and did not mention nights." We all had a good laugh over that, especially Mark, and then with many an embrace they headed out for the airport and the corporate jet. Sally and I settled in for what we expected were to be some long days and nights.

The time certainly dragged, especially as the week wore down. We had set our sights on their returning and as days went by and we heard nothing we both settled into a deepening mood of depression. It was near the end of the week and I mentioned to Sally that we should maybe consider giving up on our hopes and returning to our jobs. "Sally, I think we have to finally admit that Joseph and Rick are in fact gone. I hate to think it, especially when the arrival of the two spacecraft from the planet of the burning rocks gave us hope, but I think we would have heard something by now. I talked to Dale this morning and he has heard nothing either. He did say that everything was tentatively set for a Vegas landing, if in fact they did make contact, but he also was giving up all hope. We agreed to keep in touch, especially if anything new came up."

"Kait, as much as I love you I just can't agree with you. If you need to get back to the university I can certainly understand that but I am not going to give up hope. I, like you, are a middle-aged college professor who had finally found love and fulfillment in my otherwise dreary life. I plan on staying here at least one more week, as I have not given up hope yet. I honestly believe that they will return and my lover will again hold my head on his shoulder as we lay in perfect love and harmony together for many a night. As long as I might live I would never be able to find anyone that would even come close to the love and affection I hold for Rick. I will be happy to take you to the airport, but if you don't mind I want to remain at least another week. If you agree to stay with me I will agree to leave and return to my job also at the end of next week."

It didn't take me long to think about it and I agreed with Sally. With that settled we decided to go out to dinner at one of the fine local restaurants. We were about half way through dinner when each of our cell phones rang. We both reached for them and I was on with Dale and Sally almost screamed that it was Debbie and the news was great. They told each of us that Dale had received a contact on his special satellite phone from Rick and he told him they were headed in and asked him what the longitude and latitude were for the landing area. Dale had quickly filled them in on the plan and they both agreed it was a brilliant idea. Dale also said the Las Vegas corporate group were already moving with the tractor trailer truck and would be there to meet the spacecraft. We hung up in tears and both jumped up and gave each other an enormous embrace, much to the amazement of others in the restaurant. We were so excited we couldn't even finish our meal and rushed out to return to the ranch, even though it would be several days before they could be here. Dale said they would keep us posted, or better yet Rick and Joseph would keep us posted. We were both so excited that it was a good thing we did not have a car to drive, as I don't believe either of us was in any condition to drive. We called a cab and it took us back to the ranch.

We eagerly awaited word that all had gone well and when we had not heard in almost an hour we became worried. "Sally, I cannot understand what the delay is, we should have heard by now that they are loaded up and on their way. Do you think Rick and Joseph wanted a little down time at one of the casino's?"

"They better not be shooting dice at a crap table because if they are they are in for a rude awakening when they return here. I can guarantee that Rick, and I assume Joseph also, will be sleeping in the barn for at least a week." That broke the tension a bit and we both laughed about it. I couldn't stand not knowing any longer so I dialed Dale's number. To my surprise there was a hesitation on the phone and then I heard Joseph's voice.

"Kait, my love for you is deeper than space itself. Give us a few more minutes as we have quite a crowd here of Japanese tourists. At the same time we landed six bus loads of them arrived here at the MGM parking lot and you have never seen so much curiosity in your life. Bear with me while we put the finishing touches on our story and I will call you back shortly. Tell Sally Rick will call her in a few minutes also. With that the line went dead and with a trembling voice I filled Sally in. We both embraced, with tears coming down our faces, and sat down and Sally went to the kitchen and poured two glasses of wine and brought me one, which I sure needed at this time. Neither one of us could be quiet as we were both so excited. We talked incessantly and about twenty minutes later both of our cell phones rang. Sally went out in the kitchen so we would both have our privacy with our lovers. I quivered when I heard Joseph again.

"My darling Kait, please remember in all this excitement that these phones may not be secure, so let's keep our conversation to our love for each other." I agreed with him and thought if any intrusive government agent was monitoring cell phone calls they would just assume it was two lovers, too long apart, that were finally in touch with each other and their feelings. "Kait, I have missed you so deeply and when we are finally in each others arms I will fill you in on what has happened. I cannot wait to lay with your head on my shoulder as that is the closest to heaven I ever expect to get." I thought to myself, those are certainly code words meant to confirm to any sneaky government goon listening in that we in fact are two secret lovers. Let them eat their hearts out for want of a relationship like we have. "We will be departing wonderful Las Vegas soon and I will call you when we are about half way there. I love you so much."

"Joseph, it is so good to hear your voice. I was worried we might not be able to keep our planned rendezvous that we have both been looking forward to for so long. I love you deeply also Joseph, get some rest from your travels and I can't wait for those strong arms to be around me. My love for you is as warm as a burning rock." With that we cut the connection and about the same time Sally came back in from the kitchen. I was sure my reference to a burning rock was well received by Joseph and he fully understood the meaning in more ways than one.

As promised, they called again the next day. They could have driven it in one very long day but instead they broke it up and rested again for a full night, as they needed it so much. Sally was on the phone as long as I was and I thought she was going to take the phone to bed with her, as she was so eager to be in Rick's arms she couldn't wait another day.

We kept busy and the time went by fast. We were out on the porch enjoying the afternoon sunset with a glass of wine when we saw a tractor-trailer truck coming down the road. It wasn't unusual to see them on this highway, but this one seemed to stand out and we both arose as one and sure enough it turned into the drive to the ranch. As it pulled up to the barn we both ran across the lawn, and when Joseph and Rick got out of the truck we smothered them with our embraces and kisses. They returned the emotion many times over and it was several minutes before we could all catch our breath and start to breath normally. Rick said it was important that we tuck the space vehicle into the barn immediately so as not to arouse any more suspicion from anyone traveling along the highway, or the inquisitive drones. The fellows got out the necessary equipment, and within what seemed like only minutes it was tucked away within the hangar. They also did not want evidence of the truck here any longer than possible so Rick's operational manager from Vegas immediately bid us all a goodbye and was on his way back to his base of operation. With all that done we headed for the house and some down time. Sally and I could not wait to hear the incredible story of what had happened to them in space so after we settled in Joseph commenced to fill us in.

CHAPTER NINE

The Final Flight

"Let me just say that what I understand was your assistant's idea Kait, to land in Vegas, was an excellent one. The only downside was, as mentioned, we landed about the same time as busloads of Japanese tourists pulled into the MGM. They all seemed to buy our story that we were advertising the free drop ride at the top of the Stratosphere Casino, which was another brilliant explanation, thought up by Rick's Vegas supervisor. The only problem we encountered was the hundreds of pictures these tourists took of my craft and us. It wasn't surprising, as I have never seen tourists from China, Japan or any of those other countries in that region without their multitude of cameras. With the number of pictures they took we are somewhat concerned that someone, like your brilliant student Robert's uncle, might someday happen across one of them. Someone as well trained, as he is to see in a photo what others would not easily interpret as anything unusual, could become a major problem. We can only hope and pray that none of them ever fall into the hands of someone like him.

Rick was so fascinated with the tremendous beauty of the Universe that we ended up visiting even more galaxies than any of our other trips, and even more than I had ever seen. I'll let Rick tell his own story, but we found more populated planets and even found one where the creatures slightly resembled humans. I became so caught up in Rick's excitement that I pushed our spacecraft to the very limits. Finally we agreed to cut our trip short and head back for our appointed landing time. About half way back we began to run low on propellant, as it appeared my calculations and our unlimited enthusiasm had tended to set my mind off course. As we were coming to the end of our supply of propellant we had a choice to make, either end up being a permanent speck in space, orbiting around, or try and make it to a planet. I did some quick calculations and thought we had just enough fuel to make the planet of the burnings rocks. It was a major risk as we were closer to other planets, which we could easily make, but we had no idea if any life forms dwelled therein. Even if there were life would they be capable of helping us. We agreed to take the risk of trying to make the burning rocks planet, and as we were literally running out of fuel we skidded in for a landing with several of their UFO's guiding us in.

We did land safely, with some damage to our craft, and were welcomed with open arms. We spent some time just unwinding from our close call and nursing the bruises that we both suffered during the landing. The creatures, as you know, were cordial and helpful, and after we recovered completely they assisted me in evaluating where things stood with our craft. There was some fairly major damage, which with their help we managed eventually to repair. It took a number of months of scrounging for materials within the entire planet before it was one hundred percent again. The problem then became one of the proper materials for the repellant and none could be found on that planet. At that point we had pretty much resigned ourselves to live out the remainder of our lives on this planet with these peaceful creatures. The only other hope was that someday, before we went to our reward on one of the Heaven planets, possibly someone else from Earth would discover my secret, perhaps come here and we could solicit their help. This, of course, was wishful thinking but when I thought about you Kait, and Rick thought about his beautiful Sally, any slight glimmer of hope we seized on tightly. Rick finally came up with the idea, after he had learned to communicate with those friendly souls, that possibly one of them could take either Rick or I back to Earth. We could then bring back enough propellant to get us back home, if in fact it would still be powerful enough after the long voyage here. We held long discussions about it and I will let Rick fill you in on, as they say, the rest of the story."

"I want to say, as all of you have experienced, that the utter beauty and majesty of God's Universe is beyond human comprehension. I accept full responsibility for throwing Joseph off his routine in our travels. I could not get enough of God's handiwork. We visited so many planets where so many creatures live in total harmony with each other. I have missed you all so dearly, and of course missed my Sally more than life itself. I could not get enough of this out of this world experience and kept the pressure on Joseph constantly. I have apologized many times over for this misdeed. Being the wonderful gentleman that he is he has forgiven me. To attempt to make up for my utter disregard concerning our tight schedule, I asked, as I had learned to communicate with these inhabitants of the burning rocks planet, if they would consider taking one or both of us in their UFO's back to Earth so we could return with enough propellant to transport us back home.

Their leadership was not open to the suggestion as they said the Earth was known as one of the most hostile planets in the Universe. They said even though their machines were equipped with very sophisticated weapons, used only for defensive purposes, they did not want to expose any of their fellow creatures to potential harm. I even pleaded with them to let Joseph and I use one or two of their machines, but they firmly denied this request as they said if one of their craft fell into the hands of Earthlings it could have dire consequences. We finally resolved in our minds that this planet would be the final place that Joseph and I would ever set foot upon. It was some time later that the leadership came to us and said that two of their younger UFO operators wanted to help us out. They said these young pilots were madly in love with their opposite sex partners, for want of a better term, here on this planet. They knew how much we missed our loved ones as we had shared many an hour with them about the very sad state of our never being able to see them again. They were willing to take the risk of flying to Earth and bringing us back what we needed. As Joseph said, I think you know the rest of the story. They are such wonderful loving, caring creatures, as were all the life forms we found on other planets. Joseph, thank you again, I will remember your kindness and generosity for the rest of eternity, even when I reside on the Heaven planet with Mother Teresa."

"Rick, I think of you as a great and trusted friend but I wouldn't quite see you with Mother Teresa. Maybe the second Heaven planet, but not the most coveted." We all laughed at this and Joseph went on to outline his plans for the future. "Now that we have safely returned I would like to plan a return to space with Kait and visit the pivotal planet to see if her beloved mother and father are residing there. We need to think outside the box, however, as take off and landings from here I fear are out of the question with all the exposure of late. The fact that the sheriff, a great fellow by the way, had to file a report on activity here further jeopardizes our missions from this spot. Might I ask that we all sleep on it and tomorrow see if our collective minds have come up with any ideas? Dale and Debbie are arriving here tomorrow and I asked Dale to bring Mark along since his Vegas idea was so brilliant. I realize, Rick, you need to get back to running your firm but I hope you can give us one more day and your insight into the problem." With that we all said our good nights and headed for what I was hoping would be a night of passionate lovemaking with my handsome partner in life. We had a lot of time to make up for. In the morning we can again come back down to Earth.

I will have to say that none of the four of us looked rested in the morning when we met for breakfast although we all had smiles on our faces. We decided to go out for breakfast, as Dale, Debbie and Mark would not be here until later this morning. After a great Kansas breakfast we headed to the airport to pick up the others, as they were scheduled to return. When we all got back to the ranch we gathered around in the living room and Joseph opened the discussion.

"It will take me about a week to prepare everything for the next trip that Kait and I will be taking and we should be gone about five days. I seriously doubt we should take off from here, under the circumstances. I do believe we could land here at the end of the trip, as with time, hopefully, the authorities will have lost interest in this area. We will have to truck the craft to a secure location from where we can quietly depart. Does anyone have any ideas where that could be?" Mark was the first to speak up.

"We used Las Vegas as a landing site with the ruse that we were advertising the free drop ride at the top of the Stratosphere so I don't think it would be wise to try a take off from there. So many people twenty-four hours a day with so many lights it would hardly go unnoticed. Also, as you mentioned, a take off from here would further compromise this location. You mentioned the barge. In my opinion a mid sea take off makes the most sense. It could be trucked there but loading it on the barge would hardly go unnoticed in the busy port you mentioned. I, for one, am out of ideas at the present." Joseph asked for other thoughts and Debbie spoke up.

"Rick, I remember some time ago you and Dale talking about the used military cargo plane that your company had acquired for use in moving your company's men and materials in case of an emergency someplace that you were asked to respond to. Would it be possible to actually launch Joseph and Kait from that vehicle? You said it had a large discharge area in the rear, I, of course, don't have any idea if it would work, but just thought I would mention it." Dale looked at his Debbie with admiration in his eyes.

"Darling, talk about thinking outside the box. That plane is certainly large enough to accommodate Joseph's craft, and if we fly to forty or fifty thousand feet and then launch it would never be noticed. Unfortunately there is no way they could land there but it is certainly feasible to depart from there. What say you Joseph?"

"All I can say is without the brilliance of Mark and the Las Vegas landing and now Debbie with the use of the cargo plane, we would long ago have been permanently grounded. Thanks, Debbie, that is workable and brilliant and with Rick's approval I for one say it is a go, with of course everyone's approval. I should be ready within the week, so if it is a go all we need to do is set the date and time."

"As the CEO of this company that recently purchased the cargo plane I whole heartedly agree it is brilliant, thanks Debbie. Joseph, let me know when you will be ready and we will set it up. Dale and I have to leave for business on the west coast but we can be ready with a few hours notice. I think if we transported the craft via the tractor-trailer to the airport at night and loaded it on we would not be threatened with any inquiring eyes, especially if we keep it covered while loading. Anyone else have any input?" Mark spoke up as only Mark could.

"I have not brought this up before, but I feel as time goes on I have become a trusted member of our small group of those in the know. My brilliance, as Joseph says, in suggesting the Vegas landing I believe earns me a coveted spot in this group. Would it be to bold to ask that I be allowed to accompany Joseph into space on the next trip, since all of you have already experienced this thrill of many lifetimes? I certainly think I have earned it and that Kait's trip to find her departed parents could wait until I am given this privilege that the rest of you have experienced." Dead silence ensued after Mark's remarks. I thought I knew Mark well, but his attitude concerning what he at least thought was his right was surprising. After a few minutes of silence, with all of us looking at each other, I decided since Mark was my assistant I needed to handle this issue.

"Mark, I fail to understand your attitude in this manner. Joseph has told you and the rest of us that he will at some point in time take you on such a trip. I feel very strongly, as we have planned for some time, I wish to find my parents and tell them how much I love them. After we do that we can discuss your possible trip into the vastness of the Universe. You will have to be patient and, frankly, wait your turn. As we all know, you are a relative newcomer to this select group and even though your Las Vegas idea was brilliant it certainly does not overshadow the efforts and brilliance of Joseph and what he has achieved and the contributions of the rest of us. Very frankly, Mark, you will have to wait your turn."

We were all shocked when he stood up and almost shouted. "Because of my sexual orientation you think you can walk all over me. "Doctor Graham, I will see you back at the office when you finally return from your latest adventure. Excuse me but I will be calling a cab and be on my way." For a minute I thought Dale was going to flatten him, but Rick grabbed Dale's arm and held him back as Mark steamed out of the room. We all just sat there with looks of astonishment on our faces and wondered what had happened. Finally Rick spoke up.

"Ok folks, let's put this behind us. What triggered that outburst is unknown. Mark certainly seemed to be adjusting well to our small group and what brought this outburst on is beyond me. I say we give him some time to cool down and then you could call him Kait. In the meantime we have more important things to deal with than Mark's feelings." With that Rick turned to Dale and whispered something in his ear. I was sure it had to do with keeping an eye on Mark. I was still almost shaking from the experience and could not understand Mark's reaction. I wondered for a minute if he was jealous that here were three couples obviously so much in love with each of their partners and he was alone and thought of himself as an outcast. As I had often said, his sexual orientation was always his business, and I could not have asked for a better assistant or a warmer friend. So much for that, as it was time to move on, but it still deeply concerned me.

We all decided on a time and date for take off and Rick and Dale, since he had returned from making his phone call left for their business. They agreed they would return to the local airport with the cargo plane six days from today and we would load up Joseph's spacecraft for his and my second trip into the fantastic cosmos. We had talked about which planet in the Heaven and Hell series we would first visit to attempt to find my folks and we agreed it would be the pivotal one. I did not argue with Joseph as I was convinced my parents must have built up slightly different records of their lives on Earth in God's mind and ended up on two different planets. I was positive, however, that they loved each other so dearly that they would both choose to unite on that planet reserved for this kind of situation for eternity. I could not wait to see them and tell them what amazing parents they were and how deeply I loved them, and still love them.

The evening of the sixth day came and we headed for the airport with the craft safely tucked into the tractor-trailer truck. I was so excited I was almost shaking and Joseph, in his wisdom, put his strong arm around me and leaned down and gave me a little peck on the cheek. We discussed our return also as we had pretty much agreed upon the date and time and that we were going to land at the ranch using the diversion of a threat on the dam again. It had been some time since we used that so we felt we could get away with it this one last attempt. It had worked flawlessly in the past so there was no reason to think it would not work again.

I had tried to reach Mark several times in the past few days, with no luck. I did talk to one of the assistants to another professor and she told me that no one had seen or heard from him in some time. She did mention that one of her coworkers happened to be at the local watering hole one evening for a celebration of their birthday and thought they saw him at the bar and he was totally intoxicated. While I was on the phone with her I asked if she would check my office voice mail and e-mails and see if there was anything I should be attending to immediately. I told her I would be returning soon and would deal with Mark when I returned. She said she would check those for me and call me back. As of this trip to the airport I still have not heard from her.

As we entered the airfield my cell phone rang and it was Sara, assistant to one of the other professors at the university that I had spoken with earlier. "Dr. Graham, I'm sorry it took so long to get back to you but I was restricted from entering your office by some creepy looking men for some time. There were some people in there it seemed rummaging through your desk and paper work. I don't think they disturbed anything however, as all looked intact when I was finally allowed to enter. It looked like they had tried to enter your computer but without the password I don't think they did. Our college security personnel finally ordered them out and I did check to see if anything was demanding your attention. By the way, we still have yet to see or hear from Mark. I checked your emails and you have a lot of them on there and I quickly scanned them. The only one that caught my eye was signed, a friend, and all it said was 'be cautious, they are close to finding the answers they have been looking for.' I'm not sure what that meant but thought it might be important." I thanked her and told her that was just a coded message from an old college buddy that I keep in touch with. I think she bought my explanation, at least I hoped she did.

I filled the others in on the conversation as we arrived and were beginning to load the ship into the plane. Rick said it concerned him as his people were keeping an eye on Mark and had reported that he was spending most of his time at the bar, being totally obnoxious and loud and bragging about a secret only he knew but would not reveal. They said he was getting extremely friendly with a stranger that they had not seen before and they would keep Dale and Rick updated. Joseph expressed concern and Rick told him to relax as things were under control. I wasn't one-hundred percent convinced they were but at present we had more pressing matters to deal with.

We took off on schedule. There was no one on the ground that observed us loading the craft so we relaxed a little. I was still nervous about Mark however and asked Joseph how he felt. He said he was comfortable that Rick was on top of things and we should get ready to board the spacecraft as it would not take long to reach our designated altitude. We thanked everyone and wished them all well and said we would see them at the agreed upon time when we land at Joseph's ranch. We boarded and I again was shaking with excitement. Seeing my condition Joseph reached over and gave me a kiss and a slight hug. Looking at him and realizing my love and faith in him, I sat back and prepared for my next exploration into what I can only describe as God's handiwork. The cargo bay doors were opened and we received the thumbs up as we departed. Within seconds we were well out into space and on our way to another adventure of many lifetimes.

Joseph said, in addition to visiting the pivotal planet to find dad and mom, he also wanted to again return to the planet of the burning rocks and thank those kind creatures. I was in total agreement with this, as I also wanted to express to them my gratitude as they had done so much for us. Returning my lover to me was the greatest gift anyone had ever given me in this lifetime. It seemed to take us no time at all and we were landing on the pivotal planet. After we landed we met the person designated to keep the records for this planet and I asked them with a trembling voice if they would check their records to see if my mother and father were residing here. It seemed like it took forever, but finally they emerged and told us that in fact my mother had recently been assigned here and within a short time after my father joined her. He said he would set up a get together with them shortly so we should just relax and wait. Relax and wait was the furthest thing from my mind, but being so close to a reunion with them I had no choice. Again, Joseph was comforting and it seemed only a short time and they came walking towards us.

I embraced them both and tears streamed down my face. Joseph intervened and said how beautiful my mother was and how handsome my father was. This lightened the load and I told mother about being with her in Italy and making the decision to disconnect her from her being artificially kept alive. She hugged me and said she could hear us even though at that time she was in a vegetative state and totally agreed it was the humane thing to do. She was totally happy and content now that dad and she were together. I filled them in on our previous quest for them on the most coveted planet in the series and said we had also looked for them on several of the other planets. I told them it was then that Joseph suggested that maybe you two had not perished. "Dad, the mystery of what had happened to mom was finally solved when we found her in the hospice in Italy. What pray tell, if you want to enlighten me, is the explanation of where you have been?" Dad looked at me and then at mom with this expression on his face of should I tell her and mom just nodded and reached over and hugged him.

"Kait, let me first say that I deeply love your mother and always have. In our long life together your mother meant the world to me. I must admit though that I wandered once and mother forgave me but God did not. Life is too short however, and we made up and moved on. We loved each other and that was all that mattered between us. God, on the other hand, recorded in His book my breaking of one of His commandments and therefore I was assigned the first planet on the hell side. That planet is reserved for those of us who broke a commandment but not more than one. Mother again rescued me and we shall live in peace and harmony for eternity. Please do not think less of me Kait."

"Dad, I would never think less of you. You are my father and my hero. Life is much too short to condemn one another for brief times of weakness. I'm just so happy and content that you are together and happy. Joseph and I would like to spend a couple of days with you before we move on to the planet of the burning rocks. I love you both so deeply and thank you for always being there for me. I cannot wait to tell you of Joseph's recent experience of being lost in space with a mutual friend and what the creatures from that planet did to help save them." With that we settled in for a couple of wonderful days with my parents and so many other loving couples that had gone to their rewards before.

The time went by all too swiftly and we bid our farewells. Joseph promised mom, dad and myself that we would again return and with that we departed. I thanked Joseph for allowing me this time with them and his promise to return. A short time later, I rested most of the way, we approached the planet of the burning rocks and were led in by several of their very talented UFO pilots. When we landed we were again surrounded by many of these very wonderful, loving creatures. They didn't seem to be able to get enough of us. We spent an astonishing few days here and then had to leave for our scheduled return to the ranch.

Before we left there seemed to be many a tear shed by myself and I am sure some of these fantastic friends of ours. It was hard to break away and when we took off a number of them climbed in their UFO's and accompanied us on our way. We finally seemed to lose sight of them and shortly we were within satellite phone distance of Rick. Joseph called him and it took quite some time for him to answer. When he did answer Joseph asked him if everything was set up and on schedule and Rick was slow to respond.

"Joseph, all is set up for your scheduled landing. The diversion is in place and Dale says it should go smoothly. Feel free to proceed, as long as your burning rocks are stable." Joseph just looked at me and since the phone was on speakerphone we both just shook our heads. Finally Joseph spoke up.

"Kait, what was that all about? Do you think Rick has been into the Black Velvet a little to much or is something wrong". I think I will call him back and ask that we talk with Sally to make sure we are clear to land. Rick, can you put Sally on the line for a minute, Kait wants to talk with her?"

"She is not here right now, Joseph, she is with Dale and Debbie at the diversion point. I, frankly, think we should literally blow up the damn dam as it is long overdue with this current corrupt government that is hell bent on controlling the world."

"Joseph, what is going on with Rick on the ground, he certainly doesn't sound like himself. I am nervous about what is going on. Do you think it is safe to land?"

"Kait, I am also concerned, but frankly we have no choice, we are almost out of propellant and, frankly, even though we do have a reserve for emergency purposes, I do not want to use that now. I think everything is ok or Rick would have come right out and told us to divert. I can see the drones being pulled off so the diversion is working." I was extremely worried but Joseph seemed calm, as he always was, so I put my faith in him.

We headed in and the barn roof opened and we made a smooth landing. Joseph was about to open the hatch when we heard a loud speaker. *"EXIT YOUR VEHICLE SLOWLY, WITH YOUR HANDS IN THE AIR, OR YOUR FRIENDS WILL BE SHOT. "*

Joseph, what is going on, try to reach Rick again on the phone." Rick answered immediately.

"Joseph, we are under duress as they have guns to my head and to Sally's and have threatened to shoot either one of us, or both, if you do not exit. This entire area is surrounded by military, including tanks and thousands of troops. Fighter aircraft are now controlling the skies. Dale and Debbie, who were on assignment to set up the diversion are safe, but Sally and I are being held prisoner and they, as I said, will not hesitate to shoot us if you do not exit immediately. I strongly urge you both to come out with you hands in the air. *JOSEPH, IGNORE WHAT I JUST SAID, LEAVE HERE NOW AS THESE ANIMALS WILL STOP AT NOTHING TO KNOW YOUR SECRET."* With that there was silence and we just sat there. Finally Joseph spoke up.

Kait, my love, I am so sorry I have exposed you to danger. I hold a deep and abiding love for you and could not live with myself if anything happened to you. I believe if I am taken out of the picture entirely that you, Rick and Sally would not be harmed, as I am sure they are aware that I am the only one to hold the secret of space travel. Darling, I want you to exit and as soon as you are on the ground move away from the craft, as I plan on pulling the self-destruct button and ending it all. There is no way I will let my secret fall into the hands of our evil government and their thugs. I have thought over the years many times about this moment and have no hesitation to end it. My concern and love are for you only and not for myself. We have enjoyed our time together, even as brief as it has been. God sent you to me as He sent me the secrets of unlimited space travel. I could not ever have asked Him for more as He has blessed me, particularly with you Kait. Please hold my hand a second before you depart and someday possibly we will be united on one of the Heaven planets for eternity." The loud speaker came on again, *'YOU HAVE EXACTLY ONE MINUTE TO EXIT WITH YOUR HANDS ABOVE YOUR HEAD OR WE SHALL SHOOT` THIS WOMAN WHO IS HERE WITH RICK. THE CLOCK IS TICKING.'*

I looked at Joseph and he had tears in his eyes that were matching mine. "Joseph, I love you more than life itself and I also have thought of this moment for some time now. Please go ahead and pull that self-destruct switch as I have every intention of going with you? Even though we are not husband and wife, and may well have built up different records in God's Book of Life, I believe He will let us spend eternity together on one of the coveted planets or the pivot one. This corrupt government will never find out your secret, as it would mean the end of what little civilization this Earth enjoys. Let us pull the switch together locked in each others arms." With that the loud speaker came on again.

"YOUR TIME IS UP, EXIT OR THEY BOTH DIE."

Tears were rolling down both our faces as we reached for the self-destruct button. Joseph held me tight and we began to pull it out to end it all. All of a sudden we heard firing and it seemed to be coming from the heavens. The firing became intense and we both just looked at each other. "Kait, can that be members of Rick's team bringing the battle to these forces, I cannot believe his group would be a match for so many tanks, fighters and manpower."

"Joseph, look up, the fighters are falling to the ground in mass and it sounds like the tanks are also blowing up. What is going on?

"Kait, look, those are UFO's from the planet of the burning rocks. They must have followed us here and been observing from a distance." All of a sudden one of them appeared at the opening at the top of the barn and motioned for us to leave. Without hesitation Joseph engaged the propulsion systems reserve and we were in the sky. I looked around and the troops and fighters and tanks were being obliterated. The UFO signaled for us to follow them as we flew off into the heavens. Joseph handed me the satellite phone and screamed to call Rick. I dialed it up immediately and was elated when Rick answered. Rick, are you folks alright?"

"Kait, we love you guys, we are fine and just talked to Dale and he is on his way with our helicopter. The military is much too busy to interfere with us now so we will be long gone from here soon. The leaders of this group have both been dealt with and should spend eternity on the hellish of the Hell planets. You two rest easy wherever you settle within the Universe and maybe someday we will all meet again. God bless you both. Remember to name that first human baby to be born in space after either Sally or I, depending on whether it is a girl or boy. Don't worry about us as we have long had contingency plans and will be thinking of you two from some island in the Caribbean with a Piña Colada in our hands. God be with you." I told Rick how much we loved him and wished them God's speed and then the signal weakened. Joseph just looked at me as we followed our friends to their peaceful planet.

THE END

CREDITS

I wish to thank my significant other, Marcia Holmes, for her many hours of proofing she patiently did for me while I was writing this book. Marcia has filled a special place in my life and given me a **"second chance at love."**

As with my other four books I wish to acknowledge and thank my wonderful family, Craig, Scott, for all his computer assistance, Kirk and Jennifer for their support and encouragement while I compiled this wild story of unfettered space travel.

A special thanks to my grandsons, Tyler Parsons for his contribution to the cover design and to Kenny Romano for his input during the writing of the book.

CPSIA information can be obtained at www.ICGtesting.com
Printed in the USA
BVOW071453240313

316289BV00001B/3/P